THE GAME

THE GAME

Revised

Timothy Williams

A Conscious Press Production

First print 2007
Copyright © 2020 Timothy W. Williams

Published by Conscious Press Publications
P.O. Box 5 New Brunswick, N.J. 08903-005

All rights reserved. No part of this publication may be reproduced, stored in a retrieval system or transmitted, in any form, or by any means, electronic, mechanical, recorded, photocopied, or otherwise, without the prior written permission of both the copyright owner and the above publisher of this book, except by a reviewer who may quote brief passages in a review.

The scanning, uploading, and distribution of this book via the Internet or via any other means without the permission of the publisher is illegal and punishable by law. Please purchase only authorized electronic editions and do not participate in or encourage electronic piracy of copyrightable materials. Your support of the author's rights is appreciated.

Designed by: Vince Pannullo
Printed in the United States of America
by: One Communications LLC

ISBN: 978-0-9800759-0-8

Poem 9
Introduction 11

Chapter One 13
Chapter Two 17
Chapter Three 31
Chapter Four 35
Chapter Five 43
Chapter Six 53
Chapter Seven 61
Chapter Eight 67
Chapter Nine 75
Chapter Ten 81
Chapter Eleven 91
Chapter Twelve 97
Chapter Thirteen 105
Chapter Fourteen 109
Chapter Fifteen 113
Chapter Sixteen 117
Chapter Seventeen 119
Chapter Eighteen 127
Chapter Nineteen 135
Chapter Twenty 141
Chapter Twenty One 145
Chapter Twenty Two 151
Chapter Twenty Three 157
Chapter Twenty Four 165
Chapter Twenty Five 175

The Game - Revised 2

Chapter Twenty six 179
Chapter Twenty Seven 187
Chapter Twenty Eight 189
Chapter Twenty Nine 191
Chapter Thirty 197
Chapter Thirty One 205
Chapter Thirty Two 209
Chapter Thirty Three 219
Chapter Thirty Four 227
Chapter Thirty Five 233
Chapter Thirty Six 235
Chapter Thirty Seven 239
Chapter Thirty Eight 247
Chapter Thirty Nine 251
Chapter Forty 255
Chapter Forty One 261
Chapter Forty Two 265
Chapter Forty Three 273
Chapter Forty Four 277
Chapter Forty Five 283
Chapter Forty Six 285
Chapter Forty Seven 287
Chapter Forty Eight 291

Poem 293

This book is dedicated to all the members of my family with all my love. It is especially for the memory of my father, Theodore Williams Jr.: My brother, Charles K. Williams: My sister, Lynette F. Williams: and my maternal grandmother, Gertrude Daniels, who have become a very large part of my incentive to do something meaningful with my life.

Poem

I once lived the life of a millionaire.
I spent my money, I didn't care, and when it was gone.
I tried to find a friend, and guess what, there was no one there, but with this experience and where I've been.
I promise you all, that I'll be back again, and when those same people need a friend, then you know in your heart that I win.

Timothy Williams

Introduction

AFTER breakfast, as Theresa began to clear the kitchen table, Goldie made his way into the living room to read the morning edition of the Home News. When he was done, he placed the News Paper-back down on to the coffee table and walked over and opened the blinds.

After which, he sat back down on to his easy chair, he just sat there looking out through blinds that shielded a large picture window.

After a few moments, Goldie called out, "Come here, Baby."

Theresa appeared almost instantly. She eased up beside him in his easy chair, "Yes, Goldie."

"Baby look around yourself, and then, I just want you to take a look out of these here blinds."

Theresa replied, "Goldie, what?"

After taking a look around the elegantly decorated room, brass, glass, and various types of African artifacts, she placed her hands on to her shapely hips and had giving him an inquisitive smile. She said, "Come on, Goldie, what is it that you want me to see?"

He smiled slyly, "Hey, that this shit ain't half bad."

Theresa returned his smile and eased around in front of him and sat down on to his lap, and had giving him a big hug.

Goldie asked," What's that for?"

She looked intensely into his eyes, "It's because I remember, where, and what we've come from, and all that it took to get where we are today. Goldie, today, I appreciate it, and I owe it all to you."

He leaned forward and kissed her on the forehead, "Baby, do you know the sad part about it all.., I appreciate it…, I love.., but I cherish nothing. I'll leave here today knowing the price of everything, and everyone, but the value of nothing. However, I do have to give you credit, you have made me aware of a lot of things. I also want you to know that it's because of you that I'm beginning to come around. Today, I can honestly say that I truly value your friendship, your honesty, and your loyalty. Hell, I remember when you had a snotty nose and a face full of tears, scared to death of that big old world out there. "Do you remember?"

She placed a playful finger on to the tip of his nose and smiled, "Yeah, I remember the day we met."

"Baby, I want you to know, I'm proud of you, and it gives me great pleasure to say, today, sitting in my lap is a woman. I'm as proud of you as I' am of my work, you are a masterpiece, and I'm so glad that I got the opportunity to play a part in the making of you. I got to go to work."

Theresa rose so that he could stand.

He said, "Okay, it's Friday, big money day. Let's get it on. I'll make the necessary calls on the road. You know the drops."

As he walked over and removed his jacket from the living room closet, and began to make his way to the door to leave. Theresa, who had been standing there in the room watching him closely the whole time, called out, "Goldie," he stopped and turned to face her before leaving the room.

She said, "Thanks."

Goldie turned and walked out of the door. He knew that it had all been said, and he also knew that she had earned it.

Chapter One

GOLDIE stood out on the sidewalk in front of his hideout, and as his car warmed up. He ran his plan back and forth through his mind. He always thought before making any move that would affect life or his lifestyle for that matter. Now up drove one of the sharpest S- Type Jaguar's that he ever saw. A pretty, little single girl, jumped out with her arms full of groceries, and Goldie went right into action. He asked, "Hey, Lady, how are you?" as he walked over and removed one of the grocery bags from the young women's arms.

She looked up at him as if to be shocked and replied, "I'm fine. Thank you." The young women's name was Carla, and Goldie had thrown the ball back and forth {conversed} with her on a few different occasions in the past. He never tried to make any more out of it than that because he didn't feel that he could give her what she needed. He could give her beautiful things, but quality time would be rare and none. Goldie was a busy man, but today was different, and with the new plan, Carla would play a significant role in his life. However, Goldie knew that it would take some time.

As they approached the front door to Carla's condominium, Goldie reached over and retrieved the other grocery bag from the young woman's arms so that she could open up the front door to her place. He followed her into the house and began to survey her pad.

All of a sudden, she stopped short and before he knew it. He was right up on top of her and had bumped her lightly. Carla turned to face him rather quickly, and their eyes met, and then she asked the question, "Do you like?"

Goldie looked down intensely into her eyes, and in a serious voice, he replied, "I think that you're beautiful."

She smiled shyly, "I was talking about my place."

He smiled, "Yet, revealing that he was shocked by her words and replied, "Yeah, yeah, it's beautiful too."

Now Goldie had never been inside of her place before, he moved toward the paint easel and began to admire the few paintings that hung along the walls of her living room. He was impressed.

He said, "Wow, Baby, I didn't know that you painted." Carla politely replied, "Goldie, there's a lot to me. Would you like a drink, coffee, tea, soda?"

He smiled, "No, no, thanks, I have a few runs to make, however, I would like to see you, again. On a more personal level, you know, like, to kind of get to know each -other a little better."

Carla smiled, "I would like that."

Goldie asked, "Well, what are you doing this Saturday."

"Well, Goldie, I'm working half a day. I also have a few errands to run, but anytime after two, Saturday, afternoon, I'm free."

He stood there admiring her for a few moments, and then he began looking around her place at all of the items that were conducive to whom she was, her paint easel, and her computer. There were also black authored books that lined her bookshelves, the black artifacts, and all of the amenities.

He thought her presence in his life would be a God's, given gift. He took her hand in his, and as he led her back to the front door, he said, "Great, I'll pick you up around six.

Carla looked up into his eyes and replied, "Yeah, Well, Okay, and thank you."

As he made his way down the walkway, Carla watched him through the kitchen window, wondering: If he even thought that she was alive, or if he would even show up on Saturday. He hadn't asked for her telephone number or anything.

Now Goldie's mind was elsewhere, but after talking with Carla, he knew that he had his work cut out for him. She was beautiful and holding like the FED's, red, rich, and fertile. He also knew that thing would be lavishing in its generosity. Carla was about five feet, seven inches tall, and weighed about a hundred and thirty pounds {36-25-38} with the mental. He knew that she would be all that he would need to close a chapter in his life. That he had created and now wanted out of. He decided that Carla was going to be the one to scratch his itch of loneliness.

As he began to back his Caddie out of his parking spot, he notices Carla walking toward the car. He stopped and let his window down. She handed him a piece of paper with her telephone number on it and said, "If something should come up, or happen, and you can't make it on Saturday. This is how you can reach me.

Goldie smiled as he began to slowly back out of his parking spot, "Baby, nothings going to happen, you're stuck with me, you'll see."

As Carla made her way back toward her condominium, she was filled with wonderment and curiosity and asked herself the question. 'Who was the man that she just made plans to get together with?' In the year that Goldie lived there, she had only seen him there, three, or four times. There was incredible excitement about him, and on top of that, he was a very handsome man. She never saw him with anyone, and did know at that point, 'If he was half the man that she thought he was, she would be willing to risk it all.'

Chapter Two

AS Goldie approached the block, which was about forty minutes or so away from the hideout, he was flagged down by a young man, named, Smooth, he pulled the car over and instructed the kid to get in so that he could get off of that particular block. It was the most happening block in the town, but Goldie also knew that Remsen Avenue, in New Brunswick, was the hottest in regards to criminal activities, and police investigations.

As Goldie turned the car on to Handy Street, off Remsen, Smooth asked, "So what's up for today."

Now Smooth was one with potential, sharp at wit, and loved to make a dollar. He had been hustling for Goldie for the last six months or so. Goldie watched him closely. He seemed to be flawless, at-least ready for what he planned. Goldie replied, "Hey Man, today, I just want you to hang out with me. I have a few runs to make. I'll hit your pocket, and I'm gone."

"Okay, but Goldie, we ain't going to do no hustling today, cause it's money coming like crazy out there on the block."

Goldie glanced over at him and said, "It's always going to be out there, but you won't, if you keep focusing on the money. How many times do I have to tell you? Work on your game. That's where the money is. It's not what you make. It's what you do with what you make. Now tighten up, cause we got some rapping to do."

After a short pause of silence, Smooth asked, "Goldie, have you heard about what happen last night?"

Goldie reflected on the night before, where he stood at a crap-table, in Atlantic City, drinking Maker's Mark. He was down about thirty thousand dollars when he received the call. The voice politely said on the opposite end of the line. "It's done."

Goldie glanced over at Smooth, again, and replied, "No, I haven't heard what happen last night, you tell me."

"Well, from my understanding, Felix, his bodyguard, and two of his closes associates are dead. It's said, That they came out of one of his spots over off Lee Avenue, got into the big BMW, and somehow the car just blew up."

Goldie asked, "Are you aware that they were the competition. It's like the Spanish are taking over New Brunswick, what do we have left? The Jersey Avenue Cafe, the Elk's Club, and the Somewhere Else Bar. They have a guy on just about every hustle block in the city. Soon if you don't work with them or for them, the Bother's won't be able to work."

Smooth asked, "Goldie, what do you mean?"

"I mean: They don't mind organizing and or paying to play. The Hispanic will be able to move Brother's off the blocks that they pioneered. First off, because they are buying the blocks {based on the proceeds from small businesses that stem from drug sells, prostitution, etc.}. Second off, utilizing the law {they have willing participants, we don't}. The brother's on the Police Force will still be looking at us like we are pieces of shit, splitting our heads to the white meat, and locking us the fuck up while they build. I can't afford. We can't afford to take this shit lying down."

Smooth, slowly turned his head away and out toward the passing scenery, for Goldie had an intent stare that could kill.

Goldie stated, "Nah, look here, man. I'm on to something, something that I want to do, and you know that Goldie doesn't try to do anything. However, I'm going to need your help. The plan that I have will turn the town. Man, this is your wake up call. I'm going to make you rich."

Smooth replied, "Yeah, Goldie, yeah, I'd like that, count me in."

As Goldie pushed his ride through traffic, they rode in silence. He smiled to himself, for he knew the only way to keep his edge: Was by knowing more about what he did than anyone else. They were approaching, Joyce Kilmer, and Reed, on the other side of town. Goldie pulled the car over to the side of the road and told Smooth to sit tight. He would be right back.

Smooth sat there watching Goldie, as he disappeared into one of the three existing apartment buildings, wondering what Goldie's plan was all about.

When Goldie reached the intended apartment, he removed a small ring of keys from his pocket and opened the door, and there she sat on the living room sofa with a pillow on her lap. He called her Chocolate Thunder; she was the prettiest thing you ever wanted to see. Her name was Cathy. She stood about, five-foot, eight inches tall, and was about one hundred and twenty-eight pounds thick. He thought to himself, and Black sure is beautiful.

Now Cathy was a native of New Brunswick, and Goldie had met her while she was in High School. He should have been in some kind of school also. He was already out in the streets, trying to make a name for himself, and trying to find a way out of what was long considered a sickness. They never hooked up during that period of their lives. However Goldie would watch her, watch him, as she would make her way through the hustle block on her way home from school. It wasn't that she didn't want anything to do with him at that point in her life. His mindset was why, as fine as she was, and with all that he was in to. It wasn't until about ten years later that Goldie had run across her out in one of the happening spots of the town.

She walked over near the Juke Box, where he was standing and extended her hand in his direction.

Goldie smiled as he accepted her hand.

She returned his smile, "I'm Cathy, I was just sitting there at the bar checking you out. I wondered if you remembered me?"

Goldie kissed her on the hand, "Of course, I remember you. How could I forget?"

She blushed as the recording, Zoom, by the Commodores began to permeate the club.

A steering match ensued {he pulled her close to him}.

She had no idea that she was dealing with a much more confidant, a much more sophisticated, a much more refined, and defined, Goldie.

They have been inseparable ever since.

Goldie asked, "What's up, baby," as he closed the door to her place behind himself.

Cathy just sat there, shaking her head from side to side. Goldie took that as nothings happening, but in reality, he knew what it was, he hadn't been by to see her in a week, and three days prior, they were supposed to have a nice little quiet dinner and spend some quality time together.

Now Cathy was Goldie's pick-up lady. She made rounds and picked up his paper {money} from people that worked for him. He didn't have any problems when it came down to him getting his paper. If it was out there, she was going to get it. He knew the significance of having a sharp chick that could get out there among men and get that paper. He also knew that whenever someone was on top that there was always someone out there trying to gain what they had, trying to take that power. So he would give it to them {power}. They never realized that it wasn't available to them, based on the way that he put it out there. He knew that the workers had to believe that if they wanted to make points and or be treated like an equal: That they had to think that paying him was the most essential thing in the world, and believe me. Cathy was a real charmer.

Goldie held his arms out in her direction and gestured her over to him, she was slow-moving, but she got there. She walked into his arms and immediately began to sob, she said, "Goldie, I was worried about you. He backed up out of the embrace and looked down into her eyes and replied, "Look at you, Chump, you look beautiful with all of that water on your face. He began to kiss her tears.

Cathy asked, "How have you been? He replied, "How do I look."

"Well, where have you been?"

Goldie smiled, "Now, that's a long story."

She smiled, and right then, he knew that he had her.

He said, "Hey Girl, turn around and let me look at you."

Now Cathy's body was flawless, and the teddy that she wore didn't leave any wonder to the imagination. Goldie wanted to take her into his arms and make deep passionate love to her. However, he was already behind schedule. He explained that he had a few runs to make, and that he just wanted to touch base with her, and that he would stop by later.

Cathy asked, "Goldie, what about the money?"

He held his hands out at his side in gesture, "What about the money. It's not going anywhere, is it?"

She replied, "Well, no."

He kissed her on the mouth and said, "Alright, Baby, I'll see you a little later on, okay?"

Cathy smiled and replied, "Okay."

As Goldie made his way back to his car, he realized that Cathy was ready, overdue, and very deserving. He jumped back into his car and asked, "Smooth, are you ready?"

Smooth, looked over at him and replied, "I'm just waiting on you, and digging some of your tunes."

"Well, look here, man, I'm going to drop you off and get things in motion. He handed Smooth a hundred dollar bill and said," Buy your girl something nice, is that cool, or do you need a little more bread."

"Nah, Goldie, that's cool, and thanks."

Again, Smooth wanted to ask Goldie about working the block, but he dare not ask. Especially -after the lecture that he received from Goldie. They were approaching the block where Goldie had picked Smooth up from, and as he pulled the car over to the side of the road to drop him back off. Smooth asked, "When?"

Goldie looked over at him and smiled, and then he extended his hand and replied, "Very soon, my friend, very soon."

As Goldie pulled his ride away from the curb, he knew that it wouldn't be long before he put his plan into effect. He would put himself on top of the game, by way of everything that he knew about the game, and in success. He planned to walk away from it. He reached down and snatched his car –phone and dialed a number, and after a few rings, a voice came over the line.

Now Goldie automatically knew who it was on the other end because no-one else answered that telephone besides his-man, Jose.

Goldie said, "Jose."

Jose replied, "Yeah."

"Hey Square, what's going on up there?"

"Goldie."

"Yeah,"

"Hey Baby, how's everything?"

Goldie replied, "Just fine, my man, just fine. Look here, man, I'm in a bit of a jam."

"Well, I'm sure that it's nothing that we can't fix."

Goldie smiled, as he surveyed his surroundings while bringing his Caddie to a holt at the intersection of Remsen and George, he said, into the receiver, "You know the bakery on the corner down from the Court House. The one that we frequent, often"

Jose replied, "Yeah, I know the one."

Goldie said, "Well, I need you to order me a couple of cakes, it's my daughter and niece's birthday, and it slipped my mind."

Jose said, "Goldie, that's not a problem."

He replied, "Outstanding, I'll send someone to pick them up and Jose."

"Yeah, Goldie."

"You're a life saver man."

The line went dead.

Now Goldie had been dealing with Jose for the last five years, or so {cake was short for kilo}. Goldie's coded almost all of his telephone conversations. He knew that one could never be too careful, and trust was something that you earned with him. He didn't just give that away, and Jose' had earned Goldie's trust and respect. Jose was about five-feet seven inches tall, weighed about one hundred and forty-five pounds, and loved himself some big women. Goldie had also earned Jose's trust and respect and knew that there was nothing that Jose wouldn't do for him, if in his power.

Goldie pushed his Caddie on with a gleam in his eyes. He knew that it was time to go to work. He reached down and snatched his car telephone and dialed another number, and after a few moments, a lady's voice came over the line. Still half asleep, she said, "Hello."

He replied, into the receiver, "Hey, wake up sleepy head, we got work to do.

"Goldie?"

"Yeah, it's me."

"It's good to hear from you, but then again, it's always great to hear from you. How have you been? Goldie, where have you been? I've been worried about you, man."

Now Theresa was the type of woman that loved to ramble, but only to Goldie, out on the street, you couldn't get a peep out of her, and when Goldie first met her. He thought she was a mute.

He interjected, "Alright, Baby, I appreciate your concern, but stop rambling. We got work to do. I want you to take the gardener a check for thirty-six dollars, and tell him. I didn't like the way that he left the lawn and that I would appreciate my equipment back."

Theresa replied, "Okay, Goldie."

{He Continued) "And when you get the equipment from Joe, I want you to put an evening together for us, and I'll see you later."

She replied, "Okay, Goldie, bye."

The line went dead.

Now Theresa was a heart-stopper, brown, creamy, and rich, but more importantly she was good and true to Goldie, she knew her place and stayed in it. She was also well versed in the game. After the telephone call, Theresa began to run the conversation that she just had with Goldie back and forth through her mind. She knew that Joe was short for Jose. The check for thirty-six dollars, meant, thirty-six thousand dollars. Take it to Jose and get the equipment {two kilo}. Put an evening together for us, meant, put it together {the kilo's}, and that he would see her soon.

Now Goldie loved putting people's minds to work. He had met Theresa a few years back, at the Train station, in downtown New Brunswick, with her bags in tow and a face full of tears. She was a student at Rutgers University. However, her parents could no longer afford to send her to the University.

Goldie walked over and asked, "What is the problem," and at that point, Theresa didn't believe that sharing her problem with him could do any more harm. However, she later explained to Goldie that it was his kindness and the fact that he was a total stranger that had her to do so.

As she began to spill her story, she began to sob even harder. Goldie took her hand in his, and said, "It's okay; it's okay; you're safe now."

Theresa mustered a slight smile and replied, "Who are you, my guardian angel?"

Goldie smiled, "Let's just say that I' am. What did you say your name was?"

She froze for a moment, looking at him intensely, "I didn't, but its Theresa, my friends call me, Tee."

"Well, Ms. Tee, I would like to buy you some lunch. I don't want to leave you out here, alone, and in your present state. Well, anyway, I know a nice little spot down the street here."

Theresa smiled, "And just what would the name of this little spot be?" Goldie replied, "The Island of Breeze."

"It sounds expensive." "And don't you dare think that you don't deserve it." Again, she showed him her whites, "Okay, but what will I do with my things."

Goldie said, "We will put your things in the trunk of my car, and after we eat. I'll run you home. By the way, I'm Goldie."

Theresa, extended her hand, "Well, Goldie, it's a pleasure to meet you."

He took her hand in his and looked directly down into her eyes and said, "Believe me, the pleasure is all mine." He wanted her to draw from the sincerity of his game.

As Theresa and Goldie approached his car, her eyes lit up. She asked, "Is this your Caddie?"

Goldie reached down and opened the trunk of the car with his key, and replied, "Yes, this is one of the few cars that I have access to, but this one is mine. I own it."

As she began to hand him her things to be packed into the trunk of the car, she said, "It's beautiful."

He asked, "Do you have a license?"

Theresa replied, "Yes."

"Well, how would you like to drive yourself home?"

"Oh, Goldie, I would love to."

After a few moments, Theresa asked, "Are you serious?"

Goldie replied, "Very, now let's go and grab us a bite to eat."

Theresa and Goldie ended up having a lovely lunch and a beautiful ride to the city of Newark. During the ride, she began to tell him how unhappy she was at home. But there was one thing that Theresa said that stuck with him.

She said, "Goldie, if you're my guardian angel, your job is to save me."

He replied, "I will, Baby, but it's going to take a little time."

When Goldie got back into town that evening, he made a few telephone calls and had her a place in no time, and after getting her place all set up. He gave Theresa a call, and not only was she pleased. She has been with him ever since. She feels as though she is forever indebted to him. He saved her, for he had given her -her own. So, she had no problem with whatever Goldie may have asked of her.

After Goldie dropped Smooth off and made a few telephone calls, he road in silence, he looked down at his watch and thought, 'Wow,' where does the time go. It was like the car was driving by itself, as he re-approached Reed and Joyce Kilmer Ave. He knew

THE GAME   27

that Cathy would be waiting on him, with open arms, and a whole lot of money. Goldie couldn't think of a better place to go as he pulled the car into the parking lot and parked. He noticed Cathy getting out of her car a couple of parking spots over. She spotted him and immediately showed him her pearly whites.

As he walked over and encountered her in the parking lot, he asked, "What's going on Baby?"

Cathy quickly placed the bag that she was carrying into his arms and replied, "Ain't nothing, I just decided to go out and to get you something special. I knew that you would be back."

He looked down into her eyes, "And just how would you know that? You know, I consider myself to be unpredictable."

Cathy smiled, "Goldie, who knows you better than I do."

He returned her smiled, and rather smoothly replied, "My mother, Baby, my mother."

On the inside of Cathy's place, she rushed right into the kitchen to check the lobster that she had steaming, while out. Her place was lowly lit, and the dining room table set for two, with candles and crystal glasses. Goldie stopped in the living room and sunk into his easy-chair. He sat there messing with the buttons on the stereo system, and before long, the room was filled with the sounds of {Rose Royce, I want to get next to you}.

Now it wasn't long before everything was ready in the kitchen, and Cathy returned to the living room where Goldie sat, and said, "Give me a minute, I have a surprise for you."

Goldie looked up at her from his easy-chair and smiled as she made her way through the living room for the bedroom. He sat there, wondering what the surprise could have possibly been.

When Cathy returned to the living room, she was wearing, garter-belt, straps, crotch-less panties, and Bra, all in lace. Goldie sat there mesmerized as she made her way across the living room floor before him, with poise and grace.

Cathy walked into the kitchen and retrieved a bottle of champagne from out of the refrigerator, and then she walked over and retrieved two long stem crystal glasses from off the kitchen table. Goldie watched her closely as she made her way back toward him. He retrieved the champagne bottle from her hand and looked at the label -approvingly. He pulled her to him and sat her down on to his lap. He popped the cork on the champagne bottle and watched the bubbles matured while running down the center of her chest. He filled their glasses and proposed a toast, "To us."

Cathy quickly interjected, "Now, don't you go making no promises that you can't keep."

Goldie knew that there was only one way to avoid this type of complicated question. He removed the glass of champagne from her hand and asked, "Can I have this dance?"

She looked at him seductively and replied, "Of course".

Cathy eased into his arms, and Goldie pulled her close to him, and after a few moments of dancing to soft music. He began to nibble at her neck and to whisper into her ears.

As he felt her tremble by way of trust, she began to undress him. First, the silk-shirt that he was wearing fell to the floor, and before he knew it. His Hugo Boss slacks were down around his ankles. He stepped out of the lizard shoes that he was wearing, and Cathy had led him into the bedroom, where he had her do a Pen House layout to entice him. He eased up on to the bottom of the bed and began to kiss her slowly on her -inner thighs, and when he reached her sex. He placed his tongue on it. Cathy raised her hips off of the bed and began moving them in a circular motion while running her finger's through his hair. She began to moan, and when Goldie felt that she had peeked. He mounted her and thrust into paradise.

CHAPTER THREE

AS the sun had taken its place high above the city, the dope lines lengthened down along Remsen Avenue, but not just on Remsen. The inner workings of the Game during this time of the morning are taking place all over the world.

The dealers are out dropping drug packages off to their hustler's.

Lookout men are out getting themselves into position on, rooftops, sitting in cars with scanners, and two-way radios. Standing out on corners, porches, and out amongst those long dope lines looking for suspicious characters, robbers, and the police.

The whores are also coming in off the street corners this time of the morning in search of coffee, chewing gum, candy, and their fixes.

The robbers are out on the streets do to all of this, too. It's the opportunity of a lifetime {fast money}, and as with all rituals, the police have their positions to assume also. Patrol-men are driving through these cities, narcotic cops working the Fein's {rats}, some narcotics cops in the form of Fein's themselves. Some of them are actually out among the dope-lines{got to watch the buy and bust, undercover-sells}, surveillance crews posing as cable-men, telephone repair-men, and shooting pictures of the inner-workings of the Game and all of its player's, daily.

Goldie had once shared with Smooth that one of the most beautiful things that he has seen was the inner workings of an entire city, concerning the Game from up high in a helicopter. He shared with Smooth about the inner workings of the Game with hopes that it would inspire idealism, acquaint him with thought, create a vision, and teach him to strategize in his field of choice.

Mean while as sunlight began to creep through Cathy's bedroom window, she and Goldie laid there in the large bed. She watched him as he slept, and ran her index finger from his forehead to his chin {he opened his eyes}. She kissed him on the mouth and said, "Good Morning."

He smiled, "Heyyy, Good Morning, Baby."

Goldie, I was thinking, I could lay here forever, Baby, why don't we just put all of this behind us for a while and go away together, I Love You, and I don't want anything to happen to you."

He leaned up on to an elbow in the large bed and returned her intense look and replied,

"First off, nothing going to happen to me. Second off, I ain't got time for love, and Baby that shit sure don't pay no bills."

She playfully ran her fingernails across his chest, "You can get a job."

He sprung up into a sitting position on the bed, "A what, have you lost your damn mind this morning, Listen up, cause I'm only going to say this once. I chose this life because I know what to expect out of it. I mean, hey, what am I going to do, and after laying around here helping you starve to damn death. How long do you think that shits going to last."

Cathy dropped her head, "I, I just thought."

{He continued}, "Damn it, don't think! Let me think, cause every-time you think shit gets all fucked up."

Cathy jumped out of the bed and ran in to the bathroom.

Goldie laid back down on to the large bed-listening to her sob and all of a sudden. He got up out of bed and slipped into his silk-robe and his leather slipper's and left the bedroom for the kitchen.

He heard the bathroom door when it opened, Cathy peeped into the bedroom, no –Goldie, so she eased out into the kitchen where she found him sitting at the kitchen table looking through a magazine with coffee in hand. He acted as if he hadn't noticed her. She just stood there watching him and after a few moments without even looking up from his magazine. He held his hand out in her direction, and she eased over and slid her hand in his, and then he set her down to the kitchen table. He said, "Look, Baby, don't think that I don't understand where your coming from, and please, have no doubt about me wanting the same things that you want. It's just not the time. Anyway, I have something cooking that should get us out of this rat race forever, and when it's over, you'll play a major part in my life, forever. He asked, "Do you love me?"

She mustered a smile and replied, "You know, I do."

He kissed her on the mouth, "Then trusts me."

{He con), "Baby, go lay me some clothes out, while I shower. I have a busy day today. Oh, and Baby, it's business as usual, whenever a worker calls you. I want you to call Theresa' so she can drop off another setup. Make sure you call her, else she won't re-drop."

Cathy looked at him, disappointedly, and asked, "Goldie, do I -

He interrupted her, immediately, "Yes, you do have to work with Theresa and don't look at me that way. Cathy whatever happen to logical thinking, you're beginning to let your emotions override your better judgment, and I don't like it."

Cathy got up from the kitchen table and left the room to lay Goldie some clothes out. She knew that it was a battle that she couldn't win. She also knew that Goldie' was through talking.

As she began to leave the kitchen, he stopped her and said, "Baby, before I forget, get that paper {money} together for me."

She replied, "Okay, Goldie."

Now Cathy often wondered what Goldie did with his money, but not as much as where it went after it left her hands, but she dare not ask. Goldie never let anyone know what he did with his money or where he kept it for that matter.

Part of the money went directly into the bank, and there were also three safety deposit boxes and a little cash on hand at the hideout.

Now the way that the money went into the bank was rather simple. Goldie would use {play} Atlantic City, he would take his mother or she would go down often. She would exchange the paper (money) for chips at a variety of the different available table games. She would exchange a little here and a little there, and she would never get rated. So Atlantic City, never knew whether she brought the money with her or won it –while she was at the casino, and when she would return the chips to the casino. Often instead of accepting cash, she would request a certified check from the casino.

The money was justified –in his mother being a retired real-estate broker for the last several years and an owner of prime real estate. She was also an active investor in the stock market. So now and then, a check would be deposited into an active bank account, taxed at the end of the year, but a rather small price to pay for the clean paper to with what you choose. There were also three safety deposit box keys, two of which were held by his two sisters {one a-piece}, and the two boxes were a state away. The third key Goldie kept, and he is the only one that knows the location of that particular box.

Chapter Four

CARLA moved out from in-between satin sheets, in her panties, and bra, on to the side of the large bed as the telephone continued to ring. She reached over and retrieved the phone off the nightstand and just held the receiver up along the side of her face {still half asleep}.

The women, on the other end asked, "Carla, are you awake?"

She replied, "I' am now, and Jill, just what the hell do you want this time of the morning."

Jill smiled, "Well, first off, what's he like, and how is he, you know, like in bed. I got the message that you left on my answering machine."

Carla smiled, as memories and future visions of her and Goldie began to invade her mind, she replied, "He's the bomb, he's intelligent, charming, witty, and strong. I have never met anyone like him before in my life. He's very passionate about what he does, he's discipline, and exciting, need I go on?"

Jill rolled over in the bed and reached over on to the nightstand and retrieved a package of cigarettes, and said, "You're my partner and my girl, but I would be lying if I said, that I didn't have any reservation about this guy. She asked, "Carla, is this going to be difficult for you."

"Well, what do you want me say that he's not the bomb, that he's not every women's, man. I can't say that, however, I have made contact, and my objective is in perspective, and I haven't forgotten."

At that point, Jill lit her cigarette and said, "Just take your time, girl be-careful, and don't rush into anything with this guy."

Carla didn't bother to respond. She just placed the receiver back down on to the nightstand.

The line went dead.

Mean while after leaving Cathy's place, Goldie road through town with hopes of seeing Smooth out along the avenue {Remsen). He wanted to fill him in on his role and function with the new plan, but after not coming in to contact with him. Goldie decided that he would check in on Theresa and give Smooth a call a little later. He reached over and snatched his car-telephone and dialed Theresa's number.

Now on the outskirts of town, the ringing of the telephone startled Theresa, she was sitting there on the living room sofa, after a nice hot bubble bath in her bathrobe, painting her toenails. She reached over on to the end table and retrieved the telephone receiver, she said, "Goldie."

He replied, "Yeah, how did you know."

She smiled, "Well, you have to think, who else calls here?"

Goldie smiled as he turned the car on to Sanford Street, off Remsen, he replied, "Go –head, Baby, I love it when you pimp at me. So how did the gardener take the news?"

"With pride, Goldie, with pride."

"Okay, Baby, I'm on my way."

The line went dead.

After Goldie hung up the telephone, he rode in silence, thinking for every war that was fought and won. It was won long before it had begun, and as with war, he had a planned out come. Now all's he had to do was work his plan.

When Goldie arrived at Theresa's place, which was located in the village of North, in North Brunswick, he jumped out of the car, and no sooner than he had placed his feet down on her doorsteps. The door opened for him. Theresa stood there on the opposite side of the door on the heels of her feet. She had been waiting on her toenails to dry when he arrived. He stepped inside of her place, and she threw her arms around him and said, "I've missed you so much."

He returned her embrace, "It's only been a week."

She kissed him on the mouth, "Baby, it felt like a year. Where have you been? I have been so worried about you."

Now Goldie didn't like to be questioned, but he knew to come from her that the concern was genuine. He just overlooked the questions, and asked, "Baby, let me see that thing?"

Theresa stepped back and opened her bathrobe, revealing her birthday suit to him.

He smiled as he quickly surveyed her body while closing the door behind himself. He said, "Not that thing, Chump. However, there may be time for that thing a little later on, but right now, we have a cause that needs our attention."

Theresa returned his smile seductively, and as she closed her robe. She looked down at her feet, which she thought to be dry at that point, and left the living room to retrieve that thing {the cake}.

Goldie walked over and made himself comfortable in his easy chair and while waiting. He thought about 'how beautiful she was, and all that he had in her.'

When Theresa returned to the living room, she walked over and sat a leather carry bag down, in-between his legs, and then she walked over and closed the blinds. He looked down into the bag and immediately noticed that there was more cake in the bag than he had instructed her to go and pick up. He looked over at her and asked, "Theresa, what the hell is this?"

She walked over and sat down directly across from him on the sofa and replied, "It's two and a half cake, and if you didn't notice. I already put half of the package together."

Goldie looked back down into the bag as if what she said had made a difference, and then he looked back over at her and asked, "What the hell did I tell you to get?"

"Wait a minute, Goldie, before you get upset. I wanted to spring this on you as a surprise. The half was a gift from Jose, and he also told me to tell you. Whatever the two of you discussed, it worked out and that this Saturday. He wants you to meet him in Belmar, at the Boat Basin, peer eighty-seven, at eleven o'clock in the morning. He wants you to go out on his new boat with him for lunch and a rap session. By the way, he's bringing a friend."

He replied, "And –

" I just thought, maybe –

Goldie eased back into his easy chair and crossed his legs, "Look, don't you think a damn thing, you should have been told me about this shit. How do you know that he isn't trying to put shit on me? How many times have I told you in this game, it's all chess {nothing is done for nothing}, and the move that Jose just made was check. I think he forgot that I get the opportunity to move before he can holler 'checkmate.' Then again, in his eye's. I'm already mated.

{He cont} Now you see why I'm a loner. It's to avoid shit like this, and this is where Jose and I stand in this chess game we have been playing since the day we met. Baby, he doesn't count, he's a pawn in the game that he's trying to play. See, I didn't have to meet him to want something or to get mine for that matter. He had to meet me though because he needed me to push him around like the pawn that he is. See pawns are push people and depending upon how you set them up. They will protect you, but more importantly, in this case, he's {they're} expendable. See Jose forgot, but it's my job to remember, not only what and where I come from, but what I made out of him. I remember when he was a four or five-ounce copping, no house having, hustling in the street, little mother -fucker. See once upon a time as quick as he was getting it. I was buying it, but he had no idea at the time that I could have afforded to purchase a lot more product than I had been copping. I was getting it so quick that it made him look like a real shaker, a mover. See Baby, the easiest people to con' are people whose needs you can fulfill. I was fulfilling his needs, and he was meeting the man's needs above him. I liked working with him, I trusted him. However, after reaching a financial goal of mine, I needed to get to the next level and quickly. So I figured why not take him with me. We were tight, and I just about knew what he could and couldn't handle concerning the business. So I made sure the next move I made would be something that he couldn't handle. That would bring the big man out from behind the scene, or Jose would have to go along with the con –that I had been setting him up for in-order to stay in the game. It left him (vulnerable} open to me, teaching him how to use other people's money. I explained to him, 'how to get what I wanted on consignment.' I would pay him, he would pay the man, and in-turn he would make a profit. See, I knew he didn't want me to meet the man. So I didn't pressure him. He would have thought that I was trying to push him out of the game, and if I had given him that impression, there would have been problems. Plus, I knew who, and what I was dealing with, with him. In this game, you have to be-careful 'people will kill you behind a little bit of paper' {money}. What good is meeting the man if he kills you and takes your paper?

    Now on the deal how Jose would make out like a bandit is simple, most people never know that when they go to a drug house to cop {buy drugs}. That the workers in that house are no more than runners {their function is to go between their boss and the purchaser} Say you want to purchase ten-ounces of cocaine. The first thing that the worker says after replacing his calculator into his pocket-is, "I'll be right back." He doesn't have what you seek to cop. He is going to see the man. The worker {he} charges you say, twenty-four dollars a gram, he only pays twelve dollars a gram. So basically, he makes what the dealer makes plus a commission. Yeah, I'll tell you, the way to make money is definitely in using other people's paper. I'm not bullshitting, test the logic. What millionaire or anyone that gets real cash for that matter. What would they be doing sitting or living in a drug house? See, I made Jose, and I teach what I believe in to reproduce myself. I gave him my associate's business and everything. I blew him up at the risk of everything that he would one day gain would be mine. Baby, power is nothing when it's giving to you. You have to be the power. Okay, there's nothing that Jose wouldn't do for me, right?"

Theresa replied, "Right."

"So everything that he has is mine. I'll tell you, Jose would be willing to do more for me; than, I would have ever asked of him. See Baby, the game is big; as far as I'm concerned, the gift that Jose sent was an insult. I want you to ponder how he went about it. He gave me what he wanted me to have, nothing I needed, and it damn sure wasn't anything that I would have ever asked of him. Then to top that off -he sent the gift by you. Why didn't he just wait until Saturday, and tell me that he had a gift for me? It could have been done over lunch or during the rap session. What did he think, I would jump for joy. I know he didn't think, 'I would be impressed by this weak shit.' See, I hooked him into something big, and the power is driving him crazy. Right now, he can't see me for who I' am or what I'm worth. He can only see me for what he can get out of me, but Baby, what he doesn't know -is that I only taught him what I wanted him to know, not everything that I know, and it's going to cost him. Goldie smiled and concluded, Check mate.

Now Theresa loved to hear Goldie rap. She sat there mesmerized the whole time. She wasn't only in love with him. She was in love with his mind. Goldie sat there in his easy-chair, contemplating his next move. He was still upset with Theresa {although, he didn't show it}, and while thinking about the situation. He realized that she was well versed in the game. Yet the play that Jose just made there was no way for her to interpret it. He also knew that his fight wasn't with her, it was with him.

Theresa broke the silence, she asked, "Are we going, Saturday?"

Goldie replied, "'I' am, but you're not."

She asked, "Why, Goldie".

He looked intensely into her eyes and replied, "Saturday, you'll be working and from this point on, nobody sleeps around here. I want productivity to double".

Now Goldie hated to bust her bubble {hurt her or upset her}, but he knew that she had to pay to get something out of this experience. She had to pay to begin to take this game more seriously.

Goldie stood up out of his easy chair, "Listen, Baby, I have a few runs to make. I want you to put the rest of that thing together. I'll call you when it's time for you to make your drops, and from that point, I want you to wait on Cathy's call."

Theresa rose off of the sofa, and asked, "Goldie, why does –

He interrupted her immediately, "Because that's how it is, she is to call you whenever she receives a call from a worker and picks up the money. So you will know who to re-drop too. I mean, hey, it not like she is any bigger than you are in this thing. What is your problem?"

She looked up directly into his eyes and replied, "There is no problem, Goldie, there is none."

He smiled, "Now that's what I like to hear, give me a kiss, so that I can get out of here. Oh, and baby, I'll see you tonight."

She walked around the coffee table and kissed him on the mouth and replied, "I love you, Goldie."

Mean-while, Jose sat back in his easy-chair, in his beautifully furnished brownstone, in New York City. He was contemplating the move that he and Goldie had intended to make concerning the South. He was also trying to come up with a way to take the lead on this mass-money deal. It all balled down to Jose, not wanting to put himself back out there on Front Street. He figured that Goldie would oversee their mission and take all of the risks. While he would have reaped a portion of the benefits, and he knew that would take some smoothing over.

Chapter Five

AFTER leaving Theresa's place, Goldie decided that it would be best to implement his plan immediately. He reached over and snatched his car telephone and got Smooth on the line.

As Goldie had pulled his car out into traffic on George's Road, he spoke into the receiver, "Hey Baby, What's happening?"

Smooth replied, "Goldie."

"Yeah, and its time, Are you hungry?"

"Man, I could eat a horse."

"Well, give me about fifteen minutes. I'm in traffic."

The line went dead.

When Goldie arrived at the pick-up spot, Smooth was already there waiting for him. He jumped into the car, smiling, and said, "Let's eat."

Goldie looked over intensely at him, and replied, "Smooth, what's up? How are you, man? You didn't ask me any of that shit."

"Oh, my bad, Goldie, How are you?"

As Goldie pulled the car away from the pick-up spot, he replied, "Smooth, I have told you time and time again. Whenever you come into a set, always represent yourself with some pride and dignity. It will portray that you are respectful and that you seek and expect to be respected. Always acknowledge your brother, especially if you are somewhere you have never been before, because you may just have to come back. It can make a difference in how people perceive you. It makes a difference in how people treat you. Now, we shall dine."

After a few moments, Smooth looked over at him and smiled, "We shall dine?"

Goldie glanced over and returned his smile, "Yeah, Brother, It's a long story."

When Goldie and Smooth arrived at the Diner of Somerset, they were seated in a corner booth by a young, attractive, Spanish waitress.

As she handed both of them, menus, she asked, "What type of drinks will you have with your meals."

Smooth, looked up at the young woman from the table and replied, "I'll have, and then he stopped, abruptly. He thought about the conversation that he and Goldie had just had, and politely asked, "How are you today? I'll have two large orange juices."

She replied, "I'm fine, thank you," and then she kindly turned her attention to Goldie and asked, "Would you like a drink with your meal?"

He very calmly said, "I'll have one large orange juice, and a cup of coffee while I wait. Thank you."

As she walked away from the booth to retrieve their drinks, Smooth asked, "Goldie, what are you smiling about?"

"I'm smiling, because I thought the way you handled yourself was rather smooth. I also think that the waitress was digging you, and you didn't even notice it."

Now Goldie liked to sup {build} people up, but only in instances where there was no chance of anyone getting hurt. In reality, he liked the way that Smooth had corrected himself and thought there was hope for him yet. Goldie rapped up a storm during the meal about how the business would be conducted with the new plan in place. He said, "Smooth, I'm going to double up on you, man, and I'm going to explain to you how I want you to move it. When you get the product {drugs}, I want you to have a portion of the product cooked up. Now, whoever you have cook the product for you take good care of him, because we can use him. He's going to tell everybody about that thing {product} you miss, and after the product is cooked. I want you to go by Shonda's place, and tell her that I said to let you open up shop. She will give you the key to the basement. I want you to lock the {product} in the basement. Then take the portion of the product that you had cooked up, and I want you to pass out chips of the product to everyone who gets high out along the avenue {Remsen}. Let your clientele know where they can find you, and be sure to tell them to come to the back of the house. The basement door has a mail slot in it, despite it being located at the rear of the house. Serve them through the mail slot, and Smooth, this package is a monster. They will be coming, so I need you to be on your Ps and Qs.

{He continued} Now it shouldn't take to long for the person that you have cook the product for you to finish what little he has, be it use or sell. Tell him to stop by where you are when he's done.

Now the reason it is so important for you to choose who aids you in this process is because at your option. He can be used as your henchmen also. So we may as well put him on the payroll. It's just like I said, he's going to tell everyone about that thing that you miss.

Now when Theresa drops off the product to you, she will have a set of headsets {meaning two}, which you will be able to communicate with your henchmen through from the inside. The henchmen will stand out in front of the house or close by, and let you know, "One coming back." In-turn you will respond, "One coming out," and so forth. Hopefully, you understand how important it is for you to choose the right man for this job. Smooth this is a temporary setup, and it is going to get hot on the inside. I only need you to work for a few days. Smooth, you're my man, and much too valuable to me to lose.

Smooth could no longer conceal his smile; it felt great for him to hear Goldie tell him 'how valuable he was to him.' He also knew messing around with Goldie would allow him to touch some real money.

Now Goldie wanted Smooth to choose his own worker, because he would have to put some type of trust into that person. The worker would know his movement, he would be expendable to Goldie, and the man who would replace Smooth would be expendable also. In reality, Goldie planned to leave Smooth in that setting for the next week or so, or however long it would take for him to move a couple of cakes.

Now Shonda was a show piece, but she had four children. Which wasn't a problem for Goldie, he loved her children. He looked out for them, and from time to time he and Shonda would get together also. He was strength to her, and the help that she so desperately needed. He was also the type of man that she admired.

Now the way Shonda and Goldie met was rather ironic. One day Shonda's youngest son had gone down to the corner store, on the corner of Hale and Remsen. Goldie just happened to be out there talking to a fellow player by the name of Big Spence. The little fellow had walked up to them and asked them for a quarter. He said, "That he had been sent to the store for a loaf of bread, but he didn't have enough money." Goldie thought, it was rather ironic, because the kid couldn't have been a day over six years old. He had a little bag of candy in tow, and a mouth full of jawbreakers. Goldie reached into his jacket pocket and retrieved a twenty-dollar bill, which he handed to the kid. Then, he told the kid to take it to his mother. So she could hold on to it for him.

After which, the kid quickly disappeared from the street corner, and Goldie went back to the conversation that he was engaged in.

Now about five minutes or so later, Shonda had appeared on the scene with little man in tow. She approached Goldie, excused herself and asked, 'If she could talk to him.'

Goldie replied, "Sure, what's on your mind?"

Big Spence excused himself and had walked away toward the entrance of the corner store.

Shonda stood there displaying the twenty-dollar bill, and asked, "Did you give this to my son?"

Goldie smiled as he gave her the once over and replied, "Yes, I did. Is there a problem?"

"Well, yes, and no. Why would you give a child a twenty-dollar bill? People do not usually do things like that without an ulterior motive."

He smiled, "Well, let's just say that I've been asking questions. I hear things, and I knew you would come. By the way, I'm Goldie."

"Well, Goldie, I'm Shonda {she smiled}, and said, "I've heard a lot about you," while given him the once over. "We considered you to be a mystery man around here."

Goldie replied, "Is that so?"

Shonda's son interjected, "Mommy, is he going to be our father?"

She turned to her son and just looked at him, as if –

Goldie broke the silence and the intense stare by waving a hand between both of them and simply saying, "Earth to Shonda, Shonda to earth," and after regaining her attention. He continued, "I would like to get to know you better. Can I give you a ride somewhere or do anything for you?"

She smiled, and although somewhat still embarrassed about the question that her son asked. She replied, "I'll be fine," and had informed him that she lived right there on Hale Street, a few houses up from the corner store.

He retrieved her house and telephone number and told her that he would stop by her place later on that evening, and Shonda has been with him every since.

Now, after Goldie had dropped Smooth off at Shonda's place. He decided to stop by the flower shop on Commercial and Suydam to do something nice for Carla, she had been heavy on his mind.

As Goldie entered into the flower shop, he immediately noticed the tigress behind the sales counter. That was one of the things he hated about flower shops. They always had some beautiful young woman behind the sales counter that he could not hit on, due to him being there to purchase something for some other woman.

After making his way through the small shop, and taking time out to admire a few of the floral arrangement. He decided that it was time for him to meet the tigress.

As he approached the sales counter the young woman showed him her perfect whites, and politely said, "Hello, how can I help you, today?"

Goldie returned her smile and said, "I'll have a dozen of you."

This time she smiled, shyly.

He asked, "Where have you been all of my life? You are a doll."

She replied, "Thank you."

He looked down into her eyes, "And just what is your name, beautiful?"

She felt herself blush with embarrassment, "Its Sherry."

"Well, Sherry, I'm Goldie, and just how long have you been in love with flowers?"

"Goldie, I have always loved flowers, but this is far from a career choice. I have only been working here for the last couple of months or so. I'm a student at Rutgers, and I work here when I'm not in school."

He asked, "What are you majoring in?"

She placed her hands out on to the counter top before him revealing her nicely done finger nails, and replied, "Political Science."

"So, you would like to change the world, huh?"

"Well, I don't think that's possible, but one day. I would like to be able to say that I made a difference."

Goldie smiled, "Wouldn't we all, Baby, wouldn't we all."

Sherry asked, "Can I get you anything."

He looked into her eyes intensely and replied, "Look, Sherry, if you and I are to have something, I would like for it to begin in honesty. I have a confession, I have been watching you come in and out of this flower shop for the last ten days or so. Today, I just decided that I had to meet you at any cost." He reached over and retrieved a memo-pad and pen off the counter top and began to write as he spoke. "I would like you to take two dozen white, long stem roses, and send one dozen to this address, no card. He handed her the note pad with Carla's address on it, but the pad did not reveal Carla's name or telephone number."

{He continued.}, "It's my mother's birthday. She will know who the roses are from. The second dozen is for you. I want you to take the flowers home with you and promise to think about me, and now that I know, I'm welcome here on a more intimate level concerning you. I'll see you again, is that cool?"

Sherry smiled, "Of course, I'll think about you. How can I not, and I would love to see you again. Thank you."

After paying the young woman for the flowers, Goldie turned and walked out of the flower shop, leaving her speechless.

Sherry stood there deep in thought, wondering where he had been all of her life.

All of a sudden her thoughts were interrupted by a customer who was trying to gain her attention for the last –ten seconds or so.

She said, "Oh, I'm sorry, how can I help you?"

The customer replied, "I would like to purchase these few items."

She smiled, "That's not a problem, and again, I'm sorry."

Now Goldie chose the white roses for purity and sensuality, but more so for the beauty in the three of them, Carla, Sherry, and the roses themselves. Yes, these were the three things they all shared in common.

Goldie sat behind the wheel of his Caddie, thinking, 'why me,' but he knew somebody had to do it, and he wouldn't have it any other way. He pulled his Caddie away from the flower shop and proceeded on his way to the downtown projects. He had to see Charles to get things in motion. He snatched his car –telephone, and got Theresa on the line. He spoke in to the receiver, "Hey Baby."

She replied, "Hey Goldie."

"Look here, Baby, get those things together for me. It's time, I was thinking about the conversation we had last night. I think you should stop by the Family Learning Center, and pick up some-sort of birth-control, because we are in no position to have children."

"Okay, Goldie, if you think that's best for our situation."

"It is, Baby, it is. Hey, I got -to run."

Theresa asked, "Will I see you later?"

He replied, "Wild animals couldn't keep me away."

The line went dead.

Foot-note {coded conversation}, Smooth, would be at the Family Learning Center to pick up the package{drugs}.

Chapter Six

AT a branch of the First Fidelity Bank, in Marlboro, Carla sat in a rather elaborate office behind a large oak desk. She was looking through a few files that were on top of her desk, but Goldie seemed to be all that she was able to think about. She removed the gold-rimmed glasses that she was wearing and reared back into her desk chair and lost herself in thought about him. She didn't know what to think, and he hadn't called or anything.

All of a sudden, Hank, Carla's boss, had entered into the office in his usual, feminine, gestured way carrying new customer's individual case files. Still, upon seeing Carla, he immediately asked, "Are you alright?"

Carla mustered up a slight smile and replied, "I'm fine, thank you. Why, do you ask?"

He placed the file down on to her desk top, "Well, this morning it seemed that you had the glow of love, now you seem to be unsure. It seems you have some sort of doubt. Look at you; you're deep in thought as we speak."

Carla asked, "Hank, do you really think I'm that transparent?"

At that moment, Jill a co-worker {and friend} who was sitting there ease dropping in the office. She placed her ink-pen down on to her desk top, and slid her desk chair out from underneath her desk into a position where she could join the both of them in conversation.

Hank turned and looked over in her direction –

Carla also looked over at her, and asked, "Well, Jill is it that obvious?"

Jill smiled, "Carla, now sister girl, you know that you haven't been yourself the last couple of days or so, not only is it obvious. Why, not, just give it up and come clean."

Carla rolled her eyes at Jill, and then she stood and began clearing her desk for the day."

As she placed the contents of her desk into various draws, she replied, "And just what do the two of you know about love, anyway."

Jill took both of her hands and turned them inward toward herself, "Who me, what do I know about love."

There was a pause of silence.

Carla looked over at her and said, "Jill, you're divorced," then she looked over at Hank, "And you –

Hank interrupted her immediately, and snapped his finger with each word that he stated, he said, "Missy, don't you dare."

Carla smiled, as she reached down and retrieved her briefcase from down a-long side her desk, and said, "Look, I know your concerns are genuine, and the two of you are my closes-friends {a staring match had ensued between the three of them}.

{She continued}, "Well, I better run, it's been a-long day."

Hank asked, "Will I see you tomorrow."

As she began making her way toward the exit of the office, she replied, "Of course."

Jill looked over at Hank and said, "I still can't believe she asked us that question. She recited the question, mockingly, "What do the two of you know about love, anyway."

Carla, overhearing Jill, as she made her way through the office exit, she turned and looked back at her and stated, "Jill, it was a rhetorical question."

Mean while as Goldie stepped on to Theresa's doorstep, he removed his small key ring and opened the front door to her place.

As he entered the apartment, he noticed Theresa sitting there on the sofa, watching television, in the living room. She had a silk sheet laid across her lap.

Goldie thought, 'that's exactly what she felt like inside' {silk}.

Theresa asked, "How was your day?"

He replied, "Baby in my line of business, it can always be better. Then again, I believe that's my incentive to wake up every morning."

She smiled, "I laid your bathrobe and slippers out for you. If you're hungry, I can put you some-thing into the microwave."

As he made his way over to the sofa and kissed her on the forehead, he replied, "Baby, I'm not hungry, I ate something a little while ago."

Theresa stood up off of the sofa and said, "Okay, then I'll run you a hot bath."

Goldie smiled, "Baby, make it a shower."

She left the room to get everything set-up and ready for her man's shower. He stood there watching her as she left the room, thinking, 'Life sure is grand.'

After-which, he walked into the bedroom and removed his clothing. He slipped on his bathrobe and slippers, and headed for the shower. He wasn't in the shower two minutes before Theresa had slowly eased the shower door open, and joined him underneath a pulsating showerhead. He placed her in front of him and watched the water as it began to travel in and around the curves of her beautiful body.

She stood there, seductively.

Goldie thought, 'Wow,' as he felt his mind and body begin to come alive.

She moved toward him and began to kiss him around his neck and down his chest.

He moaned, and as he began to run his fingertips, gently, across her back. Theresa kissed him on his navel, and before he knew it. She had taken him deep within the warmth of her mouth.

Goldie exclaimed, "Ahhhhhhh –Baby," as he began to run his finger's through her hair. He loved it when she took the lead in their sexual escapades. It excited him.

After a few moments, he pulled her up to him and placed her hands on to the wall beneath a pulsating shower head. He arched her back, and slid down deep inside of her from behind, and as the water had began to run through her hair and down her back. He began to ride her-like Roy Rogers rode Trigger, hard, long, steady, and fast.

That evening when Carla got in from work, she decided to take a nice hot bubble bath, have a glass of wine, and catch up on some long overdue reading. She was in the bathtub fulfilling that planned evening when all of a sudden the doorbell rang. She thought 'Goldie,'

it had to be him. Carla jumped up out of the bathtub, grabbed her bathrobe, and rushed through the living room into the kitchen, where she stopped and got herself together before making her way around the table to the rear door of her condominium. She opens the door, and to her surprise, there stood the delivery man from the flower shop. Carla's face displayed her disappointment, and yet, she was relieved at the same time.

After the delivery man had given her the once over, he said, "I have a delivery for this address, there's no card. Will you sign for it?"

Carla, sighed, and replied, "Yes," as she walked over to the kitchen table to retrieve a pen, and a couple of dollars out of her purse to show her appreciation.

After the transaction, the delivery man thanked her and handed her the box.

She closed the door behind him and held the box close to her heart for a few moments, then she rushed over to the kitchen table where she opened the box, and to her surprise. The box contained twelve, long stemmed, white roses. She thought they're beautiful {no one had ever sent her roses before}. She rushed over to the kitchen window to see if she would see Goldie's car. She didn't see it, but she knew that the flowers were from him.

After showering, Goldie and Theresa retired to the bedroom, where she now laid with her head on his chest. She was listening to his heartbeat. She laid there wondering what made him tick. She also wondered what she could do to have him fall deeply in love with her. She felt as though she had run out of options. She had tried everything, and was willing to do anything.

Now it wasn't that Goldie didn't love his women. Hell, he was crazy about them, but even more important, he knew what he had to do to keep them. He knew that women loved strength, a man who could pay the bills, if not with his money, with hers, but with his thinking. He knew that they needed love and guidance, but even more important, he knew that they wanted to be understood. They are the most emotional-animals on the planet and everything they needed he represented.

Goldie broke the silence. He asked, "Theresa, are you awake?"

She raised her head off of his chest and looked up into his eyes. She replied, "Yes, I was just lying here, thinking."

He asked, "And just what were you thinking about?"

Theresa smiled and replied, "Us, Goldie."

"Well, let's think about us together, but later. Right now, I would like to talk about Jose and what I intend to do.

She asked, "What's your plan?"

He smiled, "I plan to act as if I know nothing. I plan to act, none the wiser, as he is since the day we met. I also plan to thank him for the gift, and in the future. I want you to continue to play your role, and any gifts, advancements, anything. I want it immediately communicated to me. I have a plan."

Theresa asked, "So Goldie, what's the plan?"

He replied, "None the wiser, Baby, none the wiser."

After a few moments, Goldie set up in thought on to the edge of the large bed.

Theresa asked, "Baby, are you okay?"

He leaned back on to the bed and kissed her on the forehead, he replied, "Baby, I'm fine. I'm going out into the living room to sit in my easy chair. I have a few telephone calls to make, and it seems to be a beautiful evening to do some thinking.

Mean-while, Carla was lying in bed playing with and admiring her roses, when the telephone rang. She reached over on to the nightstand and picked up the receiver and heard the voice that she had been dying to hear.

He said, "Hey, Doll, how are you?"

Carla replied, "Oh, I'm fine, and you?."

Goldie smiled, "Well, Angel, I'm a whole lot better now; that I've heard your voice."

She seductively, replied, "I got the roses that you sent, and they're simply beautiful. Thank you."

"Hey.., A rose for a rose. Listen, I want to talk to you about Saturday."

Carla interjected, "I knew the roses were for something other than you just being a romantic. You can't make it, Saturday, can you?"

There was a pause of silence.

Goldie wanted her to waddle in her thoughts for a few

moments, then he replied, "Sure I can, hell, I called you because I need you for the whole day. I have something planned can you take off?"

She smiled, a sigh of relief, "Well, hell, I've gotten sick before."

"Very good then, I will see you Saturday morning, your place or mine?"

"Mine, Goldie."

"Okay, Baby, I have to run. I'll talk to you later."

The line went dead.

Chapter Seven

DESPITE not sleeping well the night before, Goldie rose early the next morning and while Theresa slept. He slipped into a sweatsuit and hit the park in the development in which she lived. Goldie loved calisthenics; he worked out in his spare time. He believed that every man should be prepared for battle at all times, and if he had to go to war. He didn't want to be the one to get tired.

When Goldie arrived back at the apartment, Theresa was up and had made a nice hardy breakfast. She had noticed Goldie's car still out in the parking lot.

As he had entered into the archway of the kitchen, he said, "Good Morning, Baby."

Theresa looked up from the task of washing dishes and replied, "Good Morning."

He stood there for a few moments, admiring her, and then said, "By the way, I thought you should know, how wonderful you were last night."

Theresa smiled, "You have to realize who I was working with."

He returned her smiled, "You know what, Baby, that totally slipped my mind."

She asked, "Goldie, would you like something to eat?"

He replied, "I'll have my regular after a nice hot shower."

She walked over to the kitchen table and placed a plate, cup, glass, and a set of utensils down on to the tabletop and said, "I figured when you finished your showering, that I would warm your breakfast in the microwave and set it out for you."

Goldie disappeared into a nice hot shower and afterward had returned fully dressed to a beautiful breakfast, waffle's sausage, and eggs along with juice and coffee. That was his favorite.

After breakfast, as Theresa began to clear the kitchen table, Goldie made his way in to the living room to read the morning edition of the Home News. When he was done, he set the News Paper back down on to the coffee table, and walked over and opened the blinds.

After which, he sat back down in his easy-chair, he just sat there looking out through blinds that shielded a large picture window, and after a few moments, Goldie called out, "Come here, Baby."

Theresa appeared almost instantly. She eased up beside him in his easychair and replied, "Yes, Goldie."

"Baby, I want you to look around yourself, and then I want you to take a look out of these here blinds."

Theresa replied, "Goldie, what."

He didn't say anything; he just sat there looking out through the blinds.

After taking a look around the, elegantly, decorated room, brass, glass, and various types of African artifacts. She placed a hand on to her shapely hip and had giving him an inquisitive smile. She said, "Come on, Goldie, what is it that you want me to see?"

He smiled slyly, "Hey, that this shit ain't half bad."

Theresa returned his smile and eased around in front of him and sat down on to his lap, and had giving him a big hug.

Goldie asked, "What's that for?"

She looked intensely into his eyes and replied, "It's because I remember, where, and what, we've come from, and all that it took to get where we are today. Goldie, today, I appreciate it, and I owe it all to you."

He leaned forward and kissed her on the forehead, "Baby, do you know the sad part about it all.., I appreciate.., I love.., but I cherish nothing. I'll leave here, today, knowing the price of everything, and everyone, but the value of nothing. However, I do have to give you credit, you have made me aware of a-lot of things. I also want you to know that it's because of you that I'm beginning to come around. Today, I can honestly say that I truly value your friendship, your honesty, and your loyalty. Hell, I remember when you had a snotty nose and a face full of tears. Scared to death of that big old world out there, Do you remember?"

Theresa placed a playful finger on to the tip of his nose and smiled, "Yeah, I remember the day that we met."

"Baby, I want you to know, I'm proud of you, and it gives me great pleasure to say, today, sitting in my lap is a woman. I'm as proud of you as I' am of my work, you're a master piece, and I'm so glad that I got the opportunity to play a part in the making of you. Baby, I got -to go to work."

Theresa rose so that he could stand.

He said, "Okay, its Friday, big money day. Let's get it on. I'll make the necessary calls on the road. You know the drops."

As he walked over and removed his jacket from the living room closet, and began to make his way to the door to leave. Theresa, who had been standing there in the room watching him closely the whole time, called out, "Goldie." He stopped and turned to face her before leaving the room.

She said, "Thanks."

Goldie turned and walked out of the door. He knew that it had all been said, and he also knew that she had earned it.

On the outside of Theresa's place, Goldie jumped behind the wheel of his Caddie, and as it warmed up. He placed Freddie Jackson into the player {Good Morning, Heart ache}. He listened to the words, Freddie said, "I see you're back in town, as in the heart ache. What's new, as in it being a continuing thing? He always played music like that when he was open when he was into the sensitive of the man behind the mask.

Goldie thought, 'Well, let me put this shit a-side because this shit sure don't pay no bills.'

At that moment, he reached over and turned off the radio in the car, and had began to back out of his parking spot.

Now Theresa was watching Goldie through the kitchen window as he sat there in the parking lot. Her thoughts verbalized, and in a low voice, she said, "I got me a real man." She only wished that she had told him that during their conversation, however, she knew it was too late then. So she decided to get the things together that she would need. She also knew that it wouldn't be long before she would have received her que (call) from Goldie.

Mean while Goldie had been riding in silence for the last few minutes or so. Then, all of a sudden, he put on his war face, for it was time to do battle. He pumped himself and reached over and snatched his car telephone. He dialed a telephone number, and after a few moments, Smooth's voice came over the line. He spoke into the telephone receiver, "It's your dime."

Goldie knew that it was Smooth, and Smooth knew it was Goldie by way of what was said. Goldie said, "Go," and the line went dead {Go –meant; go to your designated pick up spot, and you had twenty minutes to get there, and wait}.

Goldie dialed another telephone number, and a few moments later. Charles came over the line, he said, "Yes," which is a helluva way to answer a telephone, but through that Goldie knew that it was him. He repeated the same procedure, he said, "Go," and the line went dead.

Goldie dialed another telephone number, and a few seconds

later. Tony came over the horn. He said, "Hello." Goldie caught the voice, and repeated the same procedure, he said, "Go." and the line went dead.

Goldie dialed another telephone number, and after the telephone had rung a few times. Finally, Mark picked up the receiver. He said, "Hello," his voice sounded as if he had just waking up. Goldie repeated the same procedure, he said, "Go," and the line went dead. Then, he got Theresa on the line, and when she answered. He repeated the same procedure, "Go," and the line went dead.

After Goldie's telephone call to Theresa, she was left in thought, but it didn't stand in the way of her getting the things she needed together and preparing to make her drops. She knew when Goldie was out there in that life. He was in a world of his own. So she promised herself the next time that she got the opportunity. She would tell him all of the things that she wanted him to know, that being the things of her heart.

Mean while Goldie had got Cathy on the line. He said, "Hey Chick, what's happening?"

She replied, "Ain't nothing, just preparing for the day.. It's Friday, and you know it's going to be busy."

As he turned the large car out into the traffic of Route Eighteen off Commercial Avenue. He smiled to himself and said, "Hey, it's good to know that you're on the ball. I called to let you know that I've made the necessary calls. It won't be long now. Are you ready?"

Cathy smiled as she reached over and retrieved her coffee cup off of the kitchen table, "Goldie, you see to that."

"Okay, Baby, let me get out of your hair, then. I'm gone."

The line went dead.

Now Goldie didn't have any other plans at the moment, so he

decided to take a ride to his hideout, check a local P.O Box, and get things ready for the following day, Saturday. He thought, 'finally, he would have some time for himself.'

Once inside of the hideout, he turned on the light switch and began to look through his mail, and to his surprise. There was a letter from a good friend, who also happens to be a fellow player. He walked over and placed his keys down on to the dining room table. Then, he stepped off into his sunken living room, where he made himself comfortable in his easy chair and began to read the letter, which read.

Hey, Big Brother,

I just thought, 'I would check in with you. I wanted you to know the storm is over, and the weather is fine. I'm waiting on you.'

Hollywood.

Now Hollywood was a fellow player from the South, he had a beautiful setup and a pretty thriving business, but it was difficult for him to keep that thing {drugs}. It wasn't because drugs are difficult to get in this country. However, longevity in this game stems from thinking, the right connections, and precise moves.

Now, this is where Goldie came in, he would furnish the entire operation. He brought Jose in because he was going to use him to do it. He figured he would make a little money, hell; everybody would make a little money.

Goldie was happy that he caught this kite (letter) before he met with Jose because he had just come up with his exit plan out of the game.

After looking through the remainder of the mail, Goldie made his way into the bedroom where he placed a DVD into the player. Then, he laid back across his king-size, water bed, thinking of a way to perfect his plan.

Chapter Eight

WHEN Goldie had awakened that afternoon to his surprise, he had slept the majority of the day, away. It was ten after four in the afternoon, and he knew that Carla would be pulling in from work at any moment. He really didn't want to see her until the following day. He didn't want to start anything that he couldn't finish. He wanted their first actual-get together to be special, of quality, and in a large quantity of time. He still had a few ends that he needed to tighten-up. So he washed up a bit, brushed his teeth, and grabbed his jacket. He figured that he would make a run for it.

On the outside of the hideout, Goldie backed his car out of his parking spot. He believed he would never make it out of the area without seeing Carla, and no sooner than he reached the end of the development-in-passing. She pulled her car up a-long side of him.

Goldie smiled as he let his car window down and said, "Hey Beautiful."

Carla showed him her whites, "Hi, Goldie."

He asked, "What's going on?"

She placed her chin on to her arm on the car door and peered over at him. She replied, "Oh, nothing, I'm just getting in from work. I was going to ask you the same thing."

"Well, I have a few runs to make after-which, I plan to rest up for our outing tomorrow
{ Saturday }."

All of a sudden, Carla got out of her car, and walked over and stuck her head into Goldie's car window and kissed him on the cheek. She said, "Thank you for the flowers, they are beautiful."

After the kiss, Goldie's body had began to turn warm, he watched her closely and replied, "They aren't as half as beautiful as you are."

Carla was wearing a sweater dress that fit every curve of her shapely body.

She felt herself, blush, with embarrassment, she said, "Why, thank you."

After sitting there admiring her for a few moments, Goldie felt the dress she was wearing had forced his hand. He asked, "How about a nightcap?"

Carla smiled at the thought of this prospect, she had been literally standing there holding her breath. Finally, she exhaled and replied, "I thought you would never ask."

He returned her smile, "Yeah, okay, I'll stop by your place upon my return."

She replied, "I'll be expecting you."

After a few moments of an awkward staring session, Carla got back into her car and continued on her way home from work.

Goldie sat there in his car for a few moments, thinking, 'Damn, I'm in love.' Carla was the only woman he had ever met, that increased his heart rate, and made his palm sweat.

When Goldie got into town that evening, his first stop was Shonda's place. He parked his car a block over and walked around to the house. He made his way to the back door, where he removed his small key ring and opened the door to the basement.

As he entered the basement, he found Smooth standing on the other side of the door with his pea-shooter in hand {gun}.

Goldie asked, "What's up, man? How's it coming?"

Smooth closed and locked the steel door behind him, and then he concealed his weapon into the small of his back. He replied, "Oh, it's been coming."

Goldie stood there for a few moments looking around the spacious room, with all of the architectural ideals he once had concerning the basement. Then, he looked over to his right into the only furnished area of the room.

Smooth walked over and took a seat on the sofa beside and end table. That held a lamp, and a forty ounce bottle of beer, unopened {rap music played, lowly}.

Goldie looked over at him intensely and said, "Smooth, I want you to lose the beer; I need you to be fully alert and able to think in this situation. I also want you to lose the music because I don't want your judgment impaired if something should happen. Right now, you need to be able to hear everything around you."

As Smooth got up off of the sofa, he retrieved the bottle of beer off the end table. Then, he walked over and turned off the radio.

{Goldie continued}, "Alright, let's shut it down, and get out of here. Let's walk and talk."

After locking the basement door behind them, Goldie and Smooth walked down toward Remsen Avenue, and it seemed that everybody knew Goldie. "Hey, Goldie, What's up, Goldie, Hey Player, and so on."

As they made their way down the avenue, Goldie decided to give Smooth, some more of this thing called game. He noticed two guys standing out on the corner in front of the Some Where Else Bar. He called Smooth's attention to them and asked, "Do they get high?"

Smooth replied, "Yeah, Goldie, you know who that is."

Goldie smiled, "That's beside the point. I asked you, 'did they get high.' My point is: If they get high, they scheme and rob. So you need to be a step ahead of them at all times."

As they approached the bar, Goldie removed two twenty-dollar bills off of his bankroll, and asked the two gentlemen "What's up, Player's?"

One of the gentlemen, replied, "Hey, hey, Goldie, what's going on, and what brings you out here tonight?"

The other gentlemen nodded.

Goldie said, cheerfully, "The same thing that brings you out here, trying to shred my oats. You guys know my man Smooth, don't you?"

The gentlemen replied, "Yeah, but we had no idea that he was your man."

Goldie smiled, "Yeah, that's my man. Look here, here's a little something for you guys."

As they entered the bar, Goldie handed each of them a twenty-dollar bill. Then, he and Smooth overheard the two gentlemen rapping on, and one of them said, "Goldie's fly as hell." The other, "That's my man."

Now on the inside of the bar, Goldie and Smooth grabbed a couple of stools at the bar, and people had immediately begun to come over and to talk with him. They were offering him drinks. Fellow players were asking, "When they were going to hang out, and it seemed as though every woman in the bar was either waving or winking at him.

When the barmaid spotted Goldie, she showed him her whites from a far and rushed right over to take his order. She placed her hands on to her hips, looking at him seductively, and said, "Hey, Stranger."

Goldie smiled, "Doll, what does a man have to do around here to get a drink?"

She placed her hands down on to the bar and looked into his eyes intensely. "Goldie, don't you start no shit with me, tonight. You know, I would have you do some real freaky shit."

He returned her intent look, "Yeah, if, given the opportunity, I bet you would."

She eased a little closer to him over the bar and said, "I would."

Goldie eased back on his barstool in acceptance of what had obviously turned out to be a stalemate. He replied, "Give everyone my warmest regards."

{which actually meant, give everyone a drink, compliments of Big Goldie}

After everyone had been served a drink in the small semi-crowded bar, Doll the barmaid returned to Goldie for payment, and as she placed Smooth and Goldies drinks down on to the bar before them. She said, "You got off rather cheap, tonight. The damage is only two hundred and thirty dollars."

As he handed Doll, two hundred and fifty dollars in three bills, he replied, "These are my people and for my people. I can never do enough."

When she returned with his change, he told her to keep it. Cause she sure as shit couldn't have him.

Doll smiled.

Goldie tapped Smooth and said, "Let's get out of here."

One the outside of the bar, Smooth asked, "Why did you just do all of those things, and just get up and leave." Goldie told him to walk and talk, because there were a few people around and Goldie knew that this thing called game wasn't for everybody.

{He continued}, "Smooth the forty dollars {two twenties} was nothing. I hit those guys off {gave them the money} because I would rather have a ruthless joker on my side than against me. It was also an opportunity to make my presence known in that which you do in the area. So they won't scheme, rob, or play games with you. If they want something from you, they will ask you. Now depending upon how you treat the people will determine how long you last, and even more important -how they will treat you. Now, whenever I'm out in the bars in this area, people always want to buy me drinks. So now and then, it's only right that I give back. With moves like that, you will have people protecting you that don't even know you. Someone can say, I don't like Goldie, and a guy that I don't even know, who got one of those drinks or that I was kind to, will say, "Goldie's cool as hell, you just have to get to know him. "Smooth, you have to pay to play. The only solution for needing is to give, and you receive out of everything that which you put into it.

As Goldie and Smooth made their way down the street from the bar, Smooth asked, "Are you going back around to the house." Goldie pointed a finger over toward his car in the distance. He replied, "Nah, I'm parked right here up the street. Smooth, call in, I want you to have one more pack. Plus, what you already have, knock it dead {get rid of it}, and shut down until tomorrow morning. I want you to go home, hang out, whatever, but I want you to do some thinking. I want you to digest some of this pimpin. Hey Man, all of this shit is real. What you know out here in these streets can determine whether you live or die. Oh, and Smooth, I'll see you in a few days you will have to call in for what you want in the morning. After then, its back to the basics, turn in, to get, same procedure."

Smooth smiled to himself, as he extended a hand in Goldie's direction, he listened, attentively, and as always Goldie's lessons were very pleasing to his ears.

Goldie accepted his hand and pulled him into an embrace. He

replied, "I'm counting on you, player. Hold the fort down, I have to run, later."

Goldie got into his car and drove off for the hideout; he knew that Carla would be waiting on him. He snatched his car telephone and got Theresa on the line.

Now when Theresa received Goldie's telephone call, she was sitting in the living room, in his easy chair, with soft music playing while looking through a few of the photo albums that she had accumulated in reference to the both of them and quality time spent together.

Goldie gave her instructions for the next couple of days to carry out in his absence, and then, he cleared the line.

Theresa sat there in his easy chair, holding the telephone alongside of her beautifully oval -shaped face. She was hoping that he knew how much she really loved and needed him.

After a few moments, she reached over and placed the cordless telephone down on to the end table, and had reverted back to the photo albums that lay upon her lap. There were all types of photographs of the two of them that ranged in span from inside to outside of the Country. We are talking, Maine to Florida, resorts, beachfronts, beaches, hot air balloon rides, and the rental of small private planes concerning travel, often. There were action parks, party boats, dinner on boats, shows, museums, protest rallies, and various marches throughout a variety of cities. There were also Casino's, in Las Vegas, and Atlantic City, and they had eaten just about everywhere. Theresa often reverted back to her past experiences and collectable-items concerning time spent with Goldie, she believed that this was one way for her to always remain close to him, even in his absence.

Chapter Nine

GOLDIE stood out on the steps of Carla's condominium, wondering what type of evening he would encounter once inside. He reached out and rung the doorbell.

Now Carla stood on the other side of the door, and watched Goldie through her kitchen window, as he had pulled his car into the parking lot, and parked. She didn't want to seem anxious, so she stood there for a few moments to regain her compos-her. She opened the door.

He smiled at the sight of her, "Hey, Baby."

Carla returned his smile, "Hi,

Goldie, I've been expecting you."

On the inside, she took Goldie's hand and led him through the kitchen into the living room. She said, "Make yourself comfortable."

He walked over and took a seat on the sofa.

Now Carla was wearing a pair of jeans that looked like they were painted on, the T-shirt that she wore revealed her breast in all of their firmness, and her nipples stood out like eyes.

Goldie thought, 'God, she's beautiful.'

Carla broke the silence as she walked over to the bar in the well-kept room. She asked, "What will you have?"

He eased back on to the sofa, making himself more comfortable and replied, "Well, now, I guess that would depend on the stock that you have behind the bar for me to choose from, besides the obvious."

She caught his pitch and smiled, "Well, besides the obvious, beer, vodka, rum, and gin. I have a nice Cognac, Sherri, several different types of wine, and a beautifully aged, bottle of champagne for a special occasion."

Goldie replied, "Well, personally, I don't believe there could be a more special occasion than a setting with me in it."

Carla reached down behind the bar along the back wall and opened the small refrigerator where she retrieved the bottle of champagne from. Then, she pushed the play button on the CD player beside the small refrigerator that was encased in a shelf of stereo components. Immediately the room filled with the sounds of Smokey Robinson {Let me be your clock}, and as she made her way around the bar carrying the bottle of champagne and two long-stemmed crystal glasses. She noticed Goldie making his way around the living room table in dance mode, the swaying of his hips, the displaying of arm movement, and working toward her with a two-step, in a grind like motion {kind of rolling his body}.

Carla's expression clearly revealed her shock. She froze and said, "Oh, my God."

Goldie met her in the middle of the living room floor, where he removed the bottle of champagne and the glasses from her hands.

She watched him curiously as he walked over and placed the items down on to the living room table, and made his way back over to where she was standing. He took her hands in his, and looked down into her eyes and said, "Wow, Baby, how did you know? I' am definitely an oldies freak, and Smokey Robinson is one of my favorites.

She smiled, "I, too, love the oldies, and Smokey is my favorite."

Goldie said, "Well, you should have no problem with a dance move like this one. He began the swaying of his hips from one side to the other.

Carla, felt herself blush with embarrassment, as she stood there watching the movement of his hips.

He raised her hands about shoulder high, and looked down at her hips and said, "Come on, Baby, work with me."

As she began to imitate his dance moves, she looked up in to his eyes and replied, "Okay, Goldie, I'm game. You got me."

He stood there holding her hands in dance mode watching the swaying of her hips, he said, in a playful manner, "That's it, Baby, you got it"

Carla broke out into light laughter.

He pulled her into an embrace and kissed her on the forehead.

At that moment, Goldie felt like if the world were to have just stopped. He would have been right where he wanted to be in the end.

After dancing with Goldie, Carla excused herself for a few moments. She left the room to retrieve a tray of hors-d"oeuvre's that she had prepared for the evening.

Goldie stood there in the middle of the living room floor, admiring her as she left the room. Then he walked over and retrieved the bottle of champagne off the living room table, and sat back down on to the sofa.

When Carla returned to the living room, she placed the tray of hors-d"oeuvre's down on to the living room table.

Goldie rose as she approached, and the two of them sat down on to the sofa together. He figured that he would get her tipsy to get the real woman out from behind the mask.

After he had given the champagne bottle the once over, he popped the cork on the bottle and said, "Now this is an exquisite bottle of champagne."

Carla smiled, revealing, she was pleased that he was pleased.

As he filled their glasses with champagne, he said, "Okay, it's obvious that we share the same taste in music and similar taste in the area of the grapes {wine}. Now you've got me curious as to what we will find next in each other that we share in the area of commonalities. We should drink to commonalities. They tapped glasses."

That evening the two of them had talked up a storm, Goldie toasted everything and after a few trips to the bar. They both ended up with their groove on.

Now Carla was the first woman that Goldie really felt that he could be himself around, but then again, Goldie thought, 'It might be that damn liquor talking.' In reality, he knew what he felt was no more than the truth, but that was just how his mind worked. He questioned everything and believed you were dead when you stopped asking why.

Goldie had learned to trust his heart long ago; he knew that the mind spent a lot of time trying to manipulate it. Think about it if you were ever in love with someone. It was in your heart, not in your head, and the things that man takes to heart. He will die for. The heart is the center of man's thinking, and Goldie knew that his heart would never stir him wrong.

The evening went beautiful, there were no complaints on either end. They laughed and talked, and had shared their points of view on a variety of different topics. The last commonality of the evening lay in protest novels concerning the black experience and situations here in this country, Richard Wright, Chester Himes, James Baldwin, etc.

Goldie sat there on the sofa knowing that this evening had to end. As he stood, he pulled Carla up beside himself and looked down into her eyes and said, "I had a wonderful time tonight."

Carla smiled, "I did too."

As Goldie started toward the front door to leave, Carla

followed close behind him. He faked a little stagger that seemed to be more real than fake. She grabbed him and asked, "Are you okay?" He turned back to face her, their eyes met, he replied, "I'm fine," and the two of them stood there looking at each other for a few moments, and then she walked into his arms and hugged him.

Goldie eased out of the embrace and said, "Hey, I better go, I'll see you in the morning. Oh, and pack an outfit."

Carla asked, "Goldie, Where are we going?"

He smiled, "Trust me."

She smiled, "I do, Goldie, I do."

Goldie took her hand in his and led her to the front door, where they kissed. After which he disappeared out into the cool night air.

Carla hung heavy on Goldie's mind that night. He knew he was in love with her. He also believed he would have no problem convincing her that she was in love too. Then, he thought about how he would get her to be his wife, and to give up everything she knew, and understood, and possibly her life, if she chose to run away with him. Goldie had a plan, but he knew if he wanted to incorporate her into that plan. That it would take more time than anticipated before he would be able to make a clean break. Another thing that lingered in the back of Goldie's mind was all that they shared in common. He knew concerning infiltration with the Panther's the oppressor sent in white women. With Malcolm X the oppressor sent in one of our own. At that moment, he only hoped that it wouldn't be this woman that the oppressor had strategically placed into his life to bring him down.

Mean-while, Carla sat deep in thought about Goldie, on the sofa in the living room. She fought as long as she could against what she knew to be true. Finally, she admitted to herself 'that she was head over heals about Goldie.' After this, she retired to her bedroom for the evening.

Chapter Ten

THE sunset high in the sky above Belmar's Boat Basin, a slight wind factor, a beautiful day for sailing.

As Goldie pulled the large car into the parking lot of the basin and parked. Carla looked over at him and smiled as her mind filled with wonderment, and her lungs began to fill with sea air. She said, "Since you still haven't told me where we are going, is it okay that I assume we have arrived?"

He returned her smile and replied, "Baby, this is only the beginning, are you game?"

She replied enthusiastically, "Goldie, I'm game."

He got out of the car and walked around to the passenger side and opened the car door for her.

As Carla exited the car, she breathed the sea air into her lungs deeply while observing the scenery around her, the people moving with purpose, a variety of boats, and the vastness of the sea itself. She said, "Goldie, it's all so beautiful."

He smiled as he placed his shades on to his face and took her hand into his, "Baby, the next couple of days are not only going to be beautiful. They are going to be memorable. Trust me."

As the both of them made their way down along the peer, Carla got the opportunity to see some of God's creations out along the rear of various fishing boats that had lived in the underworld of the powerful, dark, dangerous, Yet, beautiful sea.

Now Carla was never a very big fan of water in such a large magnitude, and the activities of the peer made her feel rather nervous. She held on to Goldie's hand tightly. However, when with him, he made her feel as though she could do, handle, or get through, anything. She jumped at the sight of a large squid that was lying out on the peer at the rear of one of the boats. Goldie placed his arm around her waist and pulled her close to him.

"Que Posa Amigo," which meant, "What's happening, my man," Jose hollered this in the company of one of his full-figured women from the rear of his boat."

Goldie looked up at him from the peer and smiled. He replied, "So far, so good, and this is my lovely lady, Carla."

Jose placed his arm around his woman as he gave Carla the once over and said, "Hi Carla, and this is my lady, Carmen."

Carla showed him her whites and replied, "I'm pleased to meet the both of you."

Goldie interjected as he looked around at the size of Jose's new boat, he said, "Wow, now this is some boat, man, and a huge upgrade from the last one."

Jose smiled, "I still have the other boat. It's just that I had a guy dying for me to have this boat."

After that statement, Carla looked over at Jose, and then back over at Goldie.

There was a pause of silence.

{He con} Holding his hands out toward the both of them, "Let me get the help to retrieve your things out of the car, and then...let's get you both onboard."

Now Jose's boat was beautiful, an eighty seven-footer. It was classified as a small yacht. The boat slept eight, and the four rooms were located in the lower level of the boat, one room in each corner of the boat, although one room had been converted into a working office.

Now in between the rooms, there was a large area with a beautiful chandelier that hung overhead. There was a bar, an entertainment center, in the entertainment area, which consisted of an amplifier, tape deck, DVD, and CD player. There was also a large LED, screened television set, complete with video hook up, and all of the latest movies and video games. There was also a dining area and a small kitchen with a hired hand for this trip. The boat was loaded.

After boarding and touring the boat, Goldie and Carla went to their cabin to slip into something a little more comfortable. They watched each-other undress. He stood there on one side of the bed in his undershorts. She stood opposite him on the other side of the bed in her panties and bra. She watched Goldie as he went through the things that he brought on board. She couldn't help feeling the excitement that he brought about in her, and after seeing his body, she just let her imagination run wild.

Now Goldie also peeped over at Carla and noticed that she was deep in thought, her eyes were fixed on him. Right then, he knew he had her, and that his callisthenic workout had paid off. He said, "Look at you such beauty should be painted, framed, and preserved for all time."

Carla smiled, shyly, as she felt herself blush with embarrassment.

Goldie thought, 'there are just no words for such a package,' as he crawled on all fours across the bed over to where she stood, and kissed her on the mouth, he said, "Come on, Baby, let's get you dressed and up on deck. I have something planned that I think you'll enjoy."

All of a sudden, the boat began to move. They were on their way out to the great beyond.

Carla said, "Goldie, I'm a little scared. I've never been out on a boat before."

He smiled, "There are a lot of things you haven't had the

opportunity to do that you are going to get to do for the first time with me. Would you like to know something new about me?"

Carla replied, "Yes, of course, Goldie, I would like to learn everything there is to know about you."

He eased up on to the edge of the bed and sat down before her. She felt a little awkward standing there before him in her panties and bra. He looked up into her eyes and said, "Baby, if I was scared of heights, I would climb. There is nothing like challenging fear and conquering it. It's the greatest accomplishment that one could ever hope to gain. This ability brings about great strength and courage, and Pumpkin I'll protect you from all things."

After Goldie and Carla had finished dressing in the lower level of the boat. He told her that he would race her upstairs to the deck, and they took off.

When Goldie stepped out on to the deck, he quickly turned around to face her and a moment or so later. Carla ran right in too his arms and said, "Goldie, that wasn't fare you took off running before you said, "Go." He chuckled as he kissed her on the forehead, and then he looked down into her eyes intensely and replied, "Baby, there is no competition between us, just incentive, and learning. When I win, Chump, you win, you dig. She showed him her whites."

Now Goldie had taken Carla' and seated her out on deck alongside of the boat and then, he told her that he would return, and in a couple of minutes or so. He returned with a couple of fishing poles, and all of the accessories necessary to do some fishing.

Carla smiled, enthusiastically, and watched the things that he did very carefully. She had never done any type of fishing before. Goldie bated their hooks and placed both of their fishing lines out into the water. They made themselves comfortable and pursued a conversation based on the do's and don'ts of relationships while watching the passing sites, and waiting for the fish to bite.

Mean-while, Jose and Carmen were down in the lower level of the boat getting into one of their sexual escapades. It was like they couldn't keep their hands off of each other.

Jose and Goldie had decided to hold their meeting in the wee hours of the morning while the women slept. They both agreed on that time because they wanted to spend quality time with their ladies the first day out at sea. They didn't feel that the interruption would be good because the women didn't know each-other and the fact; that whenever women get together. They say the damndist things.

Now Goldie and Carla had remained out on the deck enjoying each other's company. He said, "Baby, you do know that I'm into something big, don't you."

Carla replied, "apprehensively, I kind of figured that much, Goldie."

He looked into her eyes, intensely, "I also want you to know that I would never try to pull the wool over your eyes, you haven't asked me any questions, so I haven't had to lie to you. I would like to keep it that way 'right now,' I feel that some things are just better left unsaid."

She placed a hand on to his thigh and said, "Goldie, I trust and respect you. Hell, right now, my life is in your hands. If you feel that's the best thing, I will honor your decision. I don't know if you noticed or not, but I really just want to be with you.

After that statement, there was a strike at Carla's fishing pole. Goldie instructed her to pick up the pole gently....Yet, to hold the pole firmly.

{He con.}, "Now when the fish pulls at your pole, again. I want you to give the pole some-what of a jerk back toward you, but only enough to hook the fish, and after the fish is hooked. I want you to keep tension on the line. Then we work to get the fish out of the water and on to the boat. He loosened the drag on her pole, and before he knew it. The fish had taken the bate and ran with it. The reel cried out, and Carla held on to the pole as if her life depended on it. She was so excited she hollered, "I got one! I got one! Help me, Goldie, help me!" He got behind her and put his arms around her, holding the fishing pole with her while he re-tightened the drag on the pole and instructed her to crank the reel.

Now Jose and Carmen were making their way on deck, wearing silk robes, pajamas, and slippers. They had heard Carla screaming and hollering; the higher-ed hand had appeared also. Carla was so excited, that they all just stood around this scene watching her in all of her glory.

Goldie said, "Okay, Baby, we've got to get the fish out of the water."

Now behind Carla's back, Goldie had signaled for Jose to start moving the boat toward the direction of the fish. Carla cranked, and she cranked that reel. All of a sudden, the fish broke water. It was a whopper! Her eye's got big, and she screamed out, "Oh, my God!"

It made Goldie feel good to be able to give such a thrill to another human being.

Once Carla got the fish along the side of the boat, the hired hand helped Goldie gig the fish and to get it onboard the boat. The fish still fought, it flapped, jumped, and splashed water all over Carla, she turned to Goldie with the thrill of winning in her eyes. She had never caught a fish before. He hugged her tightly and had given her a big victory kiss.

Jose hollered to the hired hand, "Champagne for everyone."

Carmen walked over and congratulated Carla on her catch.

After-which, Carla looked over at Goldie and said, "The fish looks helpless, let's, let him go." He placed his arm around her, looking out toward the sea and replied, "Baby, your wish is my command."

Now, as this conversation was going on, the hired hand returned with a tray filled with glasses of champagne. They all toasted Carla's first catch and then Goldie instructed the hired hand to release the fish back into the sea. The hired hand asked, "Are you sure that's about a six and a half pound, striped bass, and it would make for one helluva meal."

Goldie replied, "I'm not, but it's what my Baby's wishes."

After all the excitement had died down, Jose looked down at his watch, and it was, two, forty- five, in the afternoon, and both parties had forgotten all about their luncheon date. He informed Goldie that they would all meet after they had cleaned themselves up for a late lunch.

Now in the cabins that the two couples occupied, they were equipped with showers. Goldie and Carla stripped stark naked and showered together. In a lot -of acts, Goldie felt that he was building trust, but then realized that it had already been established. It was like they had known each other for a lifetime.

After getting themselves all cleaned up and dressed, they all met in the dining area of the boat. Goldie and Carla were already seated at the table when Jose and Carmen arrived. They rose as Jose and Carmen approached the table. Jose seated Carmen, Carla, sat as she did, and the two gentlemen had come down together.

Jose asked, in reference to Goldie and Carla, "How are both of you doing? Do you have everything you need? Are your quarter's to your like -in?"

Goldie smiled as he eased back into his chair at the table and looked over at Carla, and then he looked over at Jose and replied, "We are fine, however, for a moment there. I thought I might have to go looking for the two of you."

Jose placed his hands down on to the table in front of him and smiled, "Well, I would like to apologize for keeping the two of you waiting {he looked over at Carmen}. I was literally tied up, you understand."

Carmen blushed with embarrassment as she covered her mouth in gesture. They all broke out into lite-laughter at the table.

(He con.}, "So Carla, are you enjoying yourself?"

She looked over at Goldie intensely and replied, "I'm having the time of my life."

Jose sat there for a few moments watching the two of them making eyes at each other at the table.

As the hired hand made his way out to the table, he asked, "What type of drinks will you all be having with your meals."

Carla looked up from the eye contact with Goldie and replied, "I'll have a glass of white wine."

Carmen replied, "I'll have the same."

Goldie replied, "The same."

Jose looked over at the hired-hand and stated, "Since we all agree on white wine. I want you to bring out a bottle of the best that I have onboard."

They made small talk while waiting for their meals, which basically turned out to be seafood platters, fish, shrimps, scallops, and fried clams. There were also lobsters, king crab legs, a host of on-trays, and a variety of different sauces.

After the meal, Goldie and Carla retired to their cabin for a nap. They laid there in each others arms, filled with wonderment and curiosity about the love making that would take place later on that evening. Neither of them could fight back these feelings anymore, for it was destiny.

Mean-while, Jose and Carmen had made their way up on deck; however, something seemed to be troubling Jose, and Carmen couldn't figure it out for the life of her. Here was a man that had the world. He just stood there looking out at the water.

Carmen asked, "What's wrong, Baby, aren't you happy?"

He placed his hands out on to the railing of the boat and looked over at her intensely, and replied, "I'm fine, I'm also pleased about a lot of things, but baby, I'm not happy, and every time I'm around Goldie, he lets me know it. Did you see the fish they caught today? Did you see how they fed each other during the meal? Did you see how they raced around here all day? You see, he is me, and I am him, but there's something inside of him that I seem to be missing."

Carmen asked, "Don't you like Goldie?"

He gave her a sly grin, "Hell, he's like a brother, and he is one helluva teacher also.

He shows me everything that I'm doing wrong, and he shows me by way of example."

She showed him her whites as he spoke of Goldie. She asked, inquisitively, "How is that, Jose?"

He replied, "Because if it's not done the way that he does it, and especially concerning the game, then it's not right. Baby, Goldie's the best! He once told me, "If I spent my whole life chasing paper, that I would miss the essence of life." He said, "Don't work the game, let the game that you know work for you." He also said, "Use your mind, there's fulfillment in it. Today, I realize I have done the total opposite. I chased paper, and I worked the game. The reality is that I almost missed the essence of life. I haven't been using my mind. So I have lacked fulfillment, and you have to have it to give it away to another human being. I watched Goldie this afternoon while you were asleep. He gave Carla such fulfillment that I could see an orgasm in her face. Yes, everything that Goldie says, and teaches me by way of example. It will always rein true."

Jose placed his arm around Carmen, and they headed for the lower level of the boat.

Chapter Eleven

AFTER Smooth readied himself to leave Shonda's house for the evening, he locked the basement door behind him. He told his girlfriend that he would be late; however, he would be home. He had just met with Cathy and had turned in his paper {money} for the evening.

As he made his way down Hale Street, he had no idea that there were two armed men that seemed to have been waiting for him out along the street. Smooth took notice of the male figure walking toward him on the sidewalk, and when they met. The gentleman hollered, "You know what it is." While the other gentleman had eased up behind him and slapped him upside the head with his pistol. Smooth staggered to the ground, and the armed gentlemen went through his pockets and beings that Smooth only had thirty dollars or so on him, again, he was hit with the pistol. Smooth lost consciousness, and the robbers had began to remove the gold chains that he had been wearing around his neck. After- which, the robbers fled the scene, as quickly as they had come.

Now Shonda had heard the commotion from inside the house and made her way outside to investigate. She immediately noticed that there was a man that laid just a couple of houses away from hers out along the sidewalk, and when she realized that it was Smooth, she screamed, "Oh, my God!" She kneeled down beside him and placed his head on her lap. She asked, "Smooth, are you alright?" He didn't respond, and tears had begun to run down her beautifully shaped face as she sat there rocking him back and forth. She cried out, "Just hold on, Smooth, I'll get help." She placed his head back down on to the sidewalk, gently, and took off running for the house. She thought, please, let him be alright.

Now Shonda really liked Smooth, but she never realized how much because they never had any type of dealings outside of the business at hand. Smooth had become just the man in the basement, which is a problem that the entire human race of people share in common. We don't realize things until it is almost or actually too late.

On the inside, Shonda grabbed the telephone in the living room off of the end table and dialed 911, and a few moments later, a woman's voice came over the line, she said, "911 Emergencies."

Shonda, who was breathing rather irregularly, replied, "I need an ambulance here in New Brunswick, between Lee, and Remsen, on Hale."

The operator said, "Ma'am, calm yourself. What is the nature of your problem? This line is for emergencies only."

Shonda screamed into the receiver, "No, you calm yourself. This is a damn emergency!"

"Ma'am, okay, I understand. What is the nature of your emergency?"

Shonda placed a hand onto her forehead trying to calm herself and replied, "There is a

Man lying out on the sidewalk, outside of my house, on Hale. He looks to have been beaten very badly."

The operator asked, "Is the victim conscious?"

She looked out of her living room window at Smooth while holding the telephone along

side of her face and replied, "Wait, no, I don't know."

"Ma'am, can you tell me what type of injuries the victim has sustained?"

The questions were beginning to frustrate Shonda, she replied sarcastically, "I don't
know, I'm not a fucking doctor. Will you people, please, just get here," and then she slammed the telephone receiver back down on the end table."

As she started for the front door to exit the house again, she noticed that she had some of Smooth's blood down the front of her housecoat. She rushed into her bedroom and removed her housecoat and nightgown. Then, she quickly slipped on a pair of fitted jeans, a Mets T-shirt, and a cap.

The reason for Shonda's clothing change was because she knew it would be best for her not to present herself to the police, as a possible suspect, an accessory, or that she may have been with the victim during the commission of the crime. She also knew that if the police could tie Smooth and her together, that a little bit of investigative work could bring forth a nightmare.

After Shonda placed her blood-stained clothing into a plastic bag, she left the house and put the plastic bag into a neighbor's garbage can. Then, she walked over and kneeled beside Smooth, thinking, 'what a waste of life, If this kid didn't make it.' She took his hand in hers, and further thought of some of the niceties concerning him. Whenever he would come by the house. He would always take time out for the children, and he would usually bring them something with him. Smooth was just a good person, and she thought 'much too good a person to die this way.'

As sirens whaled throughout the city, the houses began to light up along Hale Street, and as the meat wagon {ambulance} approached. Shonda closed her eyes and began to pray, and while praying, she was bumped by a paramedic from the meat wagon. He said, "Ma'am, you will have to step aside now, we will take over from here." The bump had startled Shonda, she looked up at the paramedic and then back down at

Smooth, and as she placed his hand back down across his midsection, she squeezed it. Then she got back on to her feet and eased into the small crowd of her neighbors that begun to gather at the scene.

The paramedics moved swiftly toward Smooth with various equipment and purpose.

As they began to work on him, they talked amongst themselves; "We have a pulse, his heartbeat is good, and his blood pressure is stable." One of the paramedics looked into Smooth's eyes with a small flashlight and said, "Possible, concussion." Then the paramedic placed a brace around Smooth's neck, and with help, he put him onto a stretcher for transport.

As the paramedics began to put Smooth into the meat wagon {ambulance}, one of the paramedics pointed over at Shonda while talking with one of the police officers that had just arrived on the scene.

{The city always dispatched white police officers to black functions, affairs, and tragedies}.

The white police officer began to approach Shonda, when he noticed a young woman who was running down the street toward the ambulance with a crowd of people behind her. The young woman was screaming, "No, No, not my Smooth!" and as she attempted to climb up into the meat wagon. The officer made a B-line and stopped her at the rear of the ambulance. He asked, "Who are you?" The young woman didn't respond. She just stood there looking up into the rear of the ambulance at what seemed to be a lifeless body. Sobbingly, she asked, "Will he be alright?" Again, the officer asked, "Who are you?" as he stood there, blocking the rear entrance to the meat wagon.

As she attempted to make her way around the police officer, she exclaimed vehemently, "I'm his wife."

The officer looked up at the paramedic in the rear of the ambulance.

The paramedic figured the young woman was just what Smooth needed, a familiar face. Since he was semi-conscious and all of his vital signs were stable. He quickly moved to the rear of the ambulance, taking the young woman by the hand and assisting her in climbing up into the ambulance.

Now Smooth's, girl, Sandra, was a hysterical wreck. She loved Smooth, they were high school sweethearts a few years back, and he was the only man that she had ever known. She didn't know what she would do without him. Smooth heard her voice and all of her cries. She sat down onto a small stationary stool beside him, and as tears began to stream down her cheeks. Smooth slowly opened his eyes and tried to speak. She covered his mouth with her finger and said, "Don't try to talk, Baby, just rest." She laid her head down on to his chest and began to sob. The tears were of hurt because he was hurt and a little of them were of joy because at that moment she knew that he was going to be alright.

The meat-wagon took Smooth to Robert Wood Johnson Hospital in New Brunswick.

Meanwhile, the white police officer was in the process of questioning Shonda, he asked,

"Ma'am, do you know the victim?"

She looked down at the bloodstain that now occupied the sidewalk where Smooth had

lain, and then she looked back up at the officer. "No, I don't, but I've seen him in the neighborhood often."

The officer asked, "Do you know why, or how, this incident has taken place?"

She looked at him intensely, and replied, "And just how would I know that? No, I don't,

Sir. I heard noises outside of my house, so I came outside to investigate, and there the victim laid." She pointed down at the blood-stained sidewalk, right where the ambulance had picked Smooth up from.

"Ma'am, are you sure that there is nothing else that you would like to tell me, or add to your story?"

Shonda placed her hands on her shapely hips and replied, "And just what is that supposed to mean? Of course, I'm sure."

As the police officer placed his pen back into his shirt pocket, he said, "Okay, Ma'am, I only have one more question for you. If {we} the Department should need to get in touch with you, again. How or where can we reach you? Do you have a number?"

She replied curtly, "You can't," as she turned and began to walk away.

The officer started to snatch her by her arm, but his partner, who was checking the perimeter of the crime scene, read it and was close enough to hear the tail end of their conversation. He said, "Let her go. We won't be able to use her because we have no case. We won't be able to get a damn thing out of the victim. Street values are a mother fucker."

The officer who questioned Shonda turned and stated, "That they are, man, that they are."

His partner walked over and placed a hand onto his shoulder. "We better get on down to the hospital."

As the two white police officers got into their patrol car, the officer on the passenger side of the vehicle broke the silence. He said, "It's just another nigga who got his head split, just another nigga."

Chapter Twelve

AFTER Goldie and Carla awoke from their evening naps, they dressed in silk pajamas and robes and made their way out to the entertainment area of the boat. They talked about the game of chess in conversation and figured what better time than right then to play. Jose had a beautiful marble chess set on board.

Now some of the tactics used in this game were irregular and ironic yet very tastefully done.

Carla stood during the chess match and removed her robe, pulling her T-shirt tightly, as she sat back down to the table, revealing protruding nipples through her pajama top that had capped her firm breasts and said, "It's your move."

Now Goldie understood this type of play. He smiled, and after moving one of his chess pieces in the match. He stood and removed his robe {she watched him closely}, then he unbuttoned his pajama top and sat back down to the table, revealing his chest and washboard stomach. He replied, "It's your move, Chump."

Carla smiled as she sat there for a few moments admiring what seemed chiseled out of stone. She exclaimed, "Touche."

Now the game that they played lasted about an hour and a half, and finally, Goldie mated her. He smiled as he eased back on to his chair and said, "You know this chessboard is a helluva mental thing, don't you?"

Carla replied, "Yeah, I know, and I almost had you too."

"Did you also know that the person that understands the many angles, options, and strategies of the game of chess, and that can relate them to life on its terms, wins. Think about it. In the game of chess, there's a king, and the king has a queen. Now the king should want a queen with a life of her own. So, she isn't always in his business, but willing to make a move if the king should need her too.

"Bishops are considered to be wisdom. If and when they see a move, their function is to notify the king and to discuss it with him, and vice versa. Bishops would be compatible to a partner or a good friend in the real world.

"Knights are no more than trained assassins. Their actual function is to enhance the Rook's ability to go straight forward and to get that paper {money}, and to get back to the king with the least amount of problems.

"And last but not least are pawns, which are actually push people, and depending upon how you set them up. They will protect you or they can be used as expenditures. Baby there are millions of pawns out there in that big old world. So I suggest that every man have or get himself some business, because the easiest people to con are people who's needs you can fulfill. This, the king can do by way of an intellectual thought process {setting up the circumstances in the lives of others}, use of money, and power. He also has the power to judge and to decide who makes it in his society. In other words, if you are not a thinker, and you do not have yourself some business, someone is liable to give you some. Baby it's all about position."

Carla sat there watching him closely. She was astonished and in awe of his wisdom.

Goldie remained silent, and seemed to have drifted off into a deep stupor.

She asked, "Goldie, are you alright?"

He smiled. "I'm fine; however, there is one other thing that I would like to share with you concerning me. I take, and I relate everything that I know about the game of chess to life on its terms, and I play life. The chessboard has never lied to me. Now, as you stated, you almost had me, you almost won. I concur with your sentiments; you have brought quite a few new and interesting moves with you to the chessboard. The game that we played was definitely exhilarating and challenging. Now I haven't lost a chess game since I was seventeen years old, and I lost that game to my first teacher, my mother. She beat on me to teach me the importance of humility and respect. She wanted me to know that I didn't have all of the answers and that I still had a great deal to learn about the game of chess, and life itself.

"There was only one other person, a childhood friend that proposed the type of challenge that you have this evening in the area of chess, and he went on to become a decorated police officer. So I'm suggesting, as we speak right now, the police are as close to me as you were to winning the chess game that we just finished playing."

Carla looked to be shocked and bewildered by this statement. Then she smiled, and asked, "Goldie what are you talking about, the police?"

He replied, "Baby, the chess board never lies." Then he just changed the subject completely, as he leaned forward on the chair that he was sitting on and asked, "Did you also know that this chessboard can talk?"

Carla smiled enthusiastically, "No, I didn't."

Goldie leaned down a little closer to the chess board and said, "Listen to it, its saying,

Let's you and I take a walk up on deck and watch the stars."

Carla playfully replied, "I bet it won't say it again, Goldie."

He looked up at her and smiled. "Come on, girl. Let's get out of here."

They both broke out into light laughter.

Now up on deck, Goldie took Carla by the hand and led her to a near-by telescope, which was located at the rear of the boat. They watched the Dippers big and small, but the Lone Stars were most important to Carla because they made her think of herself. She had shielded herself from the world for the last few years or so, but the feelings that Goldie had given to her, she never wanted to end.

Carla looked up at Goldie from the telescope and said, "I don't know what it is about you, and I don't know where to start. I'm impressed, and there's an incredible excitement about you. It's just that, I think, I'm falling in love with you."

Goldie smiled.

She said, "Please, don't make fun of me."

He placed his hands on to her shoulders and looked down into her eyes, "I'm not Baby, really,

I'm not. I'm laughing at myself because here I am trying to turn you out, and I don't think as I stand

here. It would have taken any of this shit to hear the words you just said. In other words, the jokes

on me." He dropped his head and hands before her.

Carla placed her hand underneath his chin and raised his head. She said, "Baby, don't look at it like that, because you had to come on this trip anyway. Let's just say that you brought along a companion that fell deeply in love with you."

Goldie mustered up a slight smile. "Yeah, yeah, I could do that, and Baby thank you, but that doesn't ease my conscious, because of the intent that I had in mind. However what I did do, I did to gain that which I now have." He kissed her on the forehead, "I love you too, Pumpkin. I have loved you from the beginning, and I now know that I will always love you. My cup runneth over."

Carla smiled. "Awe, Goldie, you are so sweet." He placed his hands onto her shapely hips and asked, "Baby, what do you think about the two of us getting a bottle of champagne and being fruitful and trying to multiply?"

As she looked up into his eyes, she placed her hands on top of his hands and politely removed them off of her hips.

At that moment, Goldie didn't know what to think.

All of a sudden, Carla just took off, leaving him standing there in thought, she said, "I'll race

you to the cabin."

Now Goldie didn't like to lose, and he knew that she had him beat. He smiled as he raised his head and hands toward the heavens and said, "Thank you."

Meanwhile, after getting the children back to sleep, Shonda sat on the sofa in the living room, watching the telephone that occupied one of the end tables in the room. She didn't know what to do. She had called Goldie's hideout, which was actually off-limits unless it was an extreme emergency. He was not at home, so she left a message on his answering machine. The message was simple enough, she spoke into the telephone receiver, "Terrible...Terrible... Terrible... Shonda," then she hung up the telephone. She thought about the emergency number that she had in her purse and decided to use it. Then, she realized that she would not know who or where she would be calling. She was instructed to just speak into the telephone the nature of the problem.

Now Cathy had two telephones in her place with two different telephone numbers, on the same line, one bill. One phone was for regular use, the other sat stationary on a nightstand in her bedroom hooked to an answering machine for emergencies only.

Shonda reached over onto the end table and retrieved the telephone. She dialed the emergency number, and when she heard the beep. She simply said, "Smooth's been hurt, and he's at Robert Wood Johnson Hospital," and she hung up the telephone. Then, she decided that she would go down to the hospital to see about Smooth, but only after the police had left the hospital.

Meanwhile, the beep on the emergency telephones, answering

machine had awakened Cathy, and immediately, she propped herself up on pillows in the large bed and reached over on to the nightstand, and pushed the play button on the answering machine and screened the message. She was instructed by Goldie to always listen to the message carefully, and no matter what, to remain calm. He believed it to be the basis of all things, and in that, he also believed that she would be able to think. She listened to the message again, and then she decided to call Theresa.

Now when Theresa received Cathy's telephone call, she was lying in bed deep in thought about Goldie, wondering who he had taken with him on his outing and what he was doing at that very moment.

As she reached over beside herself and retrieved the cordless telephone off the bed. She was hopeful that it was Goldie on the other end of the phone. She spoke softly into the receiver, "Goldie?"

Cathy replied, "No, it's not Goldie, it's me."

Theresa caught Cathy's voice and, immediately, her spirit dropped. She asked, "And just what the hell do you want this time of the morning?"

Now there was a lot of animosity between these two women, but working together had not been a problem. However, at that point, Theresa felt that Cathy was pushing it, calling at two-thirty in the morning. She thought, 'If it wasn't about business, she was going to let this bitch have it.'

Cathy replied, "Theresa, we have a problem."

As she sprung up into a sitting position on the large bed, she said, "What, what is it? Goldie...what happened? Is he alright?"

"Goldie's fine, it's Smooth, and he's at Robert Wood Johnson Hospital."

Now Cathy didn't know where Goldie was, but Theresa did. He only told Cathy that he

would see her in a few days. Theresa on the other hand, who

was used to handling the majority of Goldie's business told Cathy that she would call her back. She wanted to call the hospital to check on Smooth's condition. She hung up the telephone and sat there in thought for a few moments on the bed. She knew if she had to call Goldie that it damn sure better be an emergency. Plus, she didn't know whether Goldie had his cell phone with him or not. She decided if the situation wasn't too bad, that she would handle things until he returned.

After the call to information {411}, Theresa dialed the telephone number to the hospital. The telephone rang a few times, and then a lady's voice came over the line.

"Robert Wood. Can I help you, please?"

Theresa replied, "Yes, can you connect me to the emergency room?"

"One moment, please."

A few moments later, the emergency room operator came over the line, "E.R. Can I help you, please?'"

Theresa replied, "Yes, you have a patient just brought into the E.R., by way of Ambulance. I would like a rundown on his condition."

The E.R. operator replied, "Information about our patient's can only be relinquished to immediate family members."

Theresa stated into the telephone receiver, "Ma'am, I'm the patient's sister."

The operator asked, "And your name is?"

She replied, "Theresa Lyles, the patients name is Raymond Lyles."

After a few moments, the operator returned to the telephone line and said, "Doctors are with Mr. Lyles now. It seems that he was struck on the head with a blunt object, and has sustained a slight concussion."

She asked, "Will my brother be alright?

The operator replied, "Mr. Lyles should be fine. Of course, the hospital will probably like to keep him for an observational period."

Theresa smiled. "Thank you."

"Ma'am, you're welcome."

The line went dead.

Chapter Thirteen

NOW Goldie lay propped up in his undershorts on the bed, with a glass of champagne in his hand, watching Carla as she re-entered the cabin from the bathroom. She was wearing a pair of red pumps, and one of the sexiest little red teddies that he had ever seen. He also noticed that she was slightly bow-legged, which made him all the more excited.

Goldie watched her lustfully. "Hey girl, stand there and let me look at you. Wow, I don't think I knew what I was getting myself into."

Carla replied, "Well, Baby, it's a little too late for that now."

He smiled as she eased over onto the bed on top of him.

All of a sudden, he hollered, "Ho'll Baby," and poured champagne all over her beautiful

body, trying to make what happened to look to be an accident.

Carla jumped up off -the bed seemingly shocked, yet showing him her whites. She

screamed, "You did that on purpose!"

Goldie looked up at her mischievously and asked, "Now would I do something like that intentionally?"

She replied seductively. "Well, you did, and now I'll have to take it all off."

He thought, 'now that's just what I was hoping.'

As she began to come out of the teddy that she was wearing, he further thought, 'damn, everything is perfect.' He didn't remember who said 'what a man truly feels can never be expressed in words,' and it wasn't until that moment that he knew it was nothing but the truth.

Goldie laid there, examining her in her birthday suit. She blushed with embarrassment. He stood, removing his undershorts, revealing himself to her. And at that point, the lustful staring competition began.

He said softly, as he took her into his arms, and laid her down across the bed, "Baby, don't you worry about a thing. I'm going to take real good care of you, Baby, real good care of you."

Carla cried out as he eased himself down deep inside of her beautiful body and began to explore her sex. He loved the way that she whimpered and cried as he spent himself inside of her inner groove.

Meanwhile, Sandra sat at Smooth's bedside holding his hand, she said, "I thought I was going to lose you."

Smooth mustered a slight smile. "Baby, I told you that I would never leave you?" Right then, Smooth grabbed his head, revealing to Sandra that he had a splitting headache. She told him not to try to talk and to get some rest. She wondered what he had said to the police while being questioned, but Smooth didn't even remember being questioned.

All of a sudden, Shonda walked into the room. She spoke to Sandra, and then she made her way over to Smooth's bedside and took his hand in hers, "Smooth, are you okay?"

He looked up at her and smiled. "I'm okay."

Shonda said, "Good," as she walked over and placed her hand on to Sandra's shoulder, and said, "He'll be alright, I just had to come. I was worried about him, and Goldie's nowhere to be found."

Sandra replied, "Shonda, I want to thank you for coming."

Shonda sat down beside her and said, "Smooth don't you be scaring us like that anymore."

He looked over at her with a serious face and replied, "Goldie's going to be mad, isn't he?"

"Now, don't you be worrying about that right now. You just rest and get yourself better," Shonda replied.

The hospital decided to keep Smooth for a couple of days of observation.

Now Theresa sat up in the large bed and was now deep in thought after the call that she made to the emergency room. She decided that the best thing to do would be to handle the situation until Goldie returned.

Theresa picked up the telephone and got Cathy on the line. She explained to Cathy that Smooth was going to be alright and that he had a slight concussion. Then she instructed Cathy to meet her at the hospital.

Meanwhile, Goldie and Carla lay spent deep in thought in each other's arms.

Goldie broke the silence. "You know if you were to ask me to marry you. I would, don't you?"

Carla replied, "Watch it, I might. I just might."

Goldie grabbed Carla, and they went at it again.

Chapter Fourteen

WHEN Theresa entered the emergency room, to her surprise, Cathy was already there inside of the hospital. They looked each other up and down, and over, and after a few moments, Cathy broke the silence. She asked, "What's up?"

Theresa replied, "I figured that we would handle the situation ourselves, at least until Goldie returns being that Smooth isn't hurt that bad."

Cathy quickly asserted, "Alright, well, let's go in and check on him."

Theresa walked over to the information desk and told the woman her name. She also told the woman she had called an hour or so earlier in regards to a Raymond Lyles, who happened to be her brother.

The woman explained what she knew of Smooth's condition, and directed Theresa to room six, which was located in the rear of the emergency room. She gestured over to Cathy, and they made their way beyond the large wooden doors that separated the waiting room from the actual patient's examination area.

As they entered Smooth's hospital room, he lifted his head and smiled.

Cathy took the lead and walked over to where Sandra and Shonda were sitting. She said, "We have come to check on Smooth, we are friends of Goldies."

Theresa made her way bedside and asked, "Smooth, how are you?"

He replied, "I'm okay."

Sandra stood, asserting herself. "The doctors say Smooth should get some rest. He took a pretty hard hit on the head."

Cathy interjected, "Sandra, we just wanted him to know that we are here for him."

Right then, hospital transportation entered the room and informed Sandra that they would be moving Smooth upstairs to a regular hospital room. Sandra began gathering his personal belongings and decided that she was going to stay overnight with him at the hospital.

She followed closely behind transportation as Smooth was moved out of the emergency area of the hospital, which left Theresa, Cathy, and Shonda remaining in the room. Theresa suggested that they all go down to the hospital cafeteria and have a cup of tea.

Meanwhile, Goldie rose early the following morning, slipped on a sweatsuit, and made his way up on deck. It was time to do his ritual. He figured that he would work out, shower, and meet with Jose for their rap session while the women slept.

After completing his workout, while on his way to the shower. He noticed that Jose's office door was open. He looked inside and saw Jose sitting behind the large oak desk.

Jose said, "Good morning, Brother, did you sleep well?"

Goldie smiled, "Back at you, man. I had the best night's sleep of my life. If what I was doing is called sleeping. I want to do it all the time."

Jose asked, "So you are still knocking them dead, huh?"

"It's my job, Baby, it's my job. Look, I'm going to grab me a shower, and I'll meet you back here in an half."

"Hey, that's quite alright, come right in Goldie, and let's get this session over. I also know if you return to that cabin, I may not see you anymore during this trip."

As Goldie made his way into the office and sunk down on to one of the plush office chairs, he replied, "You know what, you're right."

Jose asked, and concerning the business, "Are we all set to go?"

Goldie smiled. "Yes, as a matter of fact, I have received a letter of confirmation two days before this trip. I'll be flying down some time next week to check out the scene."

Jose returned his smile. "Okay, whatever we may need, and I do mean anything. Just let me know, and together we will work out the finances and score."

Goldie sat there thinking, 'this little mother fucker thinks he's running shit.' Little does he know, he just played right into my hands? So he wants to play big shit with me, huh? Okay, you little mother fucker when the time comes. I'll push your ass to the fucken limit.

Goldie broke the silence. "You do know that this thing is going to be big, don't you?"

Jose made eye contact with Goldie and replied, "I'm in."

"Okay, I'll check the set and get back to you. Now off the record, how have you been?

It seems to me that Carmen is killing you."

Jose replied, "You got to think, what a way to die, my man. What a way to leave this fucked up ass world."

Goldie smiled, "Nah, you got to think, the world only turned out, the way that you and I made it."

Both men rose and shook hands.

Jose told Goldie to enjoy the rest of the trip because they would be pulling the boat into the dock that evening, about six.

Goldie said, "Jose..."

"Yeah, Goldie." {Again, their eyes met, and locked}

"Thanks for the gift, man."

"Goldie, you are more than welcome."

As Goldie made his way outside of the office, he noticed that the hired hand was well within ear distance of the open office door. He watched the hired hand suspiciously as he proceeded on his way back to his cabin.

Chapter Fifteen

NOW Theresa, Cathy, and Shonda had made themselves comfortable at one of the booths in the hospital cafeteria. They were discussing the incident concerning Smooth over a nice hot cup of tea. Shonda was into her spill about how worried she had been about him, while Theresa sat there trying to gather all the information that she possibly could about the incident. So she would have something for Goldie when he returned. Cathy sat there thinking, 'so this bitch is Shonda, huh.' (she knew of Shonda but had never met her before) 'I don't even know why I'm sitting here.'

Cathy broke her chain of thought and asked, "Shonda are you Smooth's sister or something?"

Shonda replied curtly, "Why, do you ask?"

Theresa caught what was about to go down, and she also knew that Cathy knew Shonda's function. So she interjected and asked, "Shonda do you have a ride home? It's getting late, and ladies, I have an early morning."

Shonda smiled, "Yes, I have a ride, but I'll be staying. I'm going to try to get upstairs and see Smooth before I leave the hospital, but, thank you anyway."

Cathy didn't say another word, she just rose and begun to walk toward the exit doors of the cafeteria.

Now on the outside of the hospital, Theresa told Cathy, "You know, you almost blew it, don't you?"

"Theresa, I thank you for what you did in there, but please don't give me that almost blew it shit, because the bitch didn't get what she had coming to her. You saw her sitting in there like she was Miss

America or somebody and shooting that weak ass story of Smooth's incident like we are stupid or something. She was holding back all she could like she would build points with Goldie for having the most original story."

"Cathy, you got a point, but was that any way to handle it? My point is, you know better, and you already know where you stand with Goldie."

Cathy smiled, "I don't know what he sees in her. I don't even know why he fucks with her."

Theresa threw a hand out before Cathy stopping her immediately. "Wait a minute, now you're going too far. With Goldie, there is always a reason for the seasons. So, who are you to question that?"

Cathy replied, "But,"

Theresa quickly interjected, "But nothing, and another thing. Whatever Goldie does, and however, he has it. Remember, he deserves it. I'll leave you with that, and good night."

Now Cathy was hot, but she knew that Theresa was right. Neither woman said another word. They both walked away in separate directions towards their cars and left the scene.

Meanwhile, Shonda was still sitting in the hospital cafeteria, she was deep in thought, not only about the incident concerning Smooth, but more so about what happen between Cathy and her. She knew that Cathy knew her function, and she also believed that Cathy knew her and Goldie had something going on too. Shonda wanted to kick Cathy's ass, but she knew that would have cost her Goldie. She knew that Goldie wanted a woman to always be a lady. He once told her, 'If someone is arguing with you or calling you out of your name, as a woman, don't say anything. The other party can't argue by themselves, and if they do who looks stupid? Plus, you ain't got no business out there fighting in no streets. However if someone does decide to try you {put their hands on you}. Do not play with them, cut their mother fucken throat.

After thinking for a few moments, she realized that she was

glad the incident did not go any further than it did because it was not the time or place. Shonda decided it was best to let the situation lye where it was…dead.

Chapter Sixteen

AFTER Goldie had showered, he walked out into the bedding area of the cabin wrapped in a bath towel, and to his surprise. Carla was up in bed laying in-between silk sheets, propped up on a couple of large throw pillows, deep in thought.

Goldie eased over and kissed her on the forehead, "Good morning, Sunshine."

She replied unenthusiastically, "Good morning, Goldie."

He picked up immediately that something was troubling her, and as he sat down beside her on the bed, he asked, "Baby, are you okay?"

"I don't know, it's just that everything goes back to normal after today, and I don't want what we have ever to end."

"So, it seems to me that you are really unsure about all that has taken place between us?"

"Well, I guess I am."

Goldie gave a reassuring smile. "Well, don't be, because I can assure you. That what we have will never end. Right now, you are one of two things in my life that truly mean something to me. I also know that I love you. You have quickly become a very significant part of my life."

Carla eased up onto the bed into his arms, "Goldie, I know that I love you, too. I guess I'm just afraid of being hurt."

He eased out of the embrace and looked down into her eyes, "Pumpkin, I told you that I would protect you from all things. I meant it, even if it takes my very life."

Carla asked, "And about marriage?"

Again, he smiled, "Baby, as people we always say what we mean, now get your pretty little self out that bed, make yourself even more beautiful, and I'll go place an order for the most beautiful breakfast that you have ever seen."

Now Goldie didn't want what they had to end either, and the feelings he had made him all the more determined to finish up his business. So he could create a life for both of them.

Meanwhile, Theresa and Cathy had continued with the instructions that Goldie left for them, just minus Smooth from the proceedings. They also knew better than to shut down his operation.

Cathy also called Theresa and thanked her whole-heartedly for what she said and done to prevent the incident between Shonda and her from going any further than it had. Theresa was very understanding and told Cathy, it really wasn't a big deal and that they would keep the incident between themselves. Now that was exactly what Cathy wanted to hear. She didn't want it to get back to Goldie that she had shown her ass, and especially not during a crisis.

Now, Theresa knew what Cathy wanted and gave it to her because she wanted to be able to tell Goldie that during a difficult time. The three of them had come together, and all went well. This was the only way they would have gained anything out of this situation in Goldie's eyes, and Theresa knew it.

Theresa and Cathy talked a while longer on the telephone, but as always, when the conversation had come to a close. They were right back where they began, and they both knew it.

Chapter Seventeen

NOW later on that evening, Goldie and Carla had said their goodbyes to Jose and Carmen, and were now sitting in the parking lot of the hideout. They planned to unpack and to have a late supper. Goldie helped Carla take her things into her place. Then, he took his personal belongings into the hideout, and while on the inside. He got Theresa on the line. He said, "Hey Girl how's everything?"

Theresa screamed into the telephone receiver, "Goldie, we've got trouble. Smooth's is hurt, and he's at Robert Wood Johnson Hospital."

"Baby, slow down, and explain what has happened to me."

"Goldie, he was jumped, robbed, or maybe even both. I really couldn't make heads or tails out of what Shonda was telling us. I can tell you that he is going to be okay and that the incident took place after Cathy made her pick up."

Goldie replied, "Very good. I'm on my way."

The line went dead.

Goldie quickly made his way over to Carla's house and explained to her something had come up and that he couldn't stay for dinner. After-which, he left her place headed for the hospital, thinking 'if something happened to that kid...' He pushed his Caddie in silence.

When Goldie arrived at the hospital, he quickly made his way to the information desk, retrieved a visitor's pass, and up he went on the elevator.

As he entered Smooth's hospital room, he found him lying in the hospital bed with his head all bandaged up. He walked over and took Sandra's hand, "Hey Sandra," then he made his way bedside. "Hey Smooth, I hear that you had to straighten a couple of guys out."

Smooth smiled. "Goldie it was more like they straightened me out, but I'm still here. Brother, I'm still here."

"Hey, and that's all that really matters."

Goldie looked over at Sandra and asked, "Do you mind if I speak to Smooth for a few minutes, alone?" He reached into his pocket and retrieved some money and handed it to her, and she left the room for the gift shop to pick up a few things.

(He continued) "Okay, Sport, now that she's gone, speak."

Smooth raised his hospital bed electronically. "Goldie, it all happened so fast. There were two of them, and although they were wearing face masks. I'm sure one of the robbers was Red, I can tell his voice anywhere. They got me for about thirty dollars and the three gold chains that I wear, one of which you gave me."

Goldie replied, "Small things to a giant. I just want you to concentrate on getting better. I'll handle the rest."

Smooth asked, "Goldie, what's our plan?"

He smiled. "First, we get you well, and then we wait."

Now Red was a well-known stick up man, and the majority of the hustlers feared him. They usually left the block whenever they saw him coming.

Goldie thought Red to be a chump, a turnout, a trick, and a sucker just someone that the environment had been bad too. He further thought the bad thing was giving Red what he deserved based on who, and what he had become. Goldie knew that Red never had a real shot at a healthy life {his circumstances had governed the choices that he made concerning life from the beginning}.

All of a sudden, Sandra reentered the hospital room. She had balloons and cards in one hand and a shopping bag in the other.

Smooth smiled as he turned his attention from Goldie to Sandra, "Look at my Baby, she loves me."

Goldie replied, "Hey, and that's just who I'm going to leave you with. I have a few runs to make." After shaking Smooth's hand and saying good-bye to Sandra, he started for the door to exit the room.

Smooth called out, "Goldie, I should be getting out of here tomorrow."

He turned to face Smooth. "Hey, I'll give you a call, and if so. I'll pick you up. Sandra keep him quiet, and Smooth get well, man."

Goldie left the hospital, smiling. The kid was going to be okay, and he hadn't lost any paper {money}. He decided to stop by Theresa's before heading back to the hideout. He rode straight through town to the sounds of Curtis Mayfield, The Super Fly Theme.

Now when Goldie arrived at Theresa's place, he opened the front door with his key.

Theresa was in the kitchen frying chicken. He snuck up behind her and kissed her on the cheek. She turned around to face him, and then she threw her arms around his neck and asked, "How did it go?"

Goldie smiled. "I'm fine, and yourself."

"I'm sorry, Baby. How are you?"

Goldie made his way over to the kitchen table and took a seat. "Baby, everything went well, but that's not what I want to discuss with you. I figured you could tell me more about what happened to Smooth, than you did over the telephone."

"I only know what Shonda told Cathy and me."

"Wait a minute. You, Shonda, and Cathy were at the hospital together?"

"Yeah, Shonda called the emergency number, and Cathy called me. I called the hospital to check on Smooth's condition, and once I found out that he was going to be okay. I called Cathy back and had her meet me at the hospital. I figured that we would handle the situation until you got back into town. I knew better than to bother you. If it was something I could handle."

Goldie said, "You know what, you're right, but then again.. You always come through for me."

Theresa walked over to the stove and began to turn the chicken. She asked, "Goldie, would you like something to eat?"

He looked up at her from the table seductively, and replied, "Of course I do, but I have something else in mind,"

She replied, "Oh, you do, huh."

Goldie smiled, "Yes, I do, but right now, I'm rather short on time. So the chicken is going to have to do."

Theresa held her fist out in Goldie's direction and shook it. She replied, " I'll get you for that."

"I'm sure of it; just get me the way I want to be got, and not the way you want to get me. Oh, and I'll have my chicken in the living room."

Theresa brought Goldie's food into the living room on a serving tray. She handed it to him and took a seat on the sofa next to his easy chair. She asked, "Goldie what are you thinking about?"

He sat the tray down on to the coffee table in front of him, "I'm thinking about getting even. Is that cool?"

Theresa placed a hand on to his thigh and looked up into his eyes, "If there's one thing that I have learned from being around you. I would say that's something that has to be done. I just want you to be careful and Goldie, you know I'm with you, don't you?"

"Baby, I have never doubted you. It's just that there are some things a man must do alone. You do understand, don't you?"

She replied, "Of course I do."

Goldie asked, "Baby, where are we at with that thing?"

"There's about a half left."

"Okay, you and Cathy finish up among the workers, and then, shut down until you hear from me. I have to run."

"Okay, Goldie."

He stood, leaving the untouched plate of chicken on the coffee table. He kissed her on the mouth and left the house.

Now the next stop for Goldie was the Jersey Avenue Cafe, which was located on Jersey Avenue in New Brunswick, and was also owned and operated by Ray and Alice two of his good friends.

As Goldie entered the bar, heads began to turn. He loved the power that he had, but it wasn't as important to him as most people thought it was. He knew they were only out to get what they could from him.

Now Goldie and Ray were cool. What he liked about Ray was that he never played on his power, yet allowed people to use their strengths against themselves as Goldie did, but what they shared in common was a love for business. Alice, on the other hand was sweet. She had high hopes and big dreams, which we all start out with, but she was one to pursue hers. Nor was she a product of the environment. This is what was so intriguing about her to him. Goldie also knew that he could learn something of substance from her, something he could keep, hold, and cherish, something that would strengthen his constitution in the area of manhood. The two of them did a lot of things together, and Atlantic City was one of their favorite places to go. But the best of times were spent alone, rapping, and in true friendship. Alice was one of the few people that cared about what happened to Goldie, not just the star...but the man.

Goldie walked over and took a seat at the bar.

Alice brought over his regular and spoke to him.

Ray hollered from the other end of the bar, "Hey, little brother."

Goldie proposed a toast. "To Ray...the man that made the price of pussy go up in my absence."

Now Ray was five-ten, light skin, and masculine.

He made his way down the bar to where Goldie was sitting and shook his hand, "Nah, brother, you got me all wrong. If a chick stays and lays. I see to it that she pays."

Goldie smiled. "Hey, maybe, I need to adopt a little bit of that in my life."

"Goldie, you ought to stop that shit."

"No really...you guys have all the luck. I'm tired of paying for the little bit of pussy I get."

Now Goldie made that statement because people were beginning to gather and one thing he had learned. If you were better than someone in the area of that which they claim to do. Always remember your kindness in that you have a chance at winning their hearts. Plus, Goldie wasn't the one with the problem, and there was no doubt in his mind that if he caught a chick-peeping 'whether or not' he would charge her for some of his pimpin.

Goldie sat there at the bar, and after having a few drinks with some of the fellows. He gestured Ray to the back office.

When the two men reached the back office, Ray took a seat behind the desk and Goldie remained standing. He asked, "Ray, you heard anything concerning my people?"

Ray replied, "Only that one of them was touch (robbed}."

Goldie gave Ray an intense look, "Any word on who may have done this?"

"If the word is out, it ain't hit the spot yet."

Goldie smiled as he extended his hand, "Okay, Big Brother, I got to run. Hopefully, I'll get to see you within the next couple of days or so."

That evening, when Goldie had returned to Carla's place, she rushed to the door to greet him.

She was worried about her man. She had never seen him that way, but then again, she figured there was still a lot to learn about him.

After the embrace, he made his way into the living room and over to the bar, where he made himself a nice stiff drink.

THE GAME   125

Carla followed close behind him. She asked, "Goldie, are you okay?"

He turned and kissed her on the forehead, "Baby, I'm fine, now that I'm here with you."

"So, what happened? Is everything alright now?"

"Baby, everything is fine. I took a small situation between family, and I made it out to be much more than it was, that's all."

Carla showed him her whites, "I'm just glad you're okay. I was worried about you."

As Goldie walked over and took a seat on the sofa. He said, "Well, aren't you sweet.

Come here, Baby. I have something to ask you."

She walked over and sat down beside him on the Sofa, "Yes Baby."

Goldie looked into her eyes intensely, "Carla, will you do a portrait of me?"

Carla replied immediately, "Goldie, that's not funny."{ She thought he was going to ask her to marry him}.

"Baby, I'm serious you do great work. I wish I were a painter. Look at you, such beauty. I would lock it away on canvas, and freeze it for eternity."

Carla returned his intent look, and after a few moments, she smiled. "Of course I'll paint you."

Goldie smiled. "Look, Baby, I got to run, I have an early morning."

As he stood up off the sofa, Carla rose also and replied, "I have an early morning too, but I was hoping that you would stay with me."

He took both of her hands in his, and kissed her on the mouth, "Now will that be for always, or for just one night?"

Carla replied, "It's your choice."

"Okay, now that we are out there in the open. How about you moving into my place? I have three bedrooms, and you have one. You can put your bedroom set in one of the spare bedrooms. Everything else is new in my place. I think you'll like it."

She asked, "Are you serious?"

Goldie replied, "When it comes to you. I'm always serious."

"Okay, then I'll take you up on your offer. I just can't move in -like tomorrow. Is that okay?"

He smiled, "Hey, that's cool."

Now Goldie knew better than to move in with any woman unless he didn't have a choice, and he had plenty of other options. The advantages of having her with him were immeasurable. He could always use the income, and if something were to come up, happen, or go wrong. He would have her to look after his things (assets}. Goldie also knew to live the way that he did was based on the help (security) he placed around him.

Being a master of the game didn't come easy, but to Goldie, it was like second nature.

Chapter Eighteen

THE following morning when Carla arrived at work, it seemed that she had walked into the atmosphere of a funeral. She made her way through the bank and into her office; no-one said a word, and everyone watched her closely.

As Carla sat down behind her desk, she noticed a file on top of it, which contained a report, two audiotapes, and a host of photos detailing her and Goldie's boat outings..

She looked over at Jill, who seemed to be preoccupied with some paperwork. Carla was holding up a few of the photographs, she asked, "What is this all about?"

Jill didn't bother to respond.

Carla walked over and dropped the file down on her desk, and again, this time raising her voice. She asked, "What is this all about?"

Jill immediately slid out from underneath her desk on the chair that she was sitting on and looked up directly into Carla's eyes. "Oh, now you're talking to me, huh?"

Carla asked, "What the hell are you talking about?"

Jill stood, "Carla, I'm your friend, your dog, your fucken partner, and me nor anyone else in the department knew where the hell you were for the last couple of days. We were fortunate that the hired hand on your little boat outing was a placed agent connected to our case. That's my fucken problem."

Carla returned the intense stare. "Listen, Jill, I appreciate your concern, but Goldie would never hurt me."

Jill screamed out, "Have you lost your damn mind?"

All of a sudden, Hank busted into the office and asked, "What the hell is going on in here?"

Both women fell silent and gave him their undivided attention.

Hank said, "Alright, Jill, you out," while pointing toward the door that he had just entered the room through. Then he told Carla to have a seat and asked, "Now what the hell is your problem?"

Carla stated, "I'll stand," as she walked over and retrieved the file on Goldie off Jill's desk. She asked, "Hank, what the hell is this all about?"

He replied, "Some of us still have to do our damn jobs."

"And just what the hell is that supposed to mean?"

"Look, Carla, I don't want to burden you any more than you already are, but the agency has procedures. So from this point on until you see Lieutenant Charles, you are confined to your desk."

As she walked over and sat down behind her desk, she asked, "And just when will that be?"

" Well, I spoke to the lieutenant about an hour ago. He said that he would be through our office sometime today and that you aren't to go back in {undercover} until he sees you, if then."

Carla jumped up from behind her desk, "And about the operation, and all of the work. My place in it."

Hank looked over at her rather intensely, and stated, "It's all off-limits until you see the lieutenant."

As Carla began to put her overcoat on, she asked, "Is the lieutenant in his office?"

"Carla, I want you to know this isn't easy for me."

Again, Carla asked, "Is the lieutenant in his office?"

Hank didn't respond.

Carla reached down and retrieved her briefcase, and as she made her way around him she said,

"If the lieutenant should call, tell him I'm on my way."

Meanwhile, as Goldie rose, he looked over at the clock on the nightstand, and after realizing the time. He quickly showered and dressed and then made his way out into the living room and took a seat on the sofa, where he got Smooth on the line. He asked, "Hey, Smooth, what's going on?"

"Hey Goldie, I can get out of the hospital anytime after twelve, today."

"Well, alright, I'll see you when I get into town. Do you need me to pick you up or anything?"

"Nah, Goldie, my Sister is going to pick me up, and drop me by the house. I'll be fine."

"I didn't know your family knew of the situation."

"They didn't, however, good news sure travels fast."

Goldie smiled. "Ain't that the truth, young blood, ain't that the truth. Look, I hope to see you later. If not, rest up and get well. I have something I must take care of."

"Goldie, you wouldn't?"

"Nah, I'll talk to you later."

The line went dead.

After the telephone call to Smooth, Goldie quickly placed another call to Jose

"Jose," Goldie said.

"Goldie."

"Yeah, it's me."

Jose asked, "What's up?"

"Hey, while we were out, I had a little problem."

"Anything drastic?"

"It may as well be because I'm using drastic measures. Jose, I need a princess."

"You got it, partner, When?"

"I mean, hey, the sooner, the better. It's still morning here. I'll pick her up around six, at the train station, in downtown New Brunswick, this evening."

"Okay, we will see you then."

Goldie quickly responded, "Jose, just the chick."

Jose sighed. "Okay, I don't understand it, but if it's what you want, cool."

"It is, Jose, and thanks,."

{A princess is a chick, a sharp chick, that will accept a mission, any mission for a fee.

They thrive off shit talkers, the so-called money getters, and they prey on the sucker. Money is their religion}.

Now when Goldie got into town that afternoon, he went straight to Cathy's house. He didn't think it would be wise to be seen too much with what he had planned.

Goldie opened the door with his key and stepped inside. Cathy sat in the living room, watching television. When she spotted Goldie, she jumped up, moved to him, and hugged him. She asked, "How are you, Baby?"

Goldie kissed her on the mouth, "I'm okay, what's up with you?"

"I'm better now. Have you heard what happened?"

"Of course I did, and I will take care of everything. So you can stop worrying your pretty little head."

Cathy asked, "Can I get you anything?"

"Yeah, you can get me a bottle of that shit{champagne}out of the rack, get us a couple of glasses, and an ice bucket. I just want to sit back in my easy chair and listen to Anita Baker, The Rapture."

"Okay, Goldie, give me your jacket and make yourself comfortable."

They sat around enjoying each others company while having a few drinks and listening to music until the latter part of the evening.

Now about five-thirty that evening, Goldie went into Cathy's bedroom where one of his safes was. He retrieved three thousand dollars, and thought, 'life was rather cheap.' After this, he kissed Cathy and told her that he would see her in a few days.

Meanwhile, Carla made her way to the city and now stood face to face with Lieutenant Charles in his office, which was located at the top of the Gate Way Building, in downtown, Newark.

Carla approached him as she had during her childhood; as if to be innocent, and full of truth. She said, "Hi, Uncle Charles."

He pointed to a chair that sat out before his desk and replied, "Don't you, Uncle Charles me. You put your ass in that chair."

She sat down and looked up at the lieutenant with tears in her eyes.

He walked over and spent the chair around to face the back wall of his office. Then he walked over and retrieved a photograph of Carla's father, Danny Jr., and himself. He pointed to a picture of Carla when she was about six years old, and then he pointed to a picture of Danny Jr., Carla's older brother. There was also a photograph of Danny Jr. and Carla together. Then he turned his focus toward a few other photographs concerning his immediate family, and he pointed Carla out.

He said, "We are all family, your father was my best friend and my partner, and upon him losing his life in the line of duty, not only was I with him. I made a promise to him that I would take care of you and Danny Jr. -as the two of you was my very own and God knows that I have tried to keep that promise."

He looked down intensely into her eyes and asked, "Do you remember how your brother died, and who was responsible for his death?"

Carla rolled her eyes, "I know who they say is responsible for Danny's death."

After Carla's statement, Lieutenant Charles walked over and sat down behind his desk, a tear trickled down his face. He looked over at her as if to say, ' this is just a sad situation.' He replied, "I thought that your objective was to bust Goldie's ass. You told me personally not only did you know he murdered Danny Jr., but you were there. So Carla, what's changed? It was written in the original report that you were there with Danny at the party the night that he was murdered. I thought this was what all of this was about, the academy, etc. Do you know that there are agents in this department of rank that pay close attention to details? I was told in the beginning that this case would be to much for you, and in any event a conflict of interest. I'm just sorry I put you in that situation."

Carla stood, "Look, Uncle Charles, I'm doing my job, and you're right. I did the academy and everything else I had to do, to get in the position I'm in now. It was true then, it's true now, and you use to believe it. Uncle Charles, what changed?"

He just sat there watching her closely.

She said, "I will never forget the night that Danny and I strolled into one of the Comfort Inn's, down along Vagina Beach. We were at the top of the hotel, and immediately upon entering the suite, a gentleman walked over and told Danny that Goldie wanted to see him in the back room. Danny told me to hang out and mingle. God knows I tried to move with him. Goldie opened the door to the backroom, and that was my first glimpse of him. At that point, Danny assured me that he would be alright and that he would be back at my side in a flash, but for some reason. I just didn't feel that he was safe, and I don't know why I felt that way. I also didn't know that he was undercover for the agency. Although, I'm assuming that Goldie did, or either he had just received that information. Anyway, about ten minutes later or so, I see Danny and two other guys come out of the backroom. He tells me to sit tight. He needed to take care of a few loose ends and that he would be back within the next hour or so. He also told me to meet Goldie, and that he was an alright dude."

Uncle Charles asked, "Did you get to meet Goldie that night?"

"No, Goldie left the party about fifteen minutes after Danny did, and that was the last time that I ever saw Danny Jr. alive. I left the party soon after. Uncle Charles, I haven't forgotten my objective, and I'm doing my job."

Uncle Charles stood up from behind his desk and walked over to the back wall of the office. He retrieved a photograph of Carla and Danny Jr., and then he turned and handed it to her, and she smiled. He said, "I just don't want to see you hurt."

Carla stood and replied, "Goldie's not going to hurt me."

Uncle Charles walked over and placed his hands on to her shoulders. "That you can never be sure of, and Goldie is a dangerous man. Why do you think the department has your team working out of a bank that believes your team is auditing the bank's financial records? It's because one leak could get you and your whole team killed. We are talking about a man who investigates everyone he gets involved with personally, and or otherwise. He has eye$_s$ and ears everywhere. He is no stranger to having people followed or planting listening devices. Baby, Goldie will kill you in the blink of an eye. Look, you get on back to work."

Carla smiled.

He returned her smile. "Don't look at me like that. You know I have no choice in letting you go back in undercover. First off, it's too late to back out now, we are in all of the right places and just about ready to go. Second off, you're going back in with or without the consent of the department.

They embraced.

Carla said, "Thanks for believing in me, Uncle Charles."

Chapter Nineteen

NOW Goldie arrived at the train station that evening about ten minutes before six, and to his surprise, there was a beautiful young woman that awaited him. He pulled his Caddie over along the side of the station, and upon seeing this young woman. He knew she had to be the princess. He got out of the car and gestured her over. She asked immediately, "Are you, Goldie?"

He replied, "Like, yeah, I'm the one."

She walked over to the car, where Goldie retrieved her over-night bag and placed it in the back seat of the car. As he opened the front passenger door for her, he asked, "And you are?"

She smiled. "I'm Tonya. My friends call me Tiny."

As Goldie pulled the car away from the train station, he asked, "Are you hungry?"

"No, I'm okay. I just want to get in and out."

Goldie smiled. "You are definitely my kind of woman."

Now Tiny was about five foot, four inches tall, a mouthful of breasts, no stomach, and one helluva ass. She also had child-like features. Goldie took one look at her and knew Red would take the bait and run with it. He said, "Okay, Tiny, we are approaching the block {Remsen}. I need you to pay close attention. Do you see that red-headed guy there," he pointed at Red. "Standing outside in front of the liquor store?"

"Yeah, I see him."

He reached into his jacket pocket and retrieved his bankroll, and after counting out one thousand dollars, he handed it to Tiny. "Okay, well, that's your target. What is the name on your identification card?"

As she rummaged through the money, she replied, "Terry Thomas."

He asked, "Is the I.D. a license?"

"It is."

Goldie pilled off another thousand dollars and said, "Okay, we are going to get you some wheels. I know a spot that will take cash as a deposit if you don't possess a major credit card. I want you to use the bullshit license when you get to the spot, give the man the required deposit, and get yourself a car.

Tiny smiled. "Hey, now that's righteous, I got to have me some wheels."

"Okay, Baby, stop bullshitting this shit ain't nothing new to you, and furthermore. What I have in mind probably won't surprise you either. I'm sure that Jose has briefed you."

Goldie continued. "Now when you get the car you will follow me back to Red's headquarters, the liquor store. At that point, I'll give you a beep, and I'm gone. I'm suggesting that you pull the car over as if you would like to cop {drugs}. Trust me, Red will make his way over to the car. The rest of the guys will back away out of fear of him. I want you to explain to him that you would like to score. You get high, yet you don't have any equipment either. You are from out of town. The objective is to get Red to go with you to a motel, and that's where I want you to set his ass on fire literally. Do you understand?"

Tiny smiled. "Goldie, believe me, I got it."

He returned her smile. "Okay, we are at the rental spot. You go ahead on in and do your thing."

The Game

As she opened the door to exit the car, Goldie reached over, placing his hand on her shoulder. She turned to face him. He said, "Oh, and another time, and possibly under different circumstances. I'm sure you know?"

Tiny smiled, "I know, I felt the same thing."

Goldie returned her smile. "Okay, I'll have Jose hit you off {pay her} when you get back to the city."

Now Goldie had let Tiny out of the car a block or so away. That way, the owner of the rental spot wouldn't be able to get a make on his car if the rental happen to get caught up.

After Tiny rented the car, she followed Goldie back to Red's headquarters, and when they arrived at the liquor store. Goldie gave her a beep and continued on his route. The hustlers out on the corner thought he was blowing at them. Goldie was actually blowing his horn at Red, he only wished that Red understood, that would have made it all the sweeter.

Tiny pulled the rental car over near the curb.

Red swayed on over to Tiny's car and asked, "What's up, Baby?"

She looked over at him through the passenger side window real innocent like and replied, "Nothing."

Red asked, "What are you doing out here all alone?"

Tiny remained silent while reaching over, pushing the passenger side door open.

He immediately thought that he had himself a victim.

As he got into the car, closing the door behind him. Tiny thought to herself 'so far, so good.' She replied, "I'm in town visiting some of my relatives. I just figured that I would sneak away and try to get myself a little something."

Red asked, "A little something like what?"

Tiny dropped her head for a few moments, pretending to be shy, and somewhat embarrassed. She looked slowly back over at him. "Oh, just a little coke, Do you get high?"

He blushed, "Yeah, sometimes, but for the most part, I'm about my business."

"Well, do you think we could get something together, and maybe, like, get a room somewhere?"

Red's heart rate increased and his eyes got big as silver dollars, "Yeah, yeah, that would be real cool. We can get some stuff right up the street here, and then we can go by my cousin's house."

Tiny looked at him intensely, and as she began to rub Red's hand gently, she said, "Look, I don't enjoy getting high around people that I don't know; plus, when I get high, I really like to enjoy myself."

He smiled, and at that point, Red was all in.

She asked, "So how much will the stuff cost me?"

"Well, Baby, that depends on how much you want to buy."

Tiny reached into her jacket pocket and removed two crispy one hundred dollar bills and stated, "How about I take you where you need to go, give you enough money to buy an eight ball, and then we go somewhere and find ourselves a room."

At that point, Red felt like God was finally paying off for all the misfortune that he had endured throughout his life. He replied, "Baby, I'm with you."

Meanwhile, Goldie was pulling into Newark's International Airport, where he had Hollywood on the line. He said, "Hey Baby, I got your kite. I need some R.N.R., so I'm on my way."

Hollywood replied, "Well, Big Brother, you know we would love to have you."

"Look man, get me a chick in mind, a round-robin. Don't do or say anything to her about me. Just point me in her direction upon my arrival."

"I can do that, Goldie, that I can do."

Goldie smiled, "Then I'm gone. I'll call you when my plane lands."
The line went dead.

Twenty minutes later or so, Goldie retrieved a shoulder bag out of the trunk of his car, paid to park his car, and quickly boarded a flight to Virginia.

{Foot-note} A round robin is a chick, with a place, car, and a job.

CHAPTER TWENTY

AFTER Tiny and Red had scored {drugs}, Red got the equipment that they needed and checked into Frank's Inn, on Route Eighteen.

The first thing Red did after entering into the confines of their private room was to start cooking the cocaine. Tiny took a seat opposite Red and commenced to watching him from the other beds in the room. She thought 'I don't know what he did, but I'm going to love doing this one.' Red's whole personality had changed. At that point, he meant no more to her than a piece of shit.

As he nervously took his first hit of the cocaine pipe, Tiny began to come out of her skirt, and by the time Red released the smoke. She had placed one leg up on the bed, allowing Red to look straight down into her love canal. He took another blast of the pipe, and this time she let the mouthful of breasts out of her button-up shirt. Red sat there looking stupid, feeling his groove and oats, yet unable to perform, and that's how cocaine affects most people, and Tiny knew it. She gestured him over as she laid back on to the bed, raising her legs while pointing down at her womb. Red moved over next to her on the bed where she took his head into her hands, and pulled it down between her legs. He licked and sucked, and she enjoyed. Tiny didn't feel that he was going to give her any of the cocaine, anyway. So she figured that she would get her thing off before she did away with him.

Red jumped up after a few minutes of what he considered to be foreplay and rushed back over to the small table where the cocaine laid. He took another hit, though this time, he did offer Tiny some of the get high. Tiny said, "I'll have some, but later. Right now, I need to freshen up, I have a surprise for you." She retrieved her overnight bag and made her way into the bathroom where she turned on the shower but didn't get into it. She arranged the things that she needed to complete her mission.

When Tiny returned from the bathroom, she sat her over-night bag down by the door, and in her hand she carried a small see through-purse. The pouch contained two pairs of handcuffs, a twelve-inch dildo, and a lighter. The dildo was filled with butane lighter fluid. She set the small purse down on to the nightstand beside the bed, and because Tiny was stark naked, Red never noticed her lay a dress out across the other bed in the room. His mind was elsewhere. He looked over at her and said, "We about to get into some real freaky shit, huh, Baby."

Tiny replied, "Whatever you like, Daddy, but first, I would like to act out a personal fantasy of mine. If you don't mind, Baby? You don't mind, do you?"

"Nah, I don't mind."

She instructed Red to bring the stuff {drugs} over into the bedding area, and after putting the stuff down on the nightstand. She told him to lay down across the bed. She removed the handcuffs from out of the pouch and handcuffed his hands to the metal bedpost. Then she began kissing him along his stomach.

Red said, "You sure know how to treat a man."

As she began pulling his pants down around his ankles and unbuttoning his shirt, Tiny replied, "Baby, just lay back and close your eyes." She repeated, "Now keep your eyes closed."

As she removed the dildo from the pouch and began squirting lighter fluid all over the exposed areas of his body, and then all over the bed. She said, "Here we go," and she struck the lighter. Red's entire body went up into ablaze. He screamed and hollered 'bitch this,' and 'bitch that.'

Tiny remained calm and moved to the other bed in the room, where she quickly slipped into the dress and grabbed her overnight bag at the door and exited the room.

Now by the time, the other guests had began to exit their rooms and gather at the scene. Tiny was pulling out of the parking lot of the Inn. She took Route Eighteen straight into downtown, New Brunswick, where she parked the rental car on a side street near the train station and quickly boarded a train headed for New York City.

CHAPTER TWENTY ONE

AS Goldie's flight had touched down at the International Airport in Virginia, a stewardess had awakened him. At that point, he thought, 'it's over, and the one that got away will stop that stick-up shit after he found out what happened to Red.' But then again, Goldie knew better.

Goldie exited the airport and took a car service into Virginia Beach. He checked into the Comfort Inn between Seventeenth and Twenty-First Street. His suite was on the tenth floor at the very top of the hotel. It was a beautiful layout; bedroom with an adjoining bathroom, kitchenette, and dining area. There was also a living room with sliding glass doors that led out to a terrace, where he could hear the sounds of the ocean.

After he checked into his hotel room, he got Hollywood on the line. He said, "Hey, Daddy 'O, I have arrived."

Hollywood replied, "Where are you, Brother? I'll slide by and pick you up."

Goldie smiled at the thought of being back in the south. "No need, I'm safe, I have already checked into a hotel for the night. I'm going to get a good night's sleep, and I'll call you in the morning."

"Okay, Goldie, I'll wait on your call."

"Hollywood, did you get a chance to check into the chick?"

"Nah, but I have someone in mind for you. She works at Brad's, she's a knockout, and she is the round-robin. Baby, this chick owns hers, and I believe that the job is for no more than kicks."

Goldie broke out into light-laughter at the thought of such

a prospect, and said, "Well, if I can't catch her, she can't be caught. Hollywood, I'm gone."

"Okay, Goldie."

The line went dead.

Now the weather had changed tremendously in Virginia, it was about sixty degrees.

Goldie removed his clothing and redressed minus the long john set, and jacket. He took the elevator down to the hotel bar and ordered a bottle of champagne, and then made his way out into the cool night air.

Now the beach wasn't crowded at all. It was late, and Goldie figured that it would be a beautiful place to do some thinking. He removed his shoes and made his way out onto the beach and took a seat. He popped the cork on the champagne bottle and toasted to the handling of his business. He sat there on the beach, thinking about all that had taken place over the last week or so.

All of a sudden, as if out of no-where, she appeared. She was out doing the same thing that he was doing. She was taking in some R.N.R., thinking, and enjoying the peacefulness of the setting. She stood there looking at him seductively. She asked, "Do you come here often?"

Goldie smiled, and thought, 'Wow.' He replied, "I come to places like this when I need to do some thinking. When I'm in search of an ideal, something concrete, something that keeps my head above water."

"Well, it seems that we share your reasoning in common. I just chose to share mine with someone."

Goldie asked, "Why me?"

"Well, it wasn't just you sitting here. I watched you come out of the hotel with a bottle of champagne. I watched you remove your shoes and make your way down on to the beach. I'm not going to lie.

I was curious, but to see you up close, and sitting here on the beach in silk socks. I'm intrigued."

He said, "Wait a minute, and just who am I talking with?"

She extended her hand and replied, "Oh, I'm sorry, I'm Sheila."

He accepted her hand. "Well, Sheila, I'm Goldie, and it is very nice to meet you. Would you care to join me?"

She showed him her whites. "I would love too."

Sheila sat down beside him, but before she sat, Goldie couldn't help but notice the gap between her legs. It looked to be big enough to throw an apple through. She was beautiful. She wore a pair of cut off jean shorts, a T-shirt, and sandals. She was light skinned and built to win.

Goldie asked, "Come on now. What are you really doing out here tonight?"

Sheila smiled. "Well, to be honest with you. I came to Virginia to start a new life. My divorce was just finalized, and I was awarded our beach house. So I decided that I would make use of it. I packed up and here I am."

"I take it that your ex-husband must have been into something big?"

"No, actually, I'm the big breadwinner. I'm an attorney, and I might add unemployed as of last Friday. He has a small detailing business."

Goldie asked, "What happened?"

"Well, last Friday was actually the day that I was supposed to return to work."

"Well, why didn't you just return to work?"

Sheila placed a hand on Goldie's knee and smiled, "I just wanted to leave everything of old and start anew. Plus, I can get a job at any law firm. I'm the best at what I do."

Goldie looked down at her hand on his knee, and then back up into her eyes, "Are you a civil or criminal attorney?"

"Well, I'm capable of doing both, but I'm in love with criminal practice."

He thought, 'Wow' again. He couldn't believe what had just fallen into his lap. He felt like he was dealt five aces in a game of five-card draw poker with duces wild. He stood taking her hand, and she rose. They walked down to the water, where he rolled up his pant's legs, and they waded out into the water about ankle high.

All of a sudden, Goldie just stopped and looked over into her eyes. He said, "Look, I've been thinking about your situation and mine. What would you say to the prospect of making a little money?"

Sheila returned the intense look curiously and replied, "First off, is it legal. Secondly, and just what would it Intel?"

He smiled, "Baby, you really wouldn't have to do anything. What I need is a place to hold up {stay}. I'll take care of everything, your mortgage if you have one, telephone bill, electric, and gas."

She looked directly into his eyes, "And may I ask, just what's involved?"

Goldie replied, confidently and was very gesticulate with his response, "Look, I'm in the business of sales. I'm expecting some products within the next week or so, which will be dispensed to various chains here in the South, and then distributed among the people."

Sheila smiled. "You make it all sound so simple."

"Well, you do know, I'm the best at what I do. There is no direct involvement. Most of the work will be done under my tutelage, and if something should go wrong. You being an attorney in all, makes sense."

Sheila replied, "It makes too much sense, that's the problem. I'll have to think about it."

At that point, Goldie figured that he would slip one by on her. He said, "Well, how about showing me where I would possibly be staying if your answer happens to be a possible, yes."

Now without even giving his question any thought, Sheila turned and pointed in the direction of her beach house. Goldie stopped and looked at the house in the distance, and then he asked her to give him a minute. He walked out into the water a few more feet, and then he removed a piece of paper from his pocket, which he slipped down into the champagne bottle, corked it, and then he threw the bottle out to sea. After this, he took Sheila's hand, and they began walking toward her beach house.

Sheila asked, "What did you just do?"

Goldie replied, "I just threw all my problems out to sea."

When they arrived at the beach house, Goldie paused, waiting on her lead, and just as he expected. Sheila had invited him into her place.

Now the house was beautiful and very well kept. There were three bedrooms and a master with it's own bathroom. At ground level, there was a dining room, kitchen, and a family room at the rear of the house. There was a large living room, with a picture window that held a beautiful view of the beach-front and the ocean. There was a finished basement, equipped with a pool table, big-screen television, a stocked bar, and out front, there was a screened-in porch

Now on the inside, Goldie immediately noticed the Sony Entertainment System and went straight to it. He loved music.

Sheila smiled, and as she left the room. She told him to make himself comfortable and that she would return momentarily.

After Goldie had found a selection of soft jazz, he grabbed a couple of throw pillows from a nearby corner and sat down on them in front of the system. Sheila returned from the kitchen and joined him on the throw pillows with a bottle of champagne, a couple of crystal glasses, fresh-cut fruit, and a can of whipped cream.

As they listened to music and talked, Goldie, fed her strawberries and cream on the throw pillows.

Now, this would have been an open-ended con for Goldie in the old days. Once he got in the door and built some sort of trust. The first time she would have left him alone in the house. He would have the opportunity to take her for everything, and if he didn't have any product (drugs) coming into town. He would still be in a position to tell her something happen or came up and that he had to send the money he did have up North.

Now by this time, he would have already slept with her and had her head over heels about his pimpin, which would have given him another option to take her by way of borrowing a few thousand dollars or so. However, this time, the poison was coming as sure as the sun would rise in the morning.

Goldie laid there on the rug with a pillow under his head. He looked over into Sheila's eyes and said, "You know I dig you, don't you?"

Sheila blushed, "I dig you too."

"Well, let's not let tonight end. I need you, I feel we need each other," He sat up and kissed her on the mouth.

Chapter Twenty Two

THE following morning, as Carla made her way into her place of work. She noticed Hank and Jill congregating outside of their office in the hallway.

As she made her way around them to enter the office, the two of them fell silent.

Hank asked, "Carla, How are you today?"

She removed her coat and placed it on to the coat rack. She replied, "I'm a lot better today than I was yesterday."

As Hank and Jill made their way into the office, Jill walked over and sat down behind her desk and asked, "So how did you make out with the lieutenant yesterday?"

Carla sat down at her desk and looked over at Jill, and then back over at Hank in the doorway, "Look, the both of you already know how I made out yesterday. So there's no need for games."

Jill stood. "What do you mean; I know how you made out? I'll have you know, I left the office right after you did yesterday. Somebody had to do the surveillance work on our primary case."

Carla leaned forward on her desk chair and asked, "What the hell do you mean surveillance? Hank, was you the one that instructed her to do the surveillance concerning Goldie?"

Jill interjected, "Who better to do so than me? Somebody had to do it. You couldn't."

Hank closed the office door behind him and walked over and told both women to calm down, and then he told Jill to sit down. He asked, "What the hell is wrong with the two of you? You two are partners or have you forgotten?"

Carla sat there, shaking her head from side to side, watching both of them closely.

Meanwhile,

Goldie was awakened by Sheila as she moved out of his embrace. They had fallen asleep, but Goldie knew that he fell asleep before she did and that she chose to lay in his clutches. If it were the other way around, Goldie would have just left her place and went back to his hotel room. He would have had to check his game to see if she would have sought after him.

Sheila rose and asked Goldie to go jogging with her that morning. He expressed that he didn't have anything to run in, which was totally unacceptable. She suggested that he retrieve a sweatsuit out of her bedroom closet and meet her out in front of her pad.

When Goldie got out in front of the house, Sheila was into some type of aerobic exercise, and then she just took off running. Goldie caught up with her and joined her in pace, and after a few minutes or so. He lost himself in thought to the world.

After Goldie and Sheila had returned from their morning run, they showered together. After which, they sat down to breakfast.

Sheila sat there at the table watching Goldie closely. She said, "Last night, I understood what you were saying, and I'm not totally sold on it. However, I would like for you to be my house guest as long as you are here in Virginia."

Goldie smiled. He sat there thinking, 'that she was going to be an even bigger challenge than he had anticipated and mainly because she was strong enough and smart enough to know that she didn't just need to settle for any man. It was also obvious that she didn't need his money. She had offered him refuge as a guest free of charge. He further thought maybe it was a smokescreen, maybe she just didn't want to get hurt, or just maybe she was trying to incorporate some of the same game that he was attempting to put down. However, there was one thing that Goldie did know, and that was that she wanted him in her bed.'

Goldie's dismissed the tape that was playing in his head, and replied, "I'll have to think about your proposal. Look, I've got to run. Will I see you later?"

Sheila smiled, "Of course, I'll be here."

He kissed her on the cheek and thanked her for a beautiful evening.

As Goldie made his way down the boardwalk, COBOL's Laws had come to mind, and he chose one to fit the situation {when in doubt, be smooth, and never show surprise}. He felt that he didn't have a lot of time to put into this situation. So he figured that he would go back to the basics, the things that he knew. One: Whenever a woman wants to pay you, do for you, or give you gifts, etc.. 'Do not sleep with her because after you're done, you are done, conquered. Sex may have been all she was interested in, and if she didn't like the way you sexed her, she would find someone else to pay.' It wasn't something that Goldie was worried about for he knew. Two: 'That a woman would pay dearly for something that she really wanted, and Sheila would accept the challenge wholeheartedly. He thought that he would make her wait until she was ready to give up, get her humble at heart, break her down like a shotgun, and then put her back together the best way he saw fit to benefit him.

After Goldie had finished doing some shopping down along the strip. He returned to the hotel and stopped at the front desk and paid for another day's stay. After which, he went up to his hotel room, where he freshened up and put on one of the outfits that he had purchased while out. Then he got Hollywood on the line.

Hollywood rolled over from beside his lady in the large bed and fumbled around on the nightstand until he got a hold of the telephone. He spoke into the receiver. "This better be good."

Goldie smiled. "Hey Wood, it's morning, it's me, and it's all good."

"Hey Goldie, where are you?"

"I'm staying at the Comfort Inn."

Hollywood smiled, thinking of all the memories that the two of them shared concerning the Comfort, and said, "Same place, huh?"

"Yeah, the little girls around here treat me pretty damn good."

Hollywood sat up on the side of the bed and said, "I bet they do, I bet they do. Look, I'll pick you up in an hour."

"Okay, Wood, cool, I'll be expecting you."

The line went dead.

After Goldie had cleared the telephone line, he placed another call to Shonda, and after a few rings. She picked up the telephone off the kitchen wall mount and said, "Goldie."

He asked, "What's going on, Baby?"

Shonda was doing some cleaning around the house when she received his call. She dropped the broom down on to the kitchen floor and replied excitedly to the sound of his voice. "I miss you."

"Baby, I miss you too."

She asked, "Did you hear about what happened to Smooth?"

"Yeah, Baby, I'm aware of the situation. How's he doing?"

"Well, he's a lot better now, he's up and around."

"Good Baby, be sure you tell him, I asked about him."

"Goldie, you know I will....Did you hear about what happened to Red?"

Goldie quickly put on his curious act and replied, "Nah, what about him?"

She interjected, "They found him out at Frank's Inn, in one of the rooms all burnt up."

"Wow, nasty, he was probably out there getting high and dropped a match or something. He was probably too high to move, you know."

Shonda was right in synch with Goldie, she said, "Yeah, probably."

Goldie smiled, "Look, I got to run. Keep it warm for me."

"Okay, Baby, bye."

The line went dead.

Chapter Twenty Three

AS Goldie made his way out of the Hotel, he was greeted by Hollywood out along the strip with a smile. The two gentlemen embraced and jumped into Hollywood's, B.M.W.

Hollywood said, "Damn, Goldie it's good to see you."

Goldie smiled. "It's good to see you too."

As Hollywood shifted the car into third gear, he said, "Look, man, I got to make a stop on Sixteenth Street for a minute. You don't mind, do you?"

"Not at all, man....I'm with you."

Hollywood asked, "Do you need a car while you're here?"

"Nah, I'm cool....I won't be here but a couple of days, if that long. I plan on staying just long enough to catch this little chick I met last night, and to put our plan into effect."

Hollywood returned his smile, "So you caught a little chick, huh?"

"It was more like she caught me, and who am I not to let some cute little chick catch me. Then again, you know she's going to have to work for it."

"I see that you're still playing."

Goldie looked over at Hollywood and said, "Man, I'm going to play till I die."

Both men broke out into laughter.

When they arrived on Sixteen Street, Hollywood didn't have to get out of the car. The gentleman that he sought awaited him. The young, thin man approached the car and dropped a wad of cash into Hollywood's lap in a smooth fashion.

Goldie just sat there, digging the scene.

Hollywood introduced the two of them. "Goldie, Sticks. Sticks, Goldie."

Sticks smiled. "I hope that this is the help that we so desperately needed."

Hollywood returned his smile. "It is, he is, and it won't be long now."

Sticks reached into the car and shook Goldie's hand and said, "If I can't move it. It can't be moved, but I got to have it, to move it. You understand!"

Goldie interjected. "Don't think, I'm not going to hold you to that....Look, we got to run. Hollywood will bring you up to speed. Oh, and the shop will be closed while I'm in town. We have a lot of planning to do. Do you need anything?"

Sticks replied, "Nah, I'm okay, and I understand, just don't forget me when this thing goes down."

Goldie made eye contact with him and said, "You got my word on it."

As Hollywood eased his BMW off the scene, he made a right off Sixteenth Street, and Goldie broke the silence.

He asked, "Hollywood, did the kid need anything? Was he as strong as he appeared to be?"

Hollywood smiled, "Goldie, the kid's okay. He's stable, and I see you still don't miss a beat."

"Hey man, I can't afford too. Cause everybody wants to dance to the beat, but nobody wants to pay the piper. At least that is until they find out that I hold the tune. Look, over lunch, we are going to rap. What do you think about our old spot, Harley's?"

Hollywood replied, "There will be players there."

"Hey man, like….the more, the merrier. That way, I can get a first-hand look at whom and what we will be dealing with."

"Goldie, you must have something pretty big in mind?"

He smiled. "Don't I always?"

Now Harley's was a well-known spot in the area of Virginia, and for one price, you could eat all that you could eat. It was also a hustler's hang out. During the lunch meal, Goldie enlightened and instructed Hollywood on how things would take place. He said, "What I would like to do is take your operation to the next level completely. Now for what I pay for the product {drugs} and what you can get for it down here. We will only fuck with dealers."

Hollywood sighed. "Goldie to be honest with you, I don't have a market for that type of shit."

Goldie smiled. "Then we will create one. Sales are something that you have to do. Shit doesn't sell itself. It can't because clientele people don't have money all the time. So naturally, I want to win your customer," he began to point around the room, "his customer, and everybody else's customer for that matter. Now the way to win the customer is by having the best quality product, the best prices, and in how you treat them."

Hollywood took a sip out of his glass and set it back down on the table. "I see your point."

"Now dig this, once we get all set up to go. The dealers you know push-up on them and find out what they are copping, and how much they are paying for it. Then in-turn, you save them a trip to the City and from trusting someone other than you to get their product for them. The way I see it is you are offering them a much better quality product, plus saving them a few bucks. Now, you don't want to save them much, though, because once you make it easier for them, and they see how quickly they can move the monster {drugs} due to its quality. They will pay our price to maintain. They will have to in order to compete with the competition, which we will be supplying also." Goldie asked, "Can you dig it?"

Hollywood looked to be having an orgasm in his face. He replied, "Not only can I dig it, I like it."

"Hey Man, soon you will be calling these same hustlers telling them you need them to take a certain amount of product from you, and even if they just copped. If the price is right, they will cop again. It's all about networking (a-net-at work)."

"Hollywood replied, "I can dig it, man. Kick that shit, kick it!"

"It's like me being able to purchase something for three cents that I know will sell for ten cents. I sell it for seven cents and in-turn I make a profit. Now you have three cents off the ten for all your players that purchase in bulk from you and being able to give prices like that you will have people that will buy just because of the profit they can turn on such a deal. Then you have all your associates that just want in on a good thing. That will cop from you just because they have got the paper {money}, and basically on your word. So, it's also important that you begin to build trust to the point that you can begin to use their paper for your initial purchase, which is truly the only way to make money. The best part about it is, if something should go wrong, you have risked none of your own paper. So yes, I say we create our own market right here in the South with what's available to us."

Hollywood smiled, "Goldie, I agree."

"Okay, now let's get out of here. Shoot me back by the hotel, and I will call you later. I want you to digest some of this pimpin, man. I want you to ingest the vision."

When Goldie got back to the hotel, he decided to hang out beach side. He thought, 'this must be heaven as he watched the string bikinis go by.'

As he walked out to the rail of the boardwalk, he noticed

Sheila approaching him. She was wearing a pair of biker shorts, a half-T, and a pretty little pair of track-Nike's. Her stomach was washboard cut, and her beautifully shaped hips were just-a-swaying. Goldie thought 'Oh my God, the gap is talking to me again.'

As Sheila cut off the distance between them, she said, "Hi Goldie, what's going on?"

He smiled, "Ain't nothing, just digging the scene. What's going on with you, Baby?"

"I'm just out for a stroll, and I decided to walk down by your hotel to see if I saw you."

Goldie slid the hair off the side of her face with a gentle hand and replied, "Wow, aren't you lucky?"

She showed him her whites, "I came by earlier, but I didn't see you. I was wondering if you would have lunch with me, but as you can see, it is a little late for lunch."

He replied, "There will be other times."

She said, "I was thinking more like dinner."

Goldie thought about playing hardball, but he realized it didn't matter because what he had planned would work with or without her at this point. He had taken his plan to another level. He replied, "Okay, we'll have dinner. I will see you around five-thirty or so."

Sheila asked, "What are you doing now?"

"I'm just going to hang out, dig the set, enjoy the sun, and then go back to my hotel room and rest up a bit before dinner."

"Do you mind, if I-"

Goldie interrupted her. "Not at all, be my guest, as you would say."

She looked up into his eyes intensely. "I said that to you."

"And I'm sure, I'm the only one you have ever said that to right?"

Sheila placed her hands on her shapely hips and replied confidently. "Yes Goldie, you are the only one."

He smiled. "Okay, Baby, I believe you." He threw his arm around her, and they began walking down the boardwalk.

They ended up having fast food out along the strip, after doing a little shopping. Then they went back to Sheila's house for an evening drink, where Goldie and Sheila sat out on the screened-in porch enjoying the beach scenery, and a bottle of champagne that Goldie had purchased while they were out.

All of a sudden, Goldie stood. He knew that it was time for him to leave. He said, "Baby, I better be going."

Sheila sat her glass down on the table and asked, "Why, Goldie?"

He replied, "Because there are a few things that need my attention."

She stood and looked up into his eyes. "Did you think about becoming my house guest?"

Goldie returned her intense stare. "I haven't given it much thought, I'm okay where I am, and at the Comfort they take care of me, and the service is excellent!"

Sheila just stood there looking at him, thinking, 'why doesn't he want to stay here? What is he getting there that I can't give him here?' She further thought any man would love to have this opportunity, but then she realized that Goldie wasn't just any man. She didn't want to, but she had to give him his props (respect). Right then, she thought about giving up on him, but she knew that she would never be able to live with herself. If she had to put Goldie down in the book as the one that got away. She really dug Goldie, but even more important, she knew that she had to have him inside of her. She said, "Goldie, I want you here with me?"

He replied, "Prove it."

Sheila asked, "How?"

"Do you accept and understand what we discussed last night, despite it not being an issue anymore because I have revised my plan?"

She looked up into his eyes and replied, "Yes."

"You know I say that because anything can happen, and there's no telling what I may need you or the spot for. Do you understand that?"

"Yes."

"See, I have only shared the things I have shared with you because I had hopes of you joining with me wholeheartedly. You know, becoming a part of me. I'm in everything for the long term. Do you understand that?"

Sheila never blinked an eye, and again she replied, "Yes."

"Then you do know if I allow you to move my things into your house. That they stay here, don't you."

This time without even thinking, Sheila blurted out, "That's fine with me."

Goldie smiled. "Okay, then give me a couple of hours. I'm going back to my hotel room. I have a few calls to make, and a few errands to run. Now, after I'm gone. there will be a message left at the front desk concerning you. They will let you into my hotel room, and I want you to move my things into your place."

Chapter Twenty Four

AFTER a nice hot shower, Jill made her way into the bedroom in her birthday suit. She walked over and retrieved her bathrobe off the bed and slipped into it. Then she reached over on to the nightstand and picked-up the telephone and flopped down on the bed. She decided to call Carla to clear the air between them. She dialed Carla's phone number, and after a few rings, she answered, "Hello."

"Hey Carla, it's me, Jill. What's up, girl?"

Carla placed the Own magazine that she was reading down on the sofa beside her and uncrossed her legs. She leaned forward on the sofa and replied, "What do you want?"

Jill asked, "What do you mean, what I want? I'm your partner, aren't I?"

"I don't know, are you? Are you the same partner who believes I wouldn't be able to handle this case? The same partner who said, I wasn't doing my job, and that the job I am doing lacks professionalism. Do you think I want or need a partner like that?"

"Look, Carla, I called to apologize, right, wrong, or indifferent. I'm sorry." A tear rolled down Jill's cheek. "I am truly sorry. I just want you to know anything that I have said or done, even concerning our differences. I have done out of a true concern for you."

Carla stood up off the sofa and said, "Look, we have been partners for almost three years now. When have I not been professional concerning a case?"

Jill replied, "Carla, this isn't just any case, and you know it."

"However, I'm doing my job, and you are right -this isn't just any case. I guess now you understand why I didn't report the boat trip and the fact that I never knew where we were going or what we were doing until we pulled into the boat basin. Jill, Goldie, is careful, even when he's careless. Please, just let me do my job!"

Meanwhile,

Goldie had made it back to his hotel room. He got Theresa on the line. He asked, "Hey, Baby. How's everything?"

"Goldie, I'm fine, and you?"

"I'm hanging. Where are we at with that thing (the product)?"

"All gone Baby."

Goldie smiled, "Okay Baby, do you need some R.N.R., or can we just push on?"

She replied, "It's up to you."

"Well, I say we push on and plan a little vacation for the both of us real soon."

"Okay, Baby."

He said, "Theresa, you know you have earned it, don't you?"

"Baby, I'm sure I have, I just can't wait."

"Look, Baby, the reason I called was because I need you to make another move. I know that's no big deal, but this time you are going to have to handle everything yourself. Can you handle that, Baby?"

"I guess I can."

"Sure you can. I'll call Jose and set everything up for you. Same pick-up spot, get the same thing, and the same time tomorrow as before. Okay, Baby?"

"Okay Goldie."

The line went dead.

After Goldie's telephone call to Theresa, she sat there in the living room of her pad, holding the telephone in both hands, and in a low voice, she said, "I love you, Goldie."

Now Goldie cleared the telephone line, and by this time, he had dialed another number and got Jose on the line.

Goldie said, "Jose."

"Yeah, Goldie."

"Look, man, I need the same thing, same spot, same time tomorrow. Can you dig it?"

"Goldie, I'll take care of it."

"Jose, Hollywood, and I hung out together today."

Jose smiled. "You're not, are you-

"I am, and everything is ready. I will call you when I get back in town. Oh, and before I forget, take care of the princess and tell her I said that she does great work."

"Goldie, you didn't, did you?"

"Nah, I'm talking about the job, but another time, some other place, and under different circumstances."

Jose smiled, "Look, man, you don't have to tell me."

"Look, I got to run, later."

"Okay, Goldie."

The line went dead.

After Goldie completed his call to Jose, he got Hollywood on the line. "Hey, Wood, what's going on?"

"Ain't nothing, taking it all in.., Look here Goldie, I'm going to get you within the hour. Hammer's going to be at Brad's tonight."

Goldie asked, "Hammer, as in dance?"

"You got it!"

"Okay, I'll meet you out in front of the hotel, later."

The line went dead.

Later on that evening, Goldie and Hollywood had met outside of the hotel at the scheduled time. Hollywood had the top down

on his BMW, and after they had cruised the strip. They proceeded to Brad's spot.

When they arrived at Brad's place, the party was already jumping, the place was packed. They didn't have tickets for the show, but Hollywood knew Brad, and upon request, Brad met Hollywood and Goldie at the front door. He welcomed them into the club with open arms, and after acknowledging them. He made his way back to his office, while Goldie and Hollywood made their way over to the bar, and that is where Goldie saw the goddess. Her name was Sylvia; she was pecan-tan, and definitely Goldie's brand. The chick was a top notch-broad, and when he first saw her, his knee caps got weak, but he got it together. Goldie took a seat on one of the bar-stools at the bar and gestured her over to him.

She asked, "Can I help you?"

Goldie seductively gave her the once over and replied, "You just did, look at you, you are beautiful." He removed a wad of paper from the inside pocket of the sports jacket he was wearing, and then he reached over tapped Hollywood, who was involved in conversation with a fellow player. Hollywood quickly turned his attention toward the bar and said, "Hey Sylvia, I would love for you to meet my brother, Goldie. He's from up North."

Sylvia showed him her whites and replied, "Hey Wood," then she extended her hand in Goldie's direction and said, "Hello, Goldie, the pleasure is all mine."

Goldie, accepted her hand, "And mine. I would like a bottle of the best champagne that you serve here at Brad's and three, long stem, crystal glasses."

`As Sylvia retracted her hand, she asked, "Why three glasses?"

He replied, "I was hoping that you would join us in one, but if you can't it's okay. I understand you being on the job and all."

Sylvia returned the intense look. "I'm not the only one working around here, and I don't guess that one will hurt. I don't usually do this, but it being the best in all."

"Hey, don't let me start you on no new habits."

She stood there looking at Goldie seductively and said, "Let's just say that I have my reasons."

Goldie smiled, "Baby, don't we all."

Now Brad's was a woodsy place, built basically in a shopping area, but very elegant and for all types of people. There was jazz some-nights, rock others, and rhythm and blues just about all of the time. However, it was Hammer's night, tonight. There was a large dance floor that would act as Hammer's stage, and where the band set up. The audience could see them after a few alterations of tables and chairs. There was also a banner that hung behind the bar that said, 'Welcome Hammer.' Goldie thought, 'Damn they are country.'

When Sylvia returned, she had a bottle of champagne and three long stem crystal glasses, which she set on the bar before them. Then she held the bottle of champagne before Goldie, label up. He nodded approvingly, and Sylvia popped the cork on the bottle and filled their glasses. Goldie proposed a toast. He looked at Sylvia intensely. "To a long and meaningful friendship." Then he glanced over at Hollywood. "To prosperity and to Hammer," who was now making his way on to the stage with his dancers? They tapped their glasses and drank.

After this, Sylvia thanked him for the drink and politely eased herself out of the equation. Goldie watched her closely as she moved out of striking distance.

Hollywood looked over at him, feeling that he was up to something and asked, "What's up, Goldie?"

"I need you to do me a favor."

Hollywood asked, "What do you need?"

Goldie smiled. "Now you know that Hammer won't be on stage all night. So when he leaves the stage. I need you to act as if something came up, anything. Tell Sylvia that you have to leave abruptly and ask her would she mind dropping your brother off at his hotel due to the emergency being in the opposite direction."

Hollywood smiled. "Goldie, you are going to owe me for this one."

"Brother, if we can pull off this one. I will owe you always."

After their brief conversation, Goldie and Hollywood got into the show. Hammer was on stage doing his thing {Can't Touch This}. Goldie thought 'Hammer was a dancing mother fucker, and for a moment he wanted to get out there and do his thing but quickly realized that it might be that damn champagne talking.

The show turned out to be fantastic, and when Hammer left the stage. Hollywood went right into his act.

After a few minutes, Sylvia made her way over to where Goldie was sitting and asked, "Goldie, what hotel are you staying at?"

Goldie fought back his smile. "Why, what's going on?"

"Goldie, your brother asked me to drop you off at your hotel. There's been some type of emergency or something."

He placed an inquisitive hand under his chin, looking as if he was deep in thought, and concerned all at the same time. "I wonder what it could have been. Why didn't he tell me?"

"I don't know after asking me to do this favor for him. He just took off, but he did say that he would call you in the morning."

Goldie dropped his head.

Sylvia placed her hand on his shoulder and asked, "Are you okay?"

"I'm fine. It's just that-"

She interjected, "Wait a minute, let me grab my things. I will tell Brad, I have to leave a little early tonight, and I will meet you out front."

Goldie asked, "Are you sure because I can-"

Sylvia smiled. "Of course, I'm sure."

Now, after Goldie got out in front of Brad's, it wasn't long before Sylvia was right at his side. She took his hand and led him to her car. Although Goldie didn't show it, he was rather shocked. She was driving a brand new Benz {S550 Sedan}. They jumped into the car and were off, talk about roomy, and a beautiful ride. Shit, Goldie thought, 'if he couldn't fuck her, he could fuck the car {ride in it and cum}.'

Now during the ride, Sylvia played jazz, and Goldie let her know that he was also a jazz fan. He liked Charlie P, Dizzy G, and Miles D, to name a few. Then he began to tell her the content of jazz, and how the music was far from being perfect, and that it consisted of a lot of improvising and how naturally anyone who could play jazz impressed him. Goldie said, "Listen to that, although separate, all of the acoustics are making one sound, and I believe that's what makes it beautiful."

Sylvia glanced over at him from the road and replied, "You must really like jazz."

"I do, but I'm versatile."

She asked, "Goldie, where are you from up, North?"

He smiled. "To be honest with you; nowhere in particular, I'm from the tri-state. I'll try them all."

Sylvia returned his smile.

"But I choose to call the Garden State home. Are you originally from Virginia?"

"No, I'm actually from up North also, but I have lived here in Virginia for the last ten years or so. My father is a doctor and has a private practice here. One day he just packed Mom and I up, and we have been here every since. I also work for my father."

Goldie said, "That must be fun."

"I'll tell you, it has its advantages."

Goldie smiled, "So you are an only child, huh?"

Sylvia looked over at him as if to be in shock and replied, "Yeah, how did you know?"

"E.S.P., Baby, it also tells me that you're spoiled. I just want to make one thing clear; I'm not going to let you just have your way with me. I'm just not."

Sylvia, not knowing how to respond, froze. Goldie smiled as if what he had said was a joke. It was a tactic in use to lay his game down. She smiled, not knowing how to take what he had said, but she knew she liked him, so she figured why blow it by flaring up.

Now Goldie was in her head and expected such confusion. It told him that she liked him enough to humble herself, and what he did, he did for control. There was one other way she could have taken it, as if this guy is crazy and when he gets out of the car. He will never have to worry about me again. However, Goldie knew the game was about gambling. He knew that she was an only child based on the statement (her father packed mom and me up).

Anyway, it was time to smooth things over, and what Goldie said now would make all the difference in her deciding what she would do.

Sylvia pulled the large car into a branch of the First Fidelity Bank, and she got out retrieving her shoulder strapped pocketbook and walked over to the night deposit drop-box. She retrieved a thick key-locked bag out of the pocketbook and dropped it into the night deposit box. Sylvia returned to the car, smiling, knowing that Goldie was curious.

He smiled. "I thought that was your pocketbook."

As she placed her bag down on the front seat of the car, Sylvia replied, "Most people do, but my pocketbook is locked in the trunk of the car. This bag is my drop bag."

Goldie said, "Brad must have some set up there. You mean to tell me, you walked out of the club tonight with all of that paper?"

She smiled. "I do it all the time."

As he returned her smile, he fell back into the comfort of the Benz and said, "Look, I'm staying at the Comfort Inn, along Virginia Beach, out on the strip."

Sylvia replied, "Okay."

When they arrived at the hotel, they parked the car in the hotel parking garage. Goldie had invited Sylvia in, and she accepted.

When they entered his hotel room to Goldie's surprise, all of his things were gone. He just smiled. He had a place to stay {Sheila's place}, a beautiful woman with him, and a hotel room for the night. Goldie took her hand in his and led her out on to the balcony. He said, "Do you know this has been the best time that I've had since arriving here in the South. I don't know, just being with you, talking about jazz, and family. See I'm an only child too. I don't guess it was as bad for you as it was for me. Yet, I feel for you. We share something beautiful in common. See, with me, circumstances and experiences have led me into a life in which I would always take for granted that I would be alone, but I also realized the life I chose didn't leave me helpless, and in that, when I'm with someone. That in itself helps me to remember all of the lonely times. So I'm offering you my friendship. I'm offering you a piece of me."

Sylvia replied, "I can appreciate you, and I accept your friendship, and I'll always cherish it. I have and do feel the same feelings that you feel. I have yearned for someone real to come my way, someone that I can let my hair down with and be myself around. Goldie, I'm actually thrilled that I met you."

Goldie moved to her, placing his arms around her and kissed her on the forehead. He retrieved her telephone number and walked her out to her car. He knew that she wanted to stay, but he also knew if he wanted to maintain and strengthen the established relationship. It would be best to let her getaway.

Chapter Twenty Five

THE following morning, Goldie arose in his hotel room alone. He showered and had room service deliver breakfast to his room. Then he got Smooth on the line.

"Hey Smooth, how's everything on that end?"

He replied, "Goldie, everything is cool. I'm back to my old self again. You do know that Red is out of the picture, don't you? I wanted to-"

"Ho'll, little Brother, thank God for small favors. You don't need that shit on your conscience."

"Yeah, Goldie, I guess you're right."

"Of course, I'm right. Look, I just called to check in on you, and to see if you were ready."

"Yeah, Goldie, I'm ready."

"Okay, you call Theresa later on today and she'll set you up."

"Okay, Goldie."

"Look, man, stay strong."

The line went dead.

Goldie sat in thought after his telephone call to Smooth, and he was trying to decide whether or not he would give up the game. In reality, he knew what would happen in the long run. He had watched it happen to so many others. He also had the logical aspects covered in regards to the game. See, he knew the hustle game was designed to get that paper as quick as one could, to get out, and to go legit! However, the more Goldie thought about it, the more he realized that the game was all that he knew, and despite not being happy. It was comfortable. He knew what to expect out of it.

Now Goldie didn't dwell on the subject matter (the game), because for once in his life. He was going to put himself first. He decided that he would win at any cost. That Morning, Goldie left his hotel room with nothing but feeling rather good. He knew if a person didn't have sense that they would never get the dollar. That statement said it all. Goldie would always be wealthy.

In other words, there were no more reasons for him to play this sick game. That his household, community, and society at large had led him too. He realized that he was finally growing up and becoming the man that he was destined to be

The Game

Revised 2

Chapter Twenty six

AS Goldie made his way down the boardwalk headed for Sheila's place. He took notice of how beautiful the beach setting was, and the inner peace that he felt at that moment.

When he arrived at Sheila's place to his surprise, she was sitting out front on the screened in-porch. He noticed that she didn't light up like she usually did, and right then, Goldie realized that she had gone too far. She was broken, she had humbled herself-to much, and in that it had torn her constitution apart in the area of women hood.

Goldie thought, 'the sad part about it was that he wouldn't be around to give her the strength and guidance that she needed. This was something that she would not only have to live with but learn to work through,' he said, "Come here, Baby."

Sheila rose and walked over into his arms, he just hugged her, thinking ' in his older age that he was getting soft.' Right then, he knew that he had to get it { paper }, and get it quick because soon the courage that he had would wither away for the game that he played due to wisdom setting in-{being able to see the whole picture, consequences}, and to be stuck in the game, lack the courage to play, and not know anything else. It would be worse than the hell that most of us are headed for.

Goldie led her into the living room, where he took a seat on a near by sofa and asked her to put on some soft music. Sheila did, and then she made her way out into the kitchen, where she retrieved a couple of cold drinks.

When she returned to the living room, she sat down on to the sofa beside him. It seemed now that he was there, she felt a little better, but to Goldie, it didn't make a bit of difference because the things that he did from that point on would be for him first. She just happened to be a part of what he was into at the time. Goldie knew that it was either "call or fold." He said, "Look Baby, later on, tonight, I'll be leaving.

Sheila asked, "Why, Goldie, why, is it something that I have done?"

"No, Baby, you haven't done anything wrong, you've been wonderful to me."

"Then, why, are you leaving?"

Goldie retrieved his cold drink off of the coffee table and replied, "Because the things that I have discussed with you need my attention. It's not like, I'm not coming back."

Sheila placed a hand on to his thigh and looked up into his eyes and said, "Goldie, right now, I need your attention."

He returned the intense stare, "Baby, don't think that I don't understand where you're coming from, but this is something that you're going to have to understand."

"Goldie, why are you doing this to me?"

"Oh, now you're the victim, you've given so damn much of yourself, huh?"

Sheila eased back as if to be shocked by his words and replied, "I think, I have giving plenty."

Goldie sat his drink back down on to the table and replied, "I'm so sick and tired of that god damn, shit. Everybody in this rotten ass world is always talking about what they give or have given. God damn it! They take to! You want to talk about a victim, damn it, look at me. Look at what, ignorance, fear, and this fuck up ass society has made me in too. If you think, I like what I do. Then you're sadly mistaken. This is the hand I was dealt. I was forced to play or die, and now that I have acquired proper knowledge, some courage, and the will to do something about it. You want me to put my plan on hold. You want me to give because you feel that you have given. You want me to let you take, but only for the sole reason of what you feel and think, and mainly for self-fulfillment. Fuck me, right!"

Sheila sat there watching him closely as he spoke and replied, "I didn't say that."

Now this time, Goldie eased way back on to the sofa and said, "You didn't have to. It's evident, and I think it's sad."

There was a pause of silence.

She said, "Goldie, I'm sorry."

He looked over at her and asked, "Why are you sorry?"

"Because....I didn't know that you felt the way you do. You always seem to be happy, and I surely didn't know you were as real as you are about what you do. It never occurred to me that this was your life."

Goldie stood up and said, "If you are going to be sorry, at least be sorry about the right things; be sorry that a little bit of curiosity, lust, this game, and that damn thing between your legs got you into this mess. That's what you should be sorry about. I'm going to shower. Is that cool?"

As tears begin to fill the wells of Sheila's eyes and stream down her beautiful face, she replied, "Yeah, Baby, go ahead."

When Goldie returned from the shower to his surprise, Sheila hadn't moved. She was sitting there thinking about the differences in their lives. Goldie was born into a bad situation and had graduated into something even worse. Whereas she had been sheltered and giving everything. Yet, she realized there laid a real man beyond the mask. He was good-hearted, smart, and a beautiful person. She also knew that he was a rarity {it is very rare that you find a man or woman with all -three of these qualities}. She admired Goldie, but she also knew those same three qualities that had drawn her to him could cost her everything.

As he walked over and took a seat beside her on the sofa, he played mentally with the idea of what she was thinking. He also knew the decision that she had to make {based on the evidence) should be hers, and hers alone, and if she couldn't make it alone. Then, she was a fool.

Goldie knew what he was doing was wrong, but he would rather know than not know because then he had the opportunity to correct it. He also felt that she deserved that same chance. Plus, he didn't want to be around no fools. He knew that they would get you kilt or in a situation that you didn't want to be in.

Sheila looked over at him and said, "Goldie."

He took her hand in his and replied, "What is it, Baby?"

"I want you to leave your things here and before you go. I'm going to give you a key to my home. Right now, I think you're the best thing that could have happen to me, and I don't intend to give up on you. Now I realize that we just met, but you put me in a position that clearly states, 'either you are with me, or you're not.' I believe I have more to gain with you, and I'm not talking finance."

Goldie asked, "Then, what are you talking about?"

"I'm talking about you as a person. I'm talking about you as a man. I'm talking about the things you represent like strength, courage, and enlightenment all of the things that I need and want in a man lie with-in you despite what you do."

Goldie leaned over and kissed her on the mouth and said, "Look, Baby, I'm going to handle my business, and I'll see you in a few days. This will give both of us some time to think and to look into what we feel. When I get back, we'll discuss it."

Sheila mustered a smile and replied, "Okay, Goldie that sounds good to me."

Goldie asked, "Are you hungry?"

"I could go for a nice cold sandwich, something with oil and vinegar on it."

Goldie eased up off the sofa and said, "Alright, Baby, I'll run out and grab us something, and while I'm gone. I want you to make my flight reservations, use Continental."

She replied, "Any specific time?"

He smiled, "You are my girl, right?"

"Yes, Goldie."

"Then use your own, discretion concerning the time. Just make sure that it's sometime tonight. I'll be back shortly."

Sheila forced a slight smile. She didn't want Goldie to leave. Yet, she replied, "Okay, Baby."

Now once outside of the house, Goldie stopped and removed his cell telephone and quickly placed a call to Carla, and on the first ring, she answered, "Hello."

"Hey Baby, how are you?"

"Goldie, I'm fine, where are you?"

He replied, "I'm in the South, something came up that I needed to handle.

Please, forgive me for not calling sooner. I should be there sometime tonight."

As tears began to fill Carla's eyes, she said, "Oh Baby, that's alright. It's just that I thought you had forgotten about me."

"Baby, now, how could I have possibly done that? I write to you every day in my mind -just to keep the sanity. I wonder how you feel, where you are, and what you're doing all the time. I'm in love with you, Pumpkin."

Carla smiled through her tears, "Goldie, I'm in love with you too."

"Hey, now that's what I needed to hear. Baby, I'll see you as soon as I can, Okay."

"Okay, Goldie."

The line went dead.

As Carla cleared the telephone line, she flopped down on to the plush living room sofa to reflect on the conversation that Jill and her had concerning her feelings for Goldie, unprofessionalism, and the case itself being a conflict of interest. At that point, Carla didn't know what to think, her emotions were in a whirlwind. She felt Jill's words as they began to flourish and come into existence. She believed that she loved Goldie, so doing her job could very well become the most challenging she ever had to do, and she knew it.

Mean while Hollywood was at the height of his career, and after rapping with Goldie, he went right into action. He was in the process of calling all of the hustlers he knew and rapping with them. He not only wanted to have a market for the stuff {drugs} when it reached him. He wanted it sold. He had also stopped by Goldie's hotel room, but to his surprise, he had checked out. Hollywood figured that he would hear from him soon, so he wanted to be ready.

Sylvia stopped Hollywood in passing and inquired about Goldie earlier that day. He thought 'damn, Goldie must have really put his thing down, but then again, every since he had known Goldie, it was always that way. He never let anyone choose him, in business, or in friendship. He always chose, and whenever he caught, he put his thing down.'

Goldie explained to Hollywood once, ' it is better to choose than to be chosen. It could save your life. It also limits the chances of being conned. If you choose someone {business or friendship} and they screw you over. There's a lesson to be learned, but if you allow someone to choose you and they screw you over. It makes you feel like a real ass, and in most cases, this is what governs how we treat one another. He did me wrong, so I'm going to do him wrong. It all stems from people not knowing and or understanding the rule of choice.

The more Hollywood thought about Goldie, their many rap sessions, and a lot of the things that he says. The more enthused he became about what he was doing.

Chapter Twenty Seven

WHEN Goldie got back to Sheila's place, she exclaimed, "That his flight would be leaving at eight, thirteen, that evening."

Now Sheila didn't want Goldie to leave, but she figured that if he had to go. She would want him to leave with her blessings.

That evening, Sheila drove Goldie to the airport, filled with apprehension.

When they arrived at the airport, after parking the car Goldie took her by the hand and led her to the gate which his plane was to depart from, and right before he got ready to board the plane. He looked over at her, and tears had begun to run down her cheeks. He took her face in his hands, kissed her, and said, "Baby don't cry, it's like I told you. I will see you in a few days {he turned and walked away}.

She called softly, "Goldie."

As he turned to face her, he replied, "Yeah, Baby."

Sheila clutched her hands tightly, and had nervously turned her feet inward and said, "You forgot something."

"Baby, and what's that?"

She walked over and handed him the key she had promised. He hugged her, turned, and boarded the flight.

Mean while, In the Garden State, Theresa and Cathy were on the telephone discussing how smooth things were going. The conversation was actually a smoke screen, Cathy had called to find out where and what Goldie was up to. She hadn't heard from him since he had left town.

Now Theresa knew this, and it wasn't like they were enemies or anything. However, Cathy hadn't been calling her either. So Theresa figured that she was up to something and although she didn't have all of the specifics about what Goldie was doing or where he was for that matter. The little information she could piece together. She would have rather died then to give it to Cathy.

Chapter Twenty Eight

CARLA hadn't stopped moving since she received the telephone call from Goldie earlier that day. She went out, and done some shopping, and while out she also stopped and got her hair and nails done.

When she returned home that evening, she was still full of energy and had begun straightening up around her place, and now she sat anticipating Goldie's arrival, his call, or something. She felt like a kid in a candy store with a limited amount of money. She didn't know what to do or how to act for that matter. It was like the first time all over again.

Mean while Smooth was back in full effect and as quick as he was getting the product. He was able to move it. He hustled by day and played the game by night. He had begun to exercise the game that was being passed down by Goldie to him.

Now Smooth knew that he had along way to go in the game, but he also knew that he had to start somewhere. He had the idea of wanting to show Goldie a few things upon his return, not so much in the area of the game, but how he had matured in the game, and he could only do that by way of implementation. So he figured that he better get some practice because Goldie wouldn't want to hear anything. He would want to see it.

Chapter Twenty Nine

WHEN Goldie's plane had landed that evening at the Newark International Airport in New Jersey, he had brought the few items that he carried with him on board the flight. So there wasn't any baggage to claim. He went straight from the plane to his car.

As he approached his Caddie, he thought, 'damn, you pretty mother fucker, I ought to marry you.' He jumped behind the wheel of his Caddie, and after clearing airport parking. He headed straight for the hideout with one thing in mind, and that was to make love to Carla.

When Goldie arrived at the hideout, the lights were off in Carla's place. However, she watched him as he had pulled into the parking lot. She was standing there, peeking out of her kitchen window, curtains.

As he approached her crib and rang the doorbell, Carla stood there, allowing him to ring the doorbell a few more times. Finally, she opened the front door and stood there as if she had just awakened.

Goldie smiled at the sight of her and said, "Hey, Baby girl."

Carla walked right into his arms and held on to him for dear life.

As he placed his arms around her, he said, "Pumpkin its okay, I'm here now, and I promise you. I will never leave you like that again.

She replied, "Goldie, I'm sorry, it's just that sometimes when thing are new, there's fear."

As she backed out of the embrace, Goldie kissed her on the forehead and said, "Baby, I understand, but you have nothing to fear with me" {this time he kissed her on the cheek}. "May you never have to look over your shoulder" {then he kissed her on the other cheek}, "Cause I'll always be there" { he kissed her on the mouth }. "I want what we have to remain forever new."

As they moved into the living room, to Goldie's surprise, on the easel, there was a portrait of him. It wasn't quite done, but it was beautiful.

Goldie smiled, "Wow, Baby, when did you start this?"

Carla returned his smile and replied, "The very same day that you left."

He walked over to the easel to get a closer look at the painting and said, "Baby, you never cease to amaze me."

She stood there watching him closely. She replied, "And I'll never stop. Can I get you anything?

Goldie turned and started toward the bedroom and replied, "Yeah Baby, you can prepare me a nice hot shower. I'm lagged out from my flight."

Carla got into stride with him and said, "I'll get us a nice hot shower ready."

They made love in the shower and the majority of that night.

Carla rose early the following morning, she kissed Goldie, and he opened his eyes. She still couldn't believe that he was there with her. He looked over and smiled at her. He said, "Damn, I thought I had died and gone to heaven, and God had assigned me, you. Carla just smiled. Look, I want you to take off from work today. We are moving you into my place. Soon, I'll want you to quit the job, and soon I plan to marry you in the islands."

Carla sprung up in bed, "Goldie, are you –

"I sure am, and the ring that I buy you this weekend should remove all doubt."

Carla placed her arms around his neck and said, "Oh, Goldie, I love you."

He began rubbing her back to assure her that he felt she needed at that moment, and replied, "I love you, too."

Now Carla was on a high, and found it impossible to get back to sleep. So she got up out of the large bed and made some breakfast, which she served Goldie in bed.

Goldie looked over the breakfast tray and said, "I sure hope that none of this stops when we are married."

She sat down on to the edge of the bed and replied, "And just what else would my wifely duties consist of?"

He smiled as he looked over into her eyes and placed his hand on to her thigh, "I'm sure there's a point to your question. However, there is one thing that I know we both enjoy doing."

Carla placed her hand on top of his and showed him her purely whites.

After breakfast, Carla removed the breakfast tray off the bed and had taken it into the kitchen.

When she returned to the bedroom, she took Goldie's hand and led him into the bathroom for a shower, where they went at it again {love making}.

After this, they dressed and planned their day.

Carla was to start packing her things, while Goldie got a moving company to move her into his place.

Now the moving company wasn't attained because she had a lot of things to move into his place. It was because Goldie wasn't into physical labor.

After seeing Goldie off at the door, Carla immediately

snatched the telephone from the kitchen wall mount and got Jill on the line. She answered, "What's up?"

Carla asked, "Is that how you answer the telephone?"

"Shit girl, I knew it was you."

Jill lit the cigarette that she intended to light upon receiving the telephone call.

Carla said, "I thought you quit smoking."

"Look, girl, what is it that you want?"

"What makes you think that I want something?"

Jill took a pull off of her cigarette and said, "You always skate around the issue when you want or need something. Now, what's on your mind?"

Carla blurted out, "Goldie asked me to move in with him. It's everything that I hoped for, you know, to get on the inside. What do you think?"

Jill rifled backed at her, "You mean; it's everything that we hoped for {to get someone on the inside}. Did you talk to Hank about this?"

"No, not yet….I thought I should run it by you first. You are my partner and besides that -if you're questioned -at-least you will be abreast on the subject matter."

Jill took another pull off her cigarette and said, "Well, let's get Hank on the three-way and handle this situation, like partners, and Carla, thanks." She clicked over and dialed Hank's telephone number.

Carla awaited their return to the telephone line. She wondered what Hank's response would be to her moving in with Goldie.

All of a sudden, Jill clicked backed over with Hank on the line. He said, "Jill, and just what can I do for you?"

Carla interjected, "It's not so much what you can do for her. We have a situation concerning our case."

Hank replied, "Well, Hello Carla, I had no idea that you were on the line too. So, what's the problem?"

Jill stated, "Goldie wants Carla to move in with him today."

Again, Carla interjected, "Jill, I can handle this, I only wanted you abreast on this matter in case you were questioned. Anyway, Hank, I'm moving in with Goldie today. It's a win, win, situation, and once we are on the inside. Its ball game and pretty much mission accomplished.

Hank replied, "Can you put the move on hold, string him along just a little bit longer. I need to run this by Lieutenant Charles, and he won't be back in his office until tomorrow."

"Well, we can't make him wait, and I can't string him along. I have no reason not to move in with him. At-least that I feel would be sufficient. After all, I felt that I was forced to accept or run the risk of arousing his suspicious nature. We all know who and what we are dealing with here."

There was a pause of silence.

Hank knew Carla was right, but he didn't want to be the one to make the decision concerning whether or not she should, could, or would move into Goldie's place.

Chapter Thirty

GOLDIE pushed his Caddie toward town and, upon arrival, the first stop he made was at Cathy's place. He figured the money that she had for him would tell it all.

When he entered her crib to his surprise, he found Cathy in the bedroom, folding some laundry. He walked over and sat down opposite her on the bed and asked, "Hey, why, so sad?"

Cathy looked up at him, "Goldie, I'm alright, I was just thinking."

He interjected, "There you go thinking, again. Just verbalize your thoughts. What's happening? Is the paper okay? Talk to me, Baby."

"Goldie, I was thinking about us and the money is fine. I love you, and I don't want anything to happen to you. I also been wondering where do we go after all of this is over?"

Goldie placed his hand under her chin and raised her head until their eyes met. He replied, "All the way to the top if you're not afraid. Baby, don't go getting weak on me now, because now is when I need you the most. There is life after all of this."

Cathy returned the intense look and asked, "Will I be apart of that life?"

Goldie placed his arms around her and pulled her close, "Baby, of course, you will."

After the embrace, Goldie made his way over to the nightstand, which was actually no more than a cover for one of his safe's. He checked the paper, and just as he expected, everything had gone well.

After which, he walked over and kissed Cathy on the mouth, and informed her that he had a few errands to run.

Cathy asked, "Will I see you tonight?"

He replied, "Baby, if not, I'll call."

Goldie left Cathy's place with the conversation they just had in mind. He thought 'when one is weak { humble and resourceful }, they're actually strong.' He knew that she would be there until the bitter end.

He rode in silence, headed for Shonda's place. He also knew Smooth would be there, and figured he would kill two birds with one stone.

When he arrived at Shonda's place, he removed his small key ring from his jacket pocket and opened the door.

Once inside, he found Shonda in the kitchen feeding the children. He placed a finger before his mouth in an attempt to silence the children that seen him before she had, which turned out to be to no avail.

When she spotted Goldie standing there in the archway of the kitchen, it startled her, and cereal flew everywhere. She didn't hear him when he entered the house. She ran over and gave him a big hug, the kids were pulling at his pants legs, and he was enjoying every moment of it. He asked, "So how are you?"

Shonda replied, "I'm fine."

Goldie smiled, "You look fine, how's the booty, Baby?"

She returned his smile, "You know you are crazy."

"Baby, I'm not crazy, I'm just real. Come on, let me look at you."

She eased back off of him and turned herself around before him, in an exquisite form-fitting silk robe, revealing sexiness in its rarest form.

{He con} "There should be a law against shit like that, let's hit the back room. I want to touch, feel, and hold what's mine for a little while."

The kids had returned to their breakfast, and Goldie took Shonda by the hand, and led her back into the bedroom. He took a seat on the edge of the bed and watched her as she lowered the shades in the room. After which, she walked over and pushed him back on to the bed and straddled him.

Now Goldie wasn't starving for any affection, but she was, and he knew it. So, he rolled around with her on the bed and played with her a little bit. He also knew that he had stayed away to long and that he had been giving her to much time to think {you can never take a break with the mind because the other party thinks too}. Right then, there was a knock at the front door.

Shonda eased out of his embrace, and after slipping her shirt back on, she left the room to get the door {bang, bang, bang}. Shonda hollered, "I'm coming." She snatched the door open, and there Smooth stood. She looked at him as if he was crazy, and his timing was really bad.

Goldie slid out of the bedroom and asked, "Hey Smooth, what's happening?"

Shonda interjected, "I don't guess any things happening now."

Goldie caught Shonda's vibe and gave her a be cool look and said, "Come on in Smooth and have a seat. Baby, get Smooth a cold drink or something."

She just stood there looking at Goldie for a few moments, and then she moved on into the kitchen. He thought, 'damn, saved by the bell.'

Goldie walked over and joined Smooth on the opposite end of the sofa and asked, "So how's business?"

Smooth replied, "I guess it's the best it can be."

Goldie leaned back on the sofa and crossed his legs. He said, "Then, that leaves room for it to get better."

Shonda returned to the living room with a couple of Coke's, which she placed on coasters before them, and then she exited the room.

Smooth took a swallow out of his Coke and replied, "Business is going to get better."

Goldie eased up on to the edge of the sofa and said, "Look, Smooth, I have something in the making. It's not up for discussion yet, but when the time comes, I would like to give all of my player's a shot at a real piece of change. Can I count on you?"

"Yeah, sure, Goldie, but what are we talking about?"

"Well, so far, it seems that I can help you double all of the paper that you have in one move.

Smooth asked, "How?"

As Shonda had re-entered the room Goldie rose, and said, "Smooth all in time, all in time. Look, I got to run. Smooth, I need you to hold the fort down."

Shonda and Smooth walked with Goldie outside of the house. Smooth made his way down into the basement, and Shonda walked with Goldie over to his car. She said, "You know you got away, don't you."

Goldie smiled, "Nah, I didn't getaway, you did, and furthermore. I'll see you a lot sooner than you think."

Shonda kissed Goldie and headed back toward the house. He just stood there watching her and thought, 'damn, look at that pretty ---'

Goldie left Shonda's house headed for Theresa's place.

When he arrived at Theresa's, he opened the door with his key, and to his surprise. He found Theresa still asleep in the bedroom. Goldie removed his jacket and hung it on the back of the bedroom door, and then he slid-up beside her on the large bed. He began to kiss her on her neck, her cheeks, her ears, and mouth.

Theresa smiled as she felt her body began to grow warm. She said, "Oh, Goldie."

He returned her smile and replied, "Baby, this is just what the doctor ordered. He told me one good shot of you would take all the pain away.

She placed a finger on to the tip of his nose, "Oh, he did, huh?"

"Baby, it's only right that a wise man seeks wise counsel when in need."

"Well, Goldie, whenever you need this shot, it will always be here for you."

He kissed her on the mouth and sat up on the bed and said, "Tee, I'll bet the house on that shot, but right now, I'm forced to let you get away."

Theresa sat up beside him in bed with her face, clearly displaying her disappointment. She asked, "Why Goldie, I don't want to get away?"

"Baby, I didn't come here for that. I came because I need a favor and some information."

Theresa asked, "Well, what can I do to help?"

"Does your Uncle Smitty still run that gambling house."

"Yeah."

"Goldie smiled as he watched her curiosity begin to grow and asked, "Is he still out to make a quick buck?"

"He will be out to make a dollar until the day he leaves this small planet."

"Good, I need you to get in touch with him, and tell him that I want to see him."

Theresa asked, "When?"

"As soon as possible! Hey, and what I have in mind is cool. I'll fill you in later, okay."

"So, I guess I won't see you tonight."

Goldie gave her a slight smile and replied, "Get your Uncle down here by tomorrow evening, and I'm all yours."

Theresa laid back on to the bed, still displaying her disappointment. She said, "Okay, Baby."

He leaned over and ran his hand down the side of her face, "Look, Baby, I'm in the mix right now, you know I would never put you on hold if I didn't have too. Come on, kiss me, I got to run."

She raised herself back up in the bed and kissed him.

After Goldie had left Theresa's house, she picked up the telephone and dialed Uncle Smitty's number, and after a few rings, he answered, "Hello."

"Hey, Uncle Smitty, how are you?"

"Who is this?"

She replied, "Its Theresa."

"Oh, Hey Baby, what can I do you for?"

Theresa smiled, based on his reply, and asked, "Can you get down to my place tomorrow evening? Goldie needs to see you. He said that it's imparative."

He replied, "Baby for you and Goldie, anything. What will you be cooking?"

"Uncle Smitty, who said anything about cooking."

"Hey, now that's a pretty damn long ride, the least you can do is feed me. It'll keep me from getting Goldie for food money, and then there's toll money. We also have to figure in gas money, and we can't forget ---"

Theresa interjected, "Okay, okay, I'm beginning to see your point, and dinner will be served around six tomorrow evening."

Uncle Smitty smiled and said, "I thought you would see things my way. I'll see you then, Bye."

"Okay, Uncle Smitty."

The line went dead.

Chapter Thirty One

ONCE Carla got everything into Goldie's place and arranged it. She thought, 'Wow, Goldie was right. His place was set up beautifully. He had a sunken in living room, which everything was white-in, from the Persian rug to the swivel blinds, and his music set up was beyond compare. He also had an elaborate smoked colored, glass, dining room set. He had a king-size water bed {specifically cut for him}, and there was also a-wall mounted big-screened, and so on.' Carla further thought, 'This must be heaven.'

As Goldie entered the hideout, he found that the house was lowly lit. He immediately noticed the few new items that complemented his new shared living space. Carla went out and brought candle holders, candles, new place mates, and had changed the kitchen curtain. He made his way through the house in search of Carla, and after finding that she wasn't in the house. He took a seat in his easy chair, in the living room, and got Theresa on the telephone.

She said, "Hello."

"Baby, it's me, Goldie....did you get a chance to speak with your Uncle Smitty?"

Theresa replied, "Goldie, it's all set up, I need you here tomorrow evening, by six, for dinner."

"Okay, Baby, I'll see you then."

The line went dead.

As Carla made her way into the hideout, to her surprise, she found Goldie sitting in his easy chair in the living room. She informed him that all of her things were now in his place, and from that point on she was all his.

Goldie rose out of his easy chair and walked over into the dining area where she stood and admired the new kitchen curtains. Then, he turned his attention to the new table set up and said, "Baby, that's just what the place needed, a feminine touch, and now it feels like a home."

Carla placed her arms around him and replied, "I'm glad that you like, and Goldie, I have something else for you. I'll be right back."

As she left the room to retrieve the gift, Goldie made his way back into the living room and sat down in his easy-chair. When Carla returned to the room, she was carrying two ring boxes. She handed one of the boxes to Goldie and withheld the other. He opened the box and said, "Wow! Baby, this is beautiful."

Carla also opened her ring box and held it out before him, and she replied, "Look at mine."

He said, "Thank you, Baby."

She leaned over and kissed him on the mouth and replied, "I just couldn't walk out of the store and leave this set of rings there."

"Look, Baby, I appreciate you, but these rings must have cost you a small fortune. How about I pay for the rings?"

Carla playfully tapped him on the shoulder and replied, "No, as far as payment goes, I used a card to pay for the rings. The card is about maxed, but Baby, we'll make it."

Goldie reached over and tapped her on the buttocks and said, "You bet your ass, we'll make it. Now come here, girl."

Carla sat down on to his lap and gave him a big kiss and a hug.

"Look, Baby, I have a passport, and either you have one,

or you will need to get one. We will need passports to leave the country. We will be married on the islands."

Carla asked, "Which one of the islands?"

"That's something I'll leave up to you."

She smiled, "Then, I choose Sunny Jamaica."

"Okay, Baby, Jamaica, it is, I have but one more question. Is Jamaica somewhere that you could live?"

"Goldie, I could live on any island with you."

"Okay, Baby, when it's time to leave, we will be leaving rather suddenly. So, if we choose to have our families at the wedding, we will have to send for them. Is that okay?"

"That's fine."

He smiled, "So, in other words this is our little secret."

Carla returned his smile and replied, "Of course."

Goldie began to rub her back as he had sunk into his easy-chair, trying to come up with a way to remove the kinks out of his exit plan.

Carla asked, "Is everything okay?"

"Baby, I'm fine. I was just thinking of you and how much better my life has gotten since you've been in it."

She smiled, "You know it gets better, don't you?"

"I don't doubt that, but if it gets any better. I won't know how to handle it."

She kissed him on the ear and said, "Now, that's why I'm here."

Goldie smiled, "Look, Baby, I know that we are not yet married. However, I want you to know that when I committed to you. I committed to you as an equal, as a partner, a friend, and a lover. I want you to be everything to me. When I'm weak, I want to be able to find strength in you. When I'm slipping, I want you to pull my coat, and when and if I should ever mess up. I will need your understanding, as well."

Carla locked eyes with him, and replied, "You've got it, always. Oh, and while I was out, I rented a couple of movies. Baby, you set them up, and I'll pop some popcorn, and then, we'll just lay back and enjoy the rest of the evening."

"Baby, you think of everything, don't you?"

As she got up out of his lap and made her way towards the kitchen, she said, "I only think of the things I think will make you happy."

Chapter Thirty Two

THE following morning, as Carla made her way into the office, to her surprise Lieutenant Charles, was there along with Hank and Jill. They all watched her from a sit-down position.

Lieutenant Charles stood up from behind Carla's desk as she made her way around it and said, "Hey, I'm glad you could make it."

As she hung her coat on the coat rack behind her desk, she replied,

"I'm on time this morning, is there a problem?"

Lieutenant Charles made his way around the desk and into a position where he could be seen by the three of them and said, "As you all know, there are codes, conduct, and procedures that are in place within the department for many reasons. Mainly for reasons of safety, and because we have come to find that our way is best, right and that they work. These procedures have saved many a life."

Carla interjected, "Does this have to do with me or the fact that I have moved in with Goldie."

Lieutenant Charles rifled back at her, "As a matter of fact, this is all about you, and your non-following procedure ass. Don't you understand that I'm not the entire department, and that requests don't just stop with me, not that you've discussed anything with me, or the department for that matter? The move that you chose to make with Goldie {Lieutenant Charles froze for a moment and then screamed out}. Damn it, and now you've got me calling him, Goldie, verses, said suspect, or ass –hole, etc."

Again, Carla interjected, "I discussed the situation with my partner, and Hank before the move went down. You were out of town, remember?"

Lieutenant Charles stood there watching her for a few moments, believing 'that she didn't have a clue as to what was going on there.' He said, "Yeah, Hank informed me of the situation that you put him in, and that he was willing to go to bat for you." He also said, "That he understood your position, yet he didn't tell you to make a move. You chose to do so. That's the part I don't understand."

Carla jumped up from behind the desk and replied, "That's not what took place. Jill, my partner, was also on the line when I talked to Hank."

Lieutenant Charles walked over and placed both hands down on to Carla's desk and looked directly into her eyes. He said, "Who, the partner that you just made abreast on the subject matter in case she was questioned about the situation."

She looked over at Jill {silence had fallen upon the room}.

Jill dropped her head, and then she looked back over at Carla and said, "It's not what it sounds like."

Carla asked, "Then what's it like?"

All of a sudden, Lieutenant Charles hollered, "Silence, Damn it, none of this shit is as it seems. I understand what took place here. I also understand everyone's position in this matter. However, that doesn't change the fact: That my ass is in a sling, right along with your asses. If we blow this operation, it's like I said, this shit doesn't just start and stop when it comes across my desk. I brought the three of you the Captain's argument, I personally concur with everything that has taking place here. Yet, I still don't like it.

Even if I didn't agree with the move that all of you have

agreed was best, willingly, or unwilling. I hadn't presented that to my superiors."

Carla asked, "So does the Captain know about all of this now?"

Lieutenant Charles mustered a slight smile and replied, "Of course he does, now, but what difference will that make if we screw this operation up. He assures me that it will be as if he never knew, and there's one more thing. We have ten days to bring them all down. The majors and the minors, everyone is in place, and there is a wealth of evidence that has been compiled. Good day."

As he turned to leave the office, Carla walked over and handed him her weekly report rather than going through the chain of command {Hank}. She also requested the passport that Goldie had instructed her to pick up for their trip.

He replied, giving her the cold shoulder, "Yeah, yeah, call me."

Later on, that evening, as Goldie headed toward town. He stopped by the first party and costume shop that he could find. He entered the shop and purchased the costume of a reverend, pants, shirt, jacket, collar, and a robe as an additional outfit.

After which, he proceeded on his way to Theresa's house.

When Goldie arrived at Theresa's place, Uncle Smitty was already there. He entered the house with his package in tow to find Theresa and Uncle Smitty sitting there in the living room engaged in conversation. He walked over and kissed Theresa on the forehead and said, "Hey, Baby." Then he walked over and shook Uncle Smitty's hand, while handed him the package with the other. He asked, "So how's everything?"

Uncle Smitty immediately began opening the package, he replied, "Goldie, I'm fine. Theresa tells me that you needed to see me."

Goldie took a seat opposite Uncle Smitty on the sofa and asked, "What do you think?"

Uncle Smitty, already knowing what Goldie had in mind, replied, "I think it's brilliant."

"Do you think you could get into Virginia, with the dress up safely?"

Uncle Smitty smiled, "Shit, if anybody can do it, I can, but Goldie black pants, black shirt, and the collar will be fine. The robe has to go."

Goldie returned the elder man's smile and replied, "Okay then, you have two days to prepare for your trip."

{He continued} "Now in two days, Theresa will be sitting outside of your house, at ten {am}, prompt. At which time you will follow her into the city. She will see my man and have you loaded, and from that point on, you will be on your own. Theresa will give you the destination of the drop after you're loaded. On arrival at the drop point, there will be someone there waiting for you, and you will know that person." Then, you will be ushered to an awaiting car where you will place the conformation call to me. That's when you will receive further instructions.

Uncle Smitty smiled, "Now you have to figure, what a reverend would receive for delivering holy water and wine to another spiritual institution.

Goldie and Uncle Smitty both just broke out into light laughter {he really admired Goldie}.

"No, seriously speaking, when Theresa gives you the drop destination, she is also going to give you two thousand dollars. If I should need you to stay, I'll handle all of the other added expenses, "Is that cool?"

"Yeah, yeah, that's cool. By the way, how much will we be moving?"

"It's not important if something should go wrong. It all carries the same amount of time."

Uncle Smitty sat there, rubbing his chin and replied, "Yeah, I see your point, now can we eat. Please?"

The three of them moved into the dining area of the house.

Goldie asked, "So Uncle Smitty, are you in?"

He replied, "I was in when I got here."

They shook hands and sat down to dinner.

After the meal, the three of them retired back into the living room, where Theresa served coffee and cake for dessert.

After which, Uncle Smitty retrieved his jacket from Theresa and said, "Well, I think I better be going. I would hate to wear out my welcome, and both of you know how I hate to eat and run." He shook Goldie's hand and told Theresa that he would see her in a couple of days.

Now, after Uncle Smitty left Theresa's, she began to straighten up around the house. Goldie just relaxed in his easy chair, while running his plan back in forth through his mind.

When Theresa was done straightening up, she walked over and took a seat on the sofa.

Goldie smiled, "Your Uncle sure is a funny guy."

Theresa broke out into light laughter and replied, "He sure is, I thought I was going to fall out when he put on that reverends collar."

"Yeah, Baby, you and I both, but what I like about your Uncle Smitty is that he's real."

Theresa replied, "Now that he is."

"Look Baby, that thing you picked up the other day (drugs} should be finished by sometime tomorrow night. Now from that point, I want everything to stop. I want you to rest up until it's time for your move with Uncle Smitty, and Tee while you are over in the city. I want you to do some shopping, spend some of that money you help me make."

She replied, "Goldie, at the moment, I don't need anything, and what I want right now, I can't have."

"Baby you can have anything you want. Sometimes it just takes time. How do you think all this has come about? We worked at it."

Now Theresa had on a skirt and blouse that showed every curve of her shapely body. She eased over and stood before Goldie {he watched her closely} and then, she leaned over and stuck her tongue into his mouth while raising her skirt and exposing her lower region and a sexy little pair of crotch-less panties.

Now, this excited Goldie, he began to slide his pants down into the direction of his ankles. He thought, 'Wow,' as he sat there erect watching her as she seductively straddled the easy chair that he had occupied. Their eyes met, she gasped, as she squatted and slowly took Goldie as deep as she possibly could inside or her beautiful body.

As Theresa began to ride his rod slowly, she moaned with pleasure.

He unbuttoned her blouse, which she allowed to slide off of her body down on to the floor. Then, he disconnected her bra, and as she continued the ride, he watched her firm breasts, jingle.

Now this excited Goldie all the more, he placed his hands on to her shapely hips, and began to guide her up and down at an intense pace until he came.

After which, they cleaned themselves up and Goldie informed her that he had to leave.

Now Theresa didn't want him to leave, she wanted to spend the night in his arms. It had been a while since they had spent any real quality time together.

Goldie returned the intense stare and said, "Baby don't look at me like that, soon all of this will be behind us, and we will have plenty of time to spend together."

"I know Goldie, but –

He quickly interrupted her, "Hey, I understand, give me a kiss so I can get out of here."

Theresa kissed him on the mouth.

Now on the ride back to the hideout, Goldie got Hollywood on the line. He asked,

"Hey, Wood, what's happening?"

"Goldie, I'm still setting up. However, I'm just about ready. The market that we intended to create, it's here."

"Hollywood, what can you do with a couple of cake?"

"I could probably throw a day and a half party, give me another day, and I will

O.D. {overdose} them on the cake."

"Look, I'll give you two additional days and let you kill them."

"Goldie, I'm looking forward to it."

"Okay, I'll reach out sometime tomorrow, later."

The line went dead.

Now, this was the move that Goldie was waiting on, the hit that he thought he would have to work up to in the South because he lacked the market needed. However, now, everything seemed to be falling into place. Goldie's biggest fear was losing Carla, and he didn't know how she would feel or what she would think when he told her that they were on the island {Jamaica} to stay. This would be without her having any knowledge of beforehand, or anything that would have taken place for that matter. At that point, Goldie didn't see any way to work the states back into their lives.

When Goldie arrived at the hideout, Carla was up lying in bed doing some reading. He moved throughout the house in silence, and after he showered, he joined her in bed, where he laid quietly in thought with his back to her.

Carla placed the book down on to the nightstand that she was reading and reached over and placed her hand on to his shoulder and asked, "Baby, what's wrong?"

Goldie turned to face her and propped himself up in the large bed, he replied, "Just thinking Baby, look, there's not much that I can tell you right now. However, I want you to have your passports ready by, Monday."

She asked, "So about a week from today?"

He smiled, "You got it. I also want you to find a travel agency and make the necessary reservation for us to leave on that Monday afternoon, for our new Island home."

Carla hugged and kissed him, "Oh, Goldie."

Goldie had no idea that all she wanted was to have him all to herself and that even in her position. She often fantasized about what it would be like to walk away from it all just to be with him.

Now Goldie didn't sleep much that night. He felt the need to perfect his plan of exit. However, upon awakening the following morning, he found that Carla had already left the house.

All of a sudden, he was hit with an idea. He reached over on to the nightstand and retrieved his coded telephone book. He figured that Robert and Stone would be able to help. When and if Goldie had problems, these were his henchmen. They would take life in a heartbeat. They dealt in arms, money, gold, jewelry, robberies, drugs, and the cheapness of lift itself, but even more important, they dealt in secrets. They were as real as they came in regards to what they chose as a profession.

Goldie dialed Robert's telephone number, and after a few rings he answered, he said, "Speak on it."

"Hey, Rob, what's happening?"

Goldie, is that you?"

"Now who else could it possibly be, especially sounding like Goldie?"

Rob knew whenever Goldie called, there was always money involved, he replied, "How the hell are you, man?"

"Goldie's good, and yourself?"

"A brother can always use a little more."

"Well, it's here, man, it's here. Look, I need to talk with you and stone."

Robert quickly responded, "When, where, and what's up?"

Goldie smiled about the conclusion of his plan, and replied, "Look, man, get Stone over to the location. I'm on my way."

"Okay, Blood, I'll be expecting you."

The line went dead.

CHAPTER THIRTY THREE

NOW Theresa was up and preparing to make her drops, but for some strange reason, Goldie was all she could think about. She felt that she was going to lose him real soon. She didn't understand why or where this premonition was coming from, and she really didn't know what to do about it, either. She felt a great sense of lose and believed after all of this without Goldie, there could be no life. She decided the first opportunity she got that she would talk with him. She gathered the things that she would need to make her drops and left the house.

Mean while Goldie had completed his meeting with Robert and Stone and was now on his way back to the hideout. He snatched his car telephone and got Jose on the line.

"Jose"

"Yeah, Goldie."

"Look, man, everything is going according to plan, and the market that I set up in the South, it's beyond what we anticipated. Yep, this is the big one. It should only take Hollywood and me, a couple of days to move in and out of there."

Now tomorrow, there will be someone traveling with my Baby {Theresa}, who will be moving as a servant of the most-high, I want him loaded. He has all of the information that he needs. He knows what we're transporting, but he isn't to know how much.

"Okay, Goldie, and the figures, what do they look like?"

"We'll discuss, I'll call you later.

The line went dead.

After Goldie's telephone call, Jose laid back across his large bed and placed his head on to Carmen's lap, smiling to himself. He was thinking 'how his plan seemed to be going the way.'

Now on the other end, Goldie was also deep in thought as he pushed his ride through traffic. He knew what Jose was thinking, and he loved his attitude of ignorance. He also knew the one that was least in the game they played would ultimately end up being the most in the end.

When Goldie got back to the hideout, he sat back in his easy chair and ran through a selection of music and anticipating all that would come to pass. He had finalized his plan, and now he would put the icing on the cake and watch it work. He got Theresa on the line.

He said, "Hey, Baby."

"Hi, Goldie."

"Look, everything is set up for you to make your move with Uncle Smitty, tomorrow, get him loaded and send him on his way. I want you to give him the money and tell him that he is to meet my man at nine o'clock tomorrow night, on the boardwalk behind the Comfort Inn, along Virginia Beach. It's between Seventeenth and Twenty First-Street, on the strip."

Theresa asked, "Will he be able to make it by nine?"

"Sure, he should be on the road by twelve noon. Hell, I've given him time to play with."

She said, "Okay, Goldie, will do, and Goldie, I love you."

"Baby, I love you too."

The line went dead.

After Goldie had called Theresa, he got Hollywood on the line.

He answered, "Yeah."

Goldie smiled, "What do you mean, yeah?"

"Oh, hey, hey, Goldie, what's going on?"

"I just called to check on you. How's it coming?"
"Goldie, it's coming along beautifully."
"The range."
Hollywood replied, "I would say, somewhere between three and four {cakes}."
"So, you're saying, "That will be taken upon arrival, right?"
"You got it, Goldie."
"Hollywood, if the price is right, do you think we could shoot for six?"
"Goldie, if the price is right, we can shoot for ten, but on a real note. I figure we could double-up on them if the price is right!"
"Well, six, it is, then, be around the house tomorrow night, and Hollywood it's up to you to find some more buyers. We can't hold it. I got –to run."
"Okay, Goldie."
The line went dead.
Goldie looked down at the Raymond Wells timepiece he was wearing and realized that it was almost time for Carla to get in from work. So, he figured he would make the final call at that point, and everything depended on that call and answer. Goldie just about knew the answer. He had put the convincer in the con long before he knew that it would all end this way.
Goldie got Jose on the line.
He said, "Jose."
Jose replied, "Yeah, Goldie."
"Look, I just got off the telephone with Hollywood, and it seems that he has
outdone himself. We are capable of moving four on arrival. I want six, I figure six would run me about twenty-three thousand

apiece. However, we are talking for you eighteen, easy. So whether you are ' in or out' on this deal, there's a profit for you.

Now being that I know this, I feel that it's only right that you give me a fair share. I say, we buy at eighteen and give Hollywood a percentage being that the profit margin is so great, but you and I will split the lot of the money between us after payouts. Give me a minute to check some figures.

Jose thought, 'that damn Goldie,' while checking a few figures of his own.

Now Jose intended to let Goldie have the equipment for about twenty-two thousand apiece. That way, he would make at least four or five grand off each cake and still be in for a cut of the overall lot of the money. He figured at twenty-two thousand that they would have spent about one hundred and thirty-two thousand, together. Then he would subtract at least four grand minimum off of each{cake}on his end, which would have left just what he had intended to spend in the first place about One hundred and eight thousand dollars. He also figured that Goldie would have given him his half of the one hundred and thirty-two thousand dollars upfront. Jose intended to get away damn near Scott-free, and Goldie would have done all of the footwork. He decided that Goldie deserved a fair share, plus there was still plenty of money to be made on this deal.

Goldie spoke into the receiver, "Jose, I figure, six, would run us about one hundred and eight-thousand, at eighteen apiece. One hundred and twenty-thousand tops."

"Now there are say, thirty six, to each one {ounces}, and at fourteen to seventeen hundred a piece, times six…We will have Virginia wide open, in likeness to prior projects, like Maryland, D.C, and the Carolina's."

Jose replied, "Not bad, Goldie, not bad at all."

"So I figure since we are not talking a lot of money to gain this type of profit. We should use the man's money."

Jose asked, "Goldie, are you talking consignment?"

"I sure am."

Now, this took Jose for a loop, because no longer was he working under the Big Man. The Big Man had brought him into the circle of the elite. So now he would be putting his own shit out there on the line.

Now Jose didn't have a problem with giving Goldie the equipment. It was just that he figured he would have received some type of money upfront. He ran the back of his hand across his forehead, thinking, ' it just wasn't his day, and to have that type of paper in anyone else's hands besides his own at that point seemed to be crazy.' He started to tell Goldie that he would make the move South with him, but that would have tipped Goldie off to what he actually felt. So he decided to go along with the program and to pray.

Now at that point, Jose could have really used a payday. The majority of his money was tied up in boats, cars, the few houses that he owned and a variety of investments. He also had the living expenses for a few of his chubby chicks. In essence, his situation wasn't as good as it seemed, and Goldie knew it.

Jose said, "Goldie….that will be fine."

Goldie smiled, "Okay, Partner, it's on, you know the time and the place, later."

The line went dead.

After Goldie hung up the telephone to his surprise, Carla was standing there before him. He said, "Hey, Sunshine."

Carla leaned over and kissed him on the mouth and replied, "Hi, Baby."

Goldie rose and placed his arms around her and pulled her close to him.

Carla asked, "What's that for?"

"Baby....that's just for being you."

"Well, who am I?"

"He kissed her along her neck, "You're Goldie's wife."

Carla said, "I 'am, aren't I?"

"You sure are, Baby. Did you take care of the business at hand?"

"First thing tomorrow morning."

Goldie smiled, "Look, Baby, do you love me?"

"Yes, of course, I love you. Why do you ask?"

"I mean, do you really love me?"

"Yes, I love you."

"Okay, Baby, I'm asking you to trust me. Now I will be leaving here tomorrow, and the next time you see me. We will be boarding the flight to the islands. Something came up that needs my attention, right away.

Carla stood there watching him closely for a few moments and replied,

"Yeah, I guess.., Okay, Goldie."

Goldie placed his hands on to her shoulders and looked directly into her eyes. He asked, "Baby, are you okay?"

"I'm fine when I got involved with you. I knew what I was up against, but you also have to realize that it's very easy for me to say, I'm alright. However, what I feel right now is something totally different. Goldie just promise me that if you don't stop what you are doing. You will at-least slow down when we return from the islands."

Goldie eased back down into his easy-chair, thinking, 'damn, she really thought I was joking about the both of us living in the islands.' He said, "Okay, Baby, I promise, but what if I told you to pack-up all of our things. The things that we would consider to be of importance, and that we would be staying in the islands."

Carla placed her hands on to her shapely hips and began shaking her head in disbelief. She had never really considered that he was serious about staying in the islands. She quickly switched on to autopilot {cop mode} to get out of her emotions. It was just too much to deal with at that moment. Things were beginning to happen to fast, and at that point, she didn't know whose side she was actually on Goldie's or the F.B.I.'s. She replied, "First off, what would we consider to be of importance?"

Goldie smiled, "clothing, money, jewelry, and all paperwork."

Carla felt that she had come to far, and giving up to much to let anything stand in the way of her having what she really wanted. At that point, she really didn't know whether it was a life with him, or to have him jailed for life. She replied, "Goldie look at me. I'm so happy, but what will we do? How will we live?"

"Baby, I have those aspects covered, I have a little money that I've been saving. I don't know, maybe we will start our own business or something. Baby, trust me, let's worry about that when the time comes. I want you to leave everything just like it is, minus what we find to be of importance. The mortgage is paid for at least another six months or so. I pay it by the year and if things don't work out. We will always have a home to come back too.

She flopped down on to the sofa beside him and laid her head on to his shoulder and replied, "Oh, Goldie, I love you so much."

"I love you too, Pumpkin. Now, next week, the day that we are leaving for the islands. I want you to take a car service to the airport, and I want you to leave your car in the parking lot. I'll garage mine and cover the couple that I have out in the lot and yours before I leave for the South, and tomorrow you will be driving me to the airport. Baby, you can forget about your job, and from that point on, everything of old will be past tense. We live for the future.

Chapter Thirty Four

As Sandra entered into the living room, she looked over at the clock that hung along the far wall in the small, elegant, well kept room. Then, she looked over at Smooth, who was sitting there on the sofa with a fist full of paper and stacks of money all over the coffee table. She asked, "Do you know what time it is?"

Smooth looked up and dropped the stack of bills that he was counting down on to the table.

Sandra asked again, "Do you know what time it is?"

He stood, "Baby, you made me lose my count. I have to get this money together for Goldie.

She snapped, "Is that Goldie's money? Smooth what the hell is going on?"

He walked over and took her hands in to his and sat her down in a nearby recliner and kneeled down in front of her. He kissed her on the mouth and replied, "Baby be cool, I'm trying to do something here that will benefit both of us, and definitely aid us in our future. Now I have to get this money together for Goldie, he assures me that whatever I can produce, he can and will double it for me. It has something to do with this new deal that he's working on."

Sandra slid up on to the edge of the recliner and asked, "Is that our money?"

Smooth smiled, "Yes, and isn't it beautiful?"

She asked, "Smooth, are you crazy? We are not investing all that we have with or in no-one. In the game, tomorrow isn't promised to anyone, and you should know that better than anybody.

Smooth eased back down on to the floor and retrieved a stack of bills off of the coffee table, and he held it up before her and replied, "Okay, we'll save a stack for a rainy day {he gave her an intense look}. Baby, I trust Goldie."

Sandra sat there in the recliner shaking her head in disbelief. She said, "Granted, you trust Goldie, well honey, I do too. However I can not, and I will not trust Goldie with our future. Smooth, Goldie's a businessman. He trusts his instincts, what he knows about people, the streets, and the game. He doesn't trust people. His life doesn't afford him that ability or luxury.

He asked, "So, what are you saying, Goldie isn't to be trusted, and that he definitely doesn't trust us?"

"No, that's not what I'm saying. I'm saying, as long as you are useful to Goldie, you are the safes person in the state of New Jersey. The questions are; what is Goldie's new plan? Where do you fit into the new plan? Have you worn out your usefulness?

Smooth got up off of the floor and sat back down on to the sofa, where he sat before the money in silence, and deep in thought about all that had been said.

Sandra called out, "Smooth" {he looked over at her}. She smiled, "You know, I got your back, don't you?"

He smiled, "Yeah, Baby, I know, let's go to bed. We'll finish this conversation in the morning."

As they made their way toward the bedroom, Sandra said, "I hope you know you're not getting any, tonight. I'm still mad at you, you were supposed to be here by, two am -- and here you come strolling in the house at seven-thirty this morning. You had me all worried about you in stuff."

Smooth placed his hands on to her shoulder's from behind and followed her into the bedroom in silence.

Mean while as Goldie had awakened in the large bed, he

noticed Carla lying on the other side of the bed watching him. She eased over into his arm and laid her head on to his chest. He kissed her on the forehead and laid back in thought about the move that they were about to make. He also took time out to think about Theresa, Cathy, Shonda, and a host of other women that he believed he could have had the opportunity to spend his life with had he chosen them. He pulled Carla close to him and smiled, realizing that none of those other women were her either.

Carla looked up into his eyes and said, "I just can't believe that any of my life is real right now."

Goldie reached down and pinched her on the thigh.

"Ouch, she exclaimed, as she playfully tapped him on the chest."

He smiled, "I just wanted to assure you that you weren't dreaming."

As he eased out of the large bed and slipped on his bathrobe, he reached over and slapped Carla on the ass.

She said, "Goldie, I'm really going to miss my life here."

He asked, "So what are you doing getting cold feet on me?"

Carla climbed out of the bed in the nude and made her way around him and replied, "Not at all, I've always wanted to live a care free life. I'll meet you in the shower."

Goldie watched her as she left the room, then he followed close behind.

After they showered, Goldie and Carla sat down to a nice hot breakfast that both of them had prepared. During the meal, they discussed the business at hand concerning passports, reservations, and the travel arrangements. After which Goldie led her into a walk-in closet in the master bedroom and handed her one of several shoe boxes that were lined with paper. He explained that the box would take care of everything and whatever was left of the money. He wanted her to put it into a shoulder bag and to carry it with her on board the plane.

Goldie asked, "Carla, do you understand what I'm saying to you?"

At that point, Carla couldn't hear anything. She was in shock, never in a million years would she have believed that he had that kind of money just lying around, despite the boat trip and all of the other beautiful things that he had.

He called out, "Carla."

"Oh, I'm sorry, Goldie."

He asked, "Baby, do you know what to do because there is no room for error?"

"She looked up into his eyes and replied, "Goldie, I'll do my part you just make sure that you're on the plane when it's time for us to leave."

"Oh, I'll be there."

She asked, "Goldie, what do you plan to do with the other boxes of money?"

He gave her an intense look, and then he smiled, "Actually there's too many boxes to just move right now, I will take care of it. I also have a little money that has been through the wash, and then there's some still in the spin-cycle. So to buy a spot in the islands won't be a problem."

Carla placed her arms around his neck and kissed him on the mouth. She said, "I'll see you around noon to take you to the airport."

"Okay, Baby, I'll see you then."

Now, after Carla left the hideout, Goldie wasn't far behind her. He left headed for Cathy's place, thinking, 'once he did what he planned to do, there would be no turning back.'

When Goldie arrived at Cathy's place, she wasn't at home.

He figured that she was probably out collecting some more of his money. He moved into the bedroom and emptied the safe, thinking, ' it was best that she hadn't been there because it would have made what he had to do all the more difficult.'

After Goldie retrieved the money, he started walking toward the door to leave Cathy's place. It was at that moment that he almost had a change of heart. Hell, these were his women that he was leaving behind, and he also knew what he was doing wouldn't last forever. At that point, Goldie believed it was time for him to do what was right in regards to creating a new life.

Once outside of Cathy's place, Goldie jumped into his car and drove away, and never once did he look back.

When Goldie arrived at his mother's, she was sitting in the living room in her favorite chair, and after a couple of trips back and forth to his car. He re-entered the moderately well-kept home, and set the boxes of money from the hideout, and the bag that he had retrieved from Cathy's place down on to the floor beside her chair. He leaned over and kissed his mother on the cheek before making his way to the kitchen and into the refrigerator. His mother thought, 'some-things never change.'

Goldie returned to the living room with a sandwich and a glass of freshly brewed ice tea. He sat down on to the end of the sofa, closes to Momma's chair, and pointed over at the money. He said, "Mom, you know what to do with that."

She looked over at him, intensely, and replied, "Yeah, I know what to do with that, but I would feel better if I knew your problem?"

"Mom, I'm fine, it's just that…Mom, I'm getting married, and I have decided to move over to the islands {Momma sat there in silence}. I'll need you to send me money as needed. I may also need you to aid me in purchasing a home {legalized money was in her name}.

Momma watched him closely and listened attentively as he spoke. She replied, "You know where the money is, and it is your money. Baby, you can have just about anything you want in the world. Who am I to deny your chance at happiness? I'm your mother, and all I can do is love you and support you in your decision. Just remember a legal way of life isn't hard, but it's not as simple as it seems either. Especially after being exposed to the game on such a vast level. It also seems that all of this has come about kind of suddenly. I want you to watch yourself."

There was a pause of silence.

Goldie asked, "So Mom, do I have your blessings?"

Momma smiled, "Yes, of course, you have my blessings. I don't even have to meet her at this point. I trust your decision making process, I trust you.

"Oh, and Ma, there's one other thing, Monday, on my way to the airport. I'm going to stop by here and drop something off, and Mom, when the wedding takes place. I will see to it that you're there. I have to run."

Goldie rose off the sofa, his Mom rose also, and he hugged and kissed his mother. He said, "Mom, I'll miss you the most." He left the house with his emotions in a whirlwind, but he was determined not to let anything stop him.

Chapter Thirty Five

WHEN Theresa arrived at Uncle Smitty's place, she parked her car across the street from his home.

Uncle Smitty spotted Theresa's car from his front room window and made his way outside of his place.

Theresa smiled; she was trying not to laugh as Uncle Smitty approached her car. He wasn't wearing the robe. However, he was wearing a pair of high water black pants, black shirt, and the reverend's collar. Yet the funniest thing to Theresa was the revealing of the white socks that he was wearing as he made his way across the street to her car. He spent around before her at the driver's side window and asked, "Well, what do you think?"

She gave him the famous once over and replied, "Uncle Smitty to be honest with you. I don't know what to think {light laughter}."

He asked, "What do you mean. You don't know what to think?"

"I mean if you're waiting for an answer from me. We better get going."

Uncle Smitty rolled his eyes at Theresa, thinking, 'what do you know anyway.' He just walked off headed for his car, which was parked about two cars up from where she parked.

When Theresa and Uncle Smitty arrived in the city, Jose was already at the pickup spot and waiting.

Uncle Smitty pulled his car behind Theresa's and parked, and as they exited their cars. Jose made his way over and asked, "Hey, Tee, how are you?"

She showed him her whites and replied, "I'm fine, and this is a friend of Goldie's, a reverend Smith."

Jose extended his hand, "I've heard of you, man. How are you, Mr. Smith?"

Uncle Smitty accepted his hand and replied, "I'm fine, thank you, sir."

Jose asked, "Is everyone here clear on role and function?"

Theresa replied, "Yes, we are clear."

Jose said, "Then let's get Mr. Smith loaded and on his way. He immediately signaled a couple of guys that were on stand by in a nearby hallway, and then he informed Mr. Smith to open the trunk of his car."

The two gentlemen walked over to Uncle Smitty's car and dropped a suitcase into the trunk of it. He slammed the trunk and walked around to the driver's side of the car and got in behind the wheel.

As Jose and the two gentlemen made their way back toward the hallway, Theresa eased up along the drivers' side of Uncle Smitty's car and handed him an envelope that contained two thousand dollars and the drop destination. He looked up at her and smiled, then said, "I better be on my way."

Theresa reached into the car and placed a hand on to his shoulder and replied, "I didn't want to tell you before, but the truth is Uncle Smitty, you make a great reverend."

He said, "Thanks, Tee."

As she turned and walked away, Uncle Smitty said, in a low voice, "Bye, Theresa." He then put the car into gear and drove off headed for the South.

Chapter Thirty Six

WHEN Goldie got back to the hideout to his surprise, Carla was back at the house and in the kitchen preparing him a special meal {lunch} for his planned trip. He stood there in the archway of the kitchen and asked, "Hey, Baby is everything cool?"

Carla heard him as he entered into the kitchen and turned away from the countertop to face him. She said, "Baby, everything is fine. We leave Monday afternoon, at three-thirty, on a Continental flight. It leaves from gate sixty, and the flight number is five seventeen."

Goldie asked, "And about your passport?"

"It's on the dining room table."

"Wow, Baby, I knew I could count on you."

Carla smiled, and then all of a sudden her facial expression changed, she asked, "Goldie, I know that you are not worried about it, but do you know how much money you gave me this morning?"

"Baby, it doesn't matter. What's mine is yours."

"Then let me rephrase the question, "Do you want me to board the flight with that type of cash in my carry on bag."

Goldie smiled, "I most certainly do. We will need that paper to get set up when we arrive on the island."

"Okay, Baby, I just thought that I would ask."

"Baby, it was a good question, now come here and hug me. Oh, and before I forget Baby, did you pack me a travel bag, because we need to get out of here soon if you intend for me to make my flight.

Carla stopped in her tracks and replied, "Baby slow down, you are already packed. Now you come here and hug me."

Goldie held a hand out before her and said, "Wait a minute, Baby, I have one more question. Are you sure that you can get all of our things to the airport that we plan to take with us?"

"Of course, I can, Goldie."

He asked, "And just how do you intend to do that?"

Carla placed her hands on to her hips and replied, "I'll pack the things we are taking with us, and I'll use the same moving company that you used to have me moved into your place. I've also made a connection with an airline company that is going to ship our things over to the island upon my arrival at the airport."

Goldie smiled, "Baby, you are sharp, now you can come and hug me."

{They embraced}

After which, Goldie left the kitchen, he walked into the dining area and retrieved her passport off of the dining room table, thinking, 'that all of this would soon be over.' He checked her passport, and then, he went into the bedroom to retrieve the travel bag that Carla had packed for him.

Now when Goldie and Carla arrived at Newark International airport, they kissed and made their goodbye a rather quick one because if they hadn't, they both would have probably changed their minds.

After Goldie had boarded the plane, Carla clung to one of the many large plate glass windows in the airport and watched his flight become airborne.

Mean while Uncle Smitty was at a filling station on the highway, he was traveling to the sounds of {Otis Redding, Sitting on the dock of the bay}. He was making good time, and everything was going according to plan. He entered the filling station to pay for his gas {self serve station} and while paying the young women. It dawned on him that he was spending his own money. His thoughts verbalized, he stomped his foot and hollered out, "That damn, Goldie," at that moment, all eyes had fallen upon him in the filling station. He asked, "What the hell are you all looking at?" He had forgotten all about his attire {the reverends collar}."

As he left out of the filling station, the few people that were inside were laughing hysterically. The young woman behind the counter asked, "What kind of reverend was he?"

Uncle Smitty cursed from the moment he entered into the filling station, until the time he left.

Chapter Thirty Seven

WHEN Goldie's plane landed at the International Airport, in Virginia, again, he took a car service, but this time he went straight to Sheila's place.

When he arrived at Sheila's place, he used the key she had given him to get into the house, and to his surprise, she wasn't at home. So he decided that he would shower and unpack the few things that he brought along with him on this trip.

Now when Goldie returned to the living room, he was dressed in something a bit more comfortable. The temperature had changed {South, verses, North}, he made his way into the kitchen and fixed himself a sandwich and after which back into the living room where he cut on the big screen television. He figured until Sheila had returned, he would just lay back and relax.

When Sheila got in that evening to her surprise, Goldie was asleep on the living room sofa. She stood there watching him breathe for a few moments. She couldn't believe that he was there.

Goldie felt her standing over top of him and opened his eyes. She was standing there in a two-piece bikini before him. She sat down on to the sofa, where he laid and hugged and kissed him. She said, "Oh, Goldie, I've missed you so much."

"Baby, I've missed you too. Can't you tell?"

Sheila smiled, "Of course I can you're back."

Goldie looked up at her lustfully and replied, "Damn, Baby, look at you."

She asked, "Would you like for me to put something on {clothing}."

He replied, "Hell no, I want you to put on some soft music, and I want to just lay here and watch you do that for me."

Sheila strolled over and retrieved a CD out of the music rack, which was located beneath the stereo system, and she bent over before him and while doing so. The bikini that she was wearing revealed her ass in its fullness as she dropped the CD into the player.

Goldie's body began to fill with excitement, and as his penis had began to stiffen. He exclaimed, "Baby stay just like that! He eased up off of the sofa and slid up behind her, and as soft music began to fill the room. He reached down and slid her bikini over to one side while allowing his pants to drop down around his ankles. He eased down as deep as he possibly could inside her beautiful body. Goldie thought, 'Lord how mercy,' and then, said, "So this is what I've been missing, huh?"

Sheila looked back at him as he began to fill her body with his hardened penis. She felt that she just had to see his facial expressions as he began to stroke her fondly.

He reached up and removed her hair from out of her face. His facial expressions excited her all the more

Sheila loved the way that her body had given him such pleasure.

He said, "Baby take your time. I'm going to take such good care of you."

Sheila cried out, "Oh Goldie," and at the sound of her voice, he ejaculated.

After the sex act, Goldie eased back on to the end of the sofa. He sat there exposed, admiring her {neither one of them, said, one word}.

As he stood up off the sofa to go and get himself cleaned up, Sheila waved him back down on to the sofa and left the room to retrieve a hot rag. When she returned to the room, she immediately began to clean up his lower extremities.

Goldie thought, 'damn, giving all of this shit up was going to be a lot more difficult than he had anticipated,' but retracted that thought quickly. He knew that he could always revert back to the game. He figured that he owed himself a chance at a life of honesty, work, play, and love.

Goldie said, "Ah –Baby that feels so good."

She asked, "But....was it good to you?"

He smiled, "Definitely! Baby, what time is it?"

Sheila looked up at the wall clock that hung above the sofa behind him, "It's ten, after eight."

He quickly said, "Look, Baby, I have to run {he began to, pull up, close up, and straighten up his clothing}. I have an appointment."

Sheila stood up off of the sofa, not really knowing what to say, she replied, "Yeah, well, okay."

He kissed her on the mouth and started for the door, but before leaving the house. He stood there in the doorway for a few moments {she watched him, closely}. He said, "I know you didn't think you were going to keep all that good pussy to yourself this time. Did you?"

Sheila smiled, "No, actually....it's been here for you since the first day we met."

Goldie returned her smile, turned, and walked out of the house.

Now out along the boardwalk, Goldie stopped and removed his cell -phone and got Hollywood on the line.

He answered, "Hello."

"Hey, Wood, its Goldie."

"Hey, Goldie, what's going on?"

"I need you to meet me in the back of the Comfort Inn, in a half-hour."

Hollywood asked, "Goldie, are you here?"

"Hey man, you know how I do it."

"Okay, Goldie, I'm on my way."

The line went dead.

After Goldie's telephone call to Hollywood, he proceeded on his way along the boardwalk toward the Comfort Inn, and upon his arrival to his surprise. He found that Uncle Smitty was already there and waiting at the drop spot. Goldie approached him out along the boardwalk and asked, "Are you looking for someone."

Uncle Smitty smiled, and extended his hand, he said, "Damn, Goldie, who would have ever thought it."

Goldie accepted his hand and replied, "I told you that you would know the person that you were to meet."

He said, "Goldie, I knew you were in on this thing. I just didn't expect to see you here."

Goldie smiled, "Guess what, nobody would."

Right then, up came Hollywood, smiling, he said, "Hey Goldie."

"Hey Wood, I want you to meet my Uncle Smitty."

Hollywood nodded at Uncle Smitty and had shaken both of the men's hands.

Goldie asked, "Hollywood, are we all set?"

"Hey, it's just like I told you."

Goldie smiled, "Alright, let's get out of this spot." He asked, "Uncle Smitty, where are you parked?"

Uncle Smitty's car was parked about a half block from the Comfort Inn, along the strip. He led them to his car and opened the trunk. Goldie reached down inside of the trunk and opened the small suitcase before them. He smiled upon seeing the product.

It looked like a trunk full of diamonds to him. He closed the small suitcase and removed it from the trunk of the car. Then he carried the suitcase over to Hollywood's car, which was parked a few cars up from Uncle Smitty's. He opened his trunk, and Goldie placed the small suitcase into his trunk and opened it. Goldie removed two cakes from the case, and then he closed the suitcase and removed it from the trunk.

Now, after Goldie had closed the trunk with his free hand, and then, he tapped on the side of the car and said, "Hollywood move out. I'll call you in the morning."

Hollywood started toward the driver's side of his car. He said, "Goldie this may be gone tonight. I wasn't bullshitting. I created a market for us, dealers only, at fourteen. Just like we talked about."

Goldie smiled, "Okay, Wood, move it. I'll call you in the morning."

Hollywood got behind the wheel of his car and started the engine. He said, "Goldie...if I'm not at the pad, ring me in the car."

Goldie replied, "Okay, Blood, later.

As Goldie walked away carrying the small suitcase toward Uncle Smitty, who was still standing out beside his car. He said, "I'm going to need you to stay, I'll be riding back up North with you in a few days. I want you to check into the Comfort Inn {Uncle Smitty looked at Goldie as if he was crazy, especially after he had spent his own money to come this far }.

{Goldie continued} "Don't worry about it. I will take care of everything when we get back up North, you got three grand coming when we reach Teresa's place. So enjoy yourself."

Now, Uncle Smitty liked the sound of the three grand, and he agreed to stay in Virginia. He actually couldn't wait to check into the Comfort Inn.

Goldie, on the other hand, left walking down the boardwalk carrying the small suitcase. He figured since nobody knew who he was, where he was, or where he was staying -that he would be safe in taking the suitcase with him back to Sheila's place.

Mean while Carla sat with Hank, Jill, and Lieutenant Charles in his office. The meeting was called by the Lieutenant on short notice after he found out that Goldie had left the state. He looked over at Hank and asked, "Did you know anything about this?"

Hank replied, "Of course not, Lieutenant."

He looked over at Carla and asked, "Why didn't you report this movement to your Superior officer{Hank}."

Carla really didn't know what to say, or what the Lieutenant would buy into at that moment. She did know that she couldn't tell him the truth, not that she knew what the truth was anymore. However, she did know that the departments plan to bring Goldie's organization down would take place in another six days and that she and Goldie had planned to leave the country in the next couple of days. She replied, "Lieutenant, I don't have to tell you how intelligent Goldie is, or how he moves. I didn't know that Goldie was going to leave the state until the moment that he was ready to leave. I took him to the airport, so I couldn't call Hank in the immediate. However since that time I've left two messages with Hank's answering service."

Lieutenant Charles reverted his attention back to Hank and asked, "Is that the truth?"

Hank confirmed that Carla made an attempt to reach out to him, and further stated, "Lieutenant, I checked my telephone messages right after you called me about this emergency meeting. So, I figured that I would share that information with you at the meeting."

Lieutenant Charles slammed his fist down on to his desk and

yelled, "Whenever we have or get someone on the inside, the department saves money on surveillance. So, what the hell am I saying to you guys?"

{The room remained silent}

"It means that we have a damn deviant, a criminal, and a suspect in a murder case at large out there without any type of surveillance on him." Again, he slammed his fist down on to his desk, and yelled, "This shit is unacceptable."

As Lieutenant Charles continued on his rampage, Carla had lost herself in thoughts of Goldie and decided not to mention her and Goldie's plan to leave the country. It was at that point that she questioned whether she would be able to do her job, effectively concerning Goldie, anymore. He had grown on her, and she knew that she had fallen deeply in love with him.

Chapter Thirty Eight

GOLDIE rose about eight o'clock the following morning, and while Sheila slept, he slipped on a sweatsuit and left the house to do some jogging.

When he got back to the house, he did a few different types of calisthenics out on the beach {he worked like a mad man), and the few women that had stopped in passing to watch him work was just the incentive that he needed to go beyond the norm -concerning his workout.

After which, Goldie made his way back into the house and up to Sheila's bedroom to look in on her, who at the time was still asleep. He made his way bedside and leaned over and kissed her on the forehead, he said, "Baby its morning."

As she opened her eyes, she began to stretch and yawn. She replied, "It is, isn't it." Sheila looked over at him and asked, "Where have you been this morning?

"I went out this morning and did a few calisthenics and some running."

"Why didn't you wake me?"

Goldie smiled, "Baby, you are going to need your strength, so I thought it would be best to let you rest."

Sheila showed him her whites.

He said, "Baby, I'm going to take a shower, dress, and make us some breakfast.

She sat up in the large bed and replied, "Goldie, I'll do it."

"Shit, you're still in bed."

As Goldie made that statement, Sheila eased out from between the silk sheets on the large bed, stark naked. He stood there, admiring her beautiful body, and as she made her way around him. When she reached the bedroom door, she said, "I'll beat you to the shower." He smiled as he stood there fully dressed for a few moments, thinking of a way to turn this upset into a victory.

As he entered the shower, Sheila threw her arms around his neck and hugged him. She said, "It's not how I played the game. It's what I was willing to do to win."

Goldie asked, "Then you admit that you were beaten."

As Sheila began to lather his body and to wash him, she asked, "What do you mean?"

Goldie smiled as he watched her move the soapy rag over his loins. He replied, "You mean to say, you didn't see what I did to get you up and out of bed this morning. So you could shower me, and feed me, after a great workout. Nah **B**aby, you're right, you win! You're showering me, and you're going to fix me a nice hot breakfast. Like now, I'm finished showering. I'll meet you down stairs."

As he left the shower, Sheila thought, 'smartass.'

Now, after Goldie had dressed, he made his way downstairs into the living room. He took a seat on the sofa and retrieved the telephone off the end table and got Hollywood on the line.

"Hello."

Goldie quickly asked, "Hollywood, where are you, man?"

Hollywood understanding the lingo, replied, "Goldie, the last movement on this pack {drugs} will take place within the hour. I also have a few more prospects. So I'll need to borrow a couple of dollars{cakes}from you. The last couple, I figure we could show some love on each one {O.Z.}, not too much though and re-hit the people that have already purchased the candy and are reaping the benefits of its presence."

Goldie smiled, "Yeah, by now, they are definitely in the money. Sounds good, and it's great to hear that you're on it."

"Goldie, I figure at this pace and level in another six months or so. I'm finished!"

"If you stick with me, man….I'll see to it! Look, we'll talk about retirement when you get here. I want you to meet me at eleven O'clock, out along the boardwalk, after your last move this morning. I want you to drop the money into a box and wrap it as if it were a gift for someone and bring it with you when you come. We will swap gifts while we exchange pleasantries."

Hollywood replied, "Okay, Goldie, I'll see you, then."

After Goldie's telephone call to Hollywood, he places another call to the Comfort Inn, where Uncle Smitty was staying.

The Hotel operator answered, "Comfort Inn. May I help you, please?"

Goldie asked for the hotel room of Mr. Charles Smith, and after a few rings, Uncle Smitty picked up the receiver and said, "Speak on it."

"Hey, Player, how's everything?"

"Goldie, I'm having a ball."

Goldie heard voices in the back ground of the call and asked, "What are you doing having a party?"

Uncle Smitty replied, "Nah, just a couple of girlfriends that I met last night."

"Well, look, I'll let you get back to them. I just called to check on you."

"Goldie, I'm fine."

"Very good, then, I'll ring you later."

The line went dead.

After Goldie had completed his telephone calls, he made his way into the kitchen, where Sheila had breakfast all laid out for him. He walked over and joined her at the kitchen table and asked, "Baby, do you have any gift-wrapping paper around the house?"

Sheila placed a hand on to her head as if to be thinking and replied, "I should, I believe there's some downstairs in the basement."

Goldie took a sip out of his glass of orange juice. Then, he reached over and retrieved his fork off the kitchen table. He said, "Look, after breakfast, I want you to grab the bag that I brought in with me last night. I want you to wrap two of the four packages that are in the bag for me."

Sheila looked over at him from across the table and asked, "What's up?"

Goldie replied, "Baby it's business."

Mean while Hollywood had just completed the last move (sell) he had to make on the pack that he had received from Goldie, and was now engaged in one of his many sells pitches to a fellow player. He said, "Look, man, I'm trying to make a move. Let's say I give you a couple of days to recoup your investment, and then, I made the price a little better for you. Would I be able to count on you for another seven or eight {OZ's}?"

The hustler smiled as he processed Hollywood's pitch and replied, "I'll tell you what if you can guarantee me a better price. I'll commit to taking at-least another five {OZ'S}."

Hollywood thought, 'I got him.' He said, "Look, man, you know you have to take more cake than that to even feel the difference in price. I'm going to count you for eight and on my next trip. I'll throw you one."

There was a pause of silence.

The player smiled, "Okay, Wood, you got me. We'll rap on it."

Hollywood extended his hand and said, "Now that's how you feel it."

Chapter Thirty Nine

CARLA rose early that morning also, and was now in the master bedroom of the hideout, packing. She figured the sooner she got it done, the better she would feel. She also couldn't believe that she decided to leave the country with Goldie either.

After she finished packing, between runs, she planned to finish Goldie's portrait, this would be her gift to him besides herself.

Carla also had a lot of thoughts running through her mind. She wasn't getting cold feet or anything, but she realized that she would be giving up a lot. She was giving up everything, but after thinking about it. She figured it to be a rather small price to pay for love and to be with someone that she wanted to be with for the rest of her life -just thinking about all that had happened between Goldie and her sent chills through her entire body. Carla couldn't wait to see Goldie board that plane with her to the Islands.

Mean while as Goldie approached the Comfort Inn, he found that Hollywood was already there waiting for him. He stood there with his gift in hand and upon meeting. They shook hands and simply exchanged gifts.

Goldie, said, "Hey Sport! How's everything?"

Hollywood smiled, "Goldie, things couldn't be better."

As Goldie led Hollywood out along the rail of the boardwalk, he said, "Look, man, as far as retirement goes. You have to ask yourself what you are willing to give to gain the retirement that you are seeking, especially in six months.

Hollywood asked, "Well, how do you think I can accomplish a six-month goal of retirement?"

There was a pause of silence.

Goldie replied, "The first thing we do is reinvest every cent that we make off this deal after payouts.

{He continued} Now there's the man that we have to pay, and then there's Jose's share. After which we take what's left and invest it all, and your share isn't like mine. So it's to your advantage to invest with me. We do our own thing, and at that point, I'll need any additional monies that you can afford to invest. I'll get you something {product}for the price that I pay for it. The more we spend, the better my price, the more you're able to acquire.

Now you won't be able to sell your product until we finish what we have, but while I'm up North during reinvestment trips. The market will be all yours, and the profit that you can to turn. I can promise you that it will be a mark you only dreamed about in the past.

Hollywood listened attentively as he spoke and then asked, "What type of prices are we talking about?"

Goldie looked out at the beach and then back over at Hollywood, he replied, "Now I know what you were paying, and how much you hated making the trip back and forth to New York, and all of the risks that was involved. What if I said, 'that I could save you three to four thousand, per –cake."

"Goldie, at that price, I'll take three {cakes}outside of the initial investment that we plan to make."

Goldie smiled, "Now, I know there's a lot of paper running through your hands, and right now you are probably wondering why I want to invest so much without a payout to you. I'm going to let you in on a secret, I'm contemplating retirement too. So, I figure -three or four more moves like the one we are planning, and in six months we will both be done."

Hollywood smiled and extended his hand. He replied, "Let's get it done."

Goldie accepted his hand and said, "Consider it done."

Now at that moment, Uncle Smitty was partying his ass off in his Hotel room. One of the women partying with him brought a radio, and the other woman had brought the pot, while Uncle Smitty was trying to buy all the liquor that he could from the Hotel bar. He turned out to be the talk of the Hotel. He had checked in as a reverend, but he was destined to leave a player.

Chapter Forty

CATHY was on the telephone with Theresa engaged in conversation, and she was in the process of explaining -that she hadn't seen Goldie in a few days, and after making her pickups upon returning home. She went into the bedroom to put the money into the safe, and to her surprise, it was empty.

Now it wasn't like she was broke or anything, the call was actually out of concern, and after all -it was Goldie's money. Cathy also told Theresa that Goldie hadn't left a note, message, or anything and that she didn't know what to think.

Theresa explained, 'that Goldie was fine, and that she didn't have to worry about him. She also told Cathy that Goldie was into something, and although she didn't know what he was into, she did know that he was safe.

After a day of sun and fun out on the beach, Goldie and Sheila had made their way back to the house and were now downstairs in the basement listening to music and shooting pool.

Goldie sat the chalk back down on to the pool table after chalking up his stick. He said, "Nine-ball, side pocket....Eight-ball, corner pocket....Baby, that's another game for me, and you know, you owe me."

Sheila interrupted him, "Goldie, that's not fare you said, you couldn't shoot pool."

"I say a lot of things."

She placed her hands on to her hips and replied, "Alright, one more game."

Goldie smiled while giving her the once over and said, "Nah, that's it for me. I think it's best that I quit while I'm ahead."

"You mean that you are not going to give me a chance to get even?"

"No, but I'll tell you what, I'll play you one more game. If I win, we make love. If you win, we still make love. However, the loser has to drink seven shots of liquor of the winner's choice."

Sheila smiled, "Okay, you're on."

Goldie removed a coin from his pocket and said, "Alright, we'll flip a coin to see who breaks. He flipped the coin into the air and said, "Heads, I win. Tales, you lose."

Sheila hollered, "Tales."

He told her, "You lose, and he broke the balls."

Mean while Hollywood was out completing a few of the product sales that he had set up, and one of the two cakes that he got from Goldie was already gone. Hollywood believed that good business was wherever you found it, and he looked everywhere for it. He hustled like he was on a mission and felt that he was finally getting a taste of the big time. At that point, he knew that he was willing to give anything to accomplish his goal of retirement.

Now Goldie and Sheila were into their third game of pool, and by now, they both seemed to be intoxicated, but not because Sheila had won any games. Goldie just decided to drink with her. He leaned over the pool table and said, "Eight-ball, side pocket.

She said, "No, Goldie....that's to easy."

He smiled, "Okay, Baby, then, I will bank the ball cross side."

Sheila walked over and stood there behind the intended pocket and raised her T-shirt, exposing her belly button before him and said, "Alright, go head."

Goldie took his que –stick and made contact with the eight

ball, and slowly but surely, the ball dropped into the side pocket. He said, "Alright, Baby that's another game."

As he made his way over to the bar, he said, "Now come on over here, so I can set up a few more drinks for you."

She called out, "Goldie {he stopped and turned to face her}. If I drink anymore, I'm going to be drunk."

He replied, "That's exactly how I want you. That way....I can take total advantage of your pretty ass."

She stood there looking at him, seductively, he leaned back on to the bar stools and said, "Drink or get naked."

Sheila began removing the T-shirt that she was wearing, which underneath she wore no bra. Her stomach was flat as a board, and her Titty's were perfectly proportioned and firm. She stood there in cut -off jean shorts and sandals. She brought the animal out of Goldie, as he watched her as she slowly removed the pair of shorts that she was wearing.

Goldie said, "Get your pretty ass up on to the pool table."

Sheila climbed up into the center of the pool table and laid out on her back with her legs spread apart. Goldie got down off the barstool that he occupied and began removing his clothing. He thought to himself, 'that Sheila had the prettiest pussy that he had ever seen.'

After removing his clothing, he climbed up in between her legs on to the pool table and began to take time with her body.

As he kneeled down over top of her admiring her beautiful body, she placed her foot into the center of his chest in a playful manner. He took her foot into his hands and placed her toes into his mouth. Her body tensed....as she made seductive eye contact with him. He smiled as he began kissing her, inner leg's, and thigh's, and when he reached her sex. He tasted her!

Sheila threw her head back and began running her fingernails across the felt-top table.

Goldie looked up into her eyes and asked, "You want me to fuck you, don't you, Baby?"

She cried out, "Yes, Goldie, I do want you to fuck me. Goldie, I really need you to fuck me right now."

Now most men as fine as she was would have never talked to her that way. They would have been pleased just to have her sexually, especially if it was for the first time. However, Goldie was just the opposite, he knew what them pretty little educated, intellectual, independent, stable chicks liked, and the majority of them were freaks anyway. He actually believed that he had an obligation to expose as many women as he possibly could to the challenge of being themselves….to deal with being excited, to seek to excite, and to express their sexuality wholeheartedly.

Goldie and Sheila laid back down on to the pool table after the first sex-act of the many to come that evening. He looked over at her knowing that it was all fantasy and lust that drove him crazy. He cared about her, and there was real love and concern, but he knew he wasn't in love with her. So Goldie made a promise to himself, as long as he was there. He would expose her to great heights, and give the word, understanding, a new meaning as it applied to her.

After a nice hot shower, Goldie and Sheila put on one set of pajamas. She put on the top of the set, and he put on the bottom. Then, Sheila prepared the large bed for sleeping.

As she climbed into the large bed, Goldie excused himself and made his way downstair into the living room to make a private telephone call. He picked up the receiver and dialed the Comfort Inn's telephone number.

The hotel operator answered, "Comfort Inn. Can I help you, please?"

Goldie asked, "May I have the room of a Charles Smith, please?"

The operator quickly replied, "The reverend?"

"Yeah, how'd you know?"

"He's the talk of the hotel. I know him because I happen to be working when he checked into the hotel as a reverend the other night."

Goldie asked, "And his room."

The operator replied, "He's not in his room right now, the last I heard -he was in the Jacuzzi with two women, and an underwater camera. Would you like to leave a message?"

"No, no, thank you."

Goldie, immediately, cleared the line and dialed Theresa's telephone number and after a few rings. She answered, "Hello."

He immediately asserted, "Theresa, this is Goldie, I need you to do something for me."

She replied, "Baby, what you need me to do?"

"I need you to call the Comfort Inn, here in Virginia, it's about your Uncle Smitty."

"Baby, is there something wrong?"

"Look, get your Uncle Smitty on the telephone and tell him, I said, "To find another hotel, and to find one quickly. Baby, your Uncle is down here showing his ass. The sad part is, he doesn't even know he's doing it."

Theresa asked, "What is it -that he's doing?"

"Everything other than what he should be doing. Listen, don't mention that though….just tell him to find another hotel, and after he checks in to calls you. Then, you can communicate where he is to me. When it's time to go back up North, I will reach out to him. Right now, I don't even want to see him."

Theresa asked, "Goldie, are you sure that everything is alright?"

"Baby, I'm fine, and everything else is going according to plan. Right now, Uncle Smitty just doesn't know what he's doing. So I have to think for him. What I'm asking you to do could save our lives."

"Then, consider it done."

"Oh, and Theresa, no matter what happens, always remember, "I love you."

"I love you too, Goldie."

The line went dead.

After the telephone call, Goldie sat there with the receiver in his lap. He was thinking about Theresa, and all she had been to him. He thought, 'God, he'd miss her.'

Meanwhile, Sheila had got impatient and decided to go downstairs in the house to see what she could do to expedite the proceedings concerning Goldie's return to the bedroom.

As she entered the living room, she walked over and sat down on the sofa beside him and asked, "Are you okay?"

Goldie mustered a smile, "Baby, I'm fine. I'm just doing some thinking."

Sheila asked, "What are you thinking about?"

"Baby, right now, I would rather not say, but I promise you before I leave the South, we will discuss it."

Sheila wasn't happy with Goldie's answer, but she accepted it. She took his hand and led him back upstairs to the bedroom.

Chapter Forty One

WHEN Goldie rose the following morning, he made his way down stairs into the living room to place a call to Hollywood, while Sheila slept.

{In the mist of conversation}

Goldie asked, "Hollywood, what's going on?"

He replied, "Goldie, I wish I could have got a hold of you last night.

"Why, what's happening?"

"Brother, I'm finished and trust me. There is a need, and there's so much more going on." Meaning; I'm out of the product, and I have more transactions to complete.

Goldie smiled, "Hey, well….ain't no need of us rappin, the same spot, in an hour, but this time. I just want you to bag the money. Now when you hit Seventeenth-Street out along the rear of the Comfort Inn, I want you to walk down toward Twenty-Fourth Street. I will be sitting out there on one of the benches. I want you to politely walk over and sit down beside me, and after a couple of moments. I want you just to get up and retrieve my bag, leaving your bag behind.

Hollywood replied, "Okay, Goldie, I'll see you in an hour."

The line went dead.

After a nice hot shower, Goldie made his way back into the bedroom to dress and to his surprise, Sheila was up lying in the large bed looking lovely as ever, despite just waking up.

Goldie asked, "Hey Love, how do you feel this morning?"

Sheila smiled, "I'll make it."

"So you admit I worked you over pretty good last night."

"No Goldie, You took advantage of me last night."

"I intended to take advantage of you, to love you, and to maim your soul. Look, Baby, this conversation we'll pick-back-up-on-upon my return, I have to make a run. He leaned over the large bed and kissed her on the mouth before he exited the bedroom.

Now when Goldie had arrived on Twenty-Forth Street, he took a seat on one of the benches out along the boardwalk, and as he had began to survey his surroundings. He noticed Hollywood with his bag in tow as he approached the scene.

Hollywood smiled at the site of Goldie and immediately began to assess the situation and to come up with the most efficient way to execute their plan. He quickly picked up on the fact that Goldie had placed his carry bag down on to the center of the bench that he occupied. Hollywood walked over and took a seat on the bench beside Goldie's carry bag and placed his bag down between Goldie and his bag.

Goldie said, "Good day."

Hollywood replied, "It's going to be."

"Hey, I want to be out of here by tomorrow morning. Jose gets his shipment on the first Monday of every month. We can get it fresh, and I can be back here by Wednesday evening. Do you think that's possible?"

Hollywood smiled, "Man, watch me work!"

As Goldie stood and retrieved the bag that Hollywood had placed down on to the bench beside him. He smiled and stated, "Enough said," then he walked away headed back down the boardwalk.

Mean while Uncle Smitty was checking into the Holiday Inn, which was about ten blocks down from the Comfort Inn, along the Virginia Beach strip.

Now Theresa hadn't mentioned anything to Uncle Smitty about why Goldie wanted him to change hotels. So Uncle Smitty was none the wiser, and the two women that were partying with him the whole time. He ended up bringing them with him to the new hotel. He was also drunk and talking shit.

Chapter Forty Two

AS Goldie made his way back down the boardwalk toward Sheila's place, he removed his cell telephone and placed a call to Carla at the hideout. She answered, "Hello."

"Hey Baby, how's everything going?"

Carla's -face -lit -up at the sound of Goldie's voice. She replied, "We are all set. The moving company will be here tomorrow, around noon. The things that we are taking with us are already packed, and after the moving truck is loaded, the movers will be following me to the airport."

Goldie smiled, "Well, it seems that everything is in order, but then again, I never doubted your ability to handle the situation."

Carla exclaimed, "Oh, and Goldie, the car service should arrive here at the house around one-thirty. So that will give me plenty of time to check our luggage, and to pay the additional freight -fee for the extra weight that we will be shipping through the moving Company."

He asked, "Carla….do, you know why I called you?"

She was hesitant about responding, and she was hoping that everything was alright with him and that their trip was still going to take place. She replied, "No, I guess I don't know why you called me."

Goldie smiled, "I called you because I needed to hear your voice. Carla, I called you because I love you."

As a sense of relief invaded her body, she replied, "Well, I'm glad you called, and I love you too." She asked, "Goldie, are you sure that everything is alright?"

"Baby, everything is fine. I'll see you tomorrow, okay."
Carla called out, "Goldie."
He listened attentively.
She continued, "Baby, I can't wait."
After Goldie had cleared the line, he stood there holding his phone for a few moments, after which he headed back toward Sheila's place.

When he arrived at Sheila's, he found that she was up and in the kitchen preparing breakfast. She greeted him with a kiss and sat him down to the breakfast table for some idol -chit –chat. She asked, "How did things go?"

Goldie didn't reply, he just sat there watching her as she placed his breakfast plate down on to the kitchen table before him, and as Sheila backed away from the table. She placed her hands on to her hips and asked, "Goldie, did you hear me?"

{Now Goldie didn't like to be questioned}

He placed his fork back down on to the table and lunged up out of his chair at her. This scared Sheila, Yet it excited her (she began to breathe heavy).

Goldie spent her around opposite himself, and had her spread her legs apart like the police often do to the brothers of the urban -communities.

As she placed her hands on to the kitchen sink for balance, the short gown that she was wearing eased up, exposing her buttocks.

He took Sheila's breast into his hands from behind and had began to caress them. Her breathing had become erratic {which turned Goldie on}.

As she began to arch her back, by way of pushing her ass back toward him. He place a finger down between her legs 'feeling for her wet -spot.'

Sheila moaned…

At that moment, Goldie's trousers had dropped down around his ankles. He took his penis into his hand and as he entered into her beautiful body. She cried out, which always gave him great pleasure.

After Goldie and Sheila cleaned themselves up, both of them sat back down to the breakfast table. At that point, Goldie found it challenging to find the words that he wanted to say to Sheila, so he just blurted out, "You do know that I'm leaving, don't you."

Sheila mustered a slight smile, "Goldie, I'm not going to argue with you about your decision to leave. However, I do want you to promise me that you will return."

He sighed with relief and smiled, "Baby, that I can do. I also thought that you should know that in my absence. I'm going to miss the hell out of you. After all, it was you that had shown me, 'that there is more to life than just what I do,' and for that, I will always be grateful to you."

They ate their breakfast in silence, after which, Goldie retired into the living room where he had falling asleep on the sofa, but before falling asleep. He visualized all that he would bring forth into reality when he got to Jamaica, which turned out to be a beautiful dream.

Goldie visualized Carla, a child, and himself setup royally in Jamaica. He saw a house with six to eight bedrooms in it, a few car garages, indoor and outdoor swimming pools, a nursery where Carla could grow all types of tropical flowers, a Doberman name, Satan, and all of this on about fifty acres of land.

Sheila sat there in the living room watching him as he slept, thinking, 'that she must have really put that thing on him.' She smiled, and decided to let him sleep. She also figured that he would need his rest.

When Goldie had awakened, he found Sheila in the kitchen and asked, "Why did you let me sleep the day away."

She smiled and explained, 'that she thought he really needed his rest.'

Goldie thought, 'that she must really think that she put that thing on me.'

Sheila went on to explain, 'that she went out and did some shopping, and while out how she had run into an old girlfriend and that they had lunch together.

At that moment, Goldie looked down at his watch and quickly made his way into the living room, where he placed a call to Hollywood, and after a few rings, he answered, "Yeah."

Goldie asked, "Hollywood, What's going on?"

"It seems there is so much to do and so little time to do it in. I'm sitting on one {cake}, and it seems that I've run out of options."

" Now....that doesn't sound like the Hollywood that I know."

"Yeah, I know, but Goldie, we both know that there are days like this."

"Yeah, but that doesn't mean give up, either. I'll tell you what, Let me see if I can make your day. Now, this is what you call a sacrifice play, the additional forty-two grand, that you are going to give me to get you two cakes, at twenty-one thousand apiece, while I'm up North. I'll just need you to give it to me, and you keep that last one (cake}. Now what you can do is put Sticks {hustler} back into your program. You take no risk while I'm gone, and you make a profit way beyond your personal investment, and if you work with it (cut the product} even much more. Plus, our market is all yours to do it in until I return."

There was a pause of silence.

Hollywood replied, "Goldie, I don't know....then, I'll be paying forty-two thousand, for one cake."

"Hey, in this, I also loose about twenty five-grand. Shit, you still gain. The sacrifice that you and I are making here is to strengthen our partnership and business."

"Yeah, I see your point."

"Look, if we don't get this paper together, we are going to miss the deal of a lifetime, and you do know that tomorrow is the first Monday of the month, don't you?"

"Yeah, Goldie, I know (pause}, Count me in."

Goldie smiled to himself, "Okay Hollywood, meet me at the Comfort Inn, in an hour, bring the money, and let's go by Brad's and have a drink. I have to see Cilvia before I leave the South."

"Okay, Goldie, I'll see you in an hour."

The line went dead.

After the telephone call, Goldie showered and dressed, and then, he left the house headed for the Comfort Inn, where he was to meet Hollywood.

Now upon their arrival at Brad's, Goldie and Hollywood were greeted by Brad, himself.

Goldie immediately noticed Cilvia behind the bar serving drinks, and that Brad had a nice jazz band playing that evening.

Goldie and Hollywood made their way through the semi-crowded club

and up to the bar. Cilvia was in the midst of serving a customer when she turned and spotted Goldie, she immediately showed him her whites.

As they took stools at the bar, Cilvia made her way over with a bottle of the clubs best Champaign and three long-stemmed glasses. She held the bottle out before Goldie label up {he sat there admiring her} and after his nod of approval. Cilvia filled their glasses.

She said, "Hi, Goldie, how are you?"

He smiled, "Hey, Baby, I'm cool."

Cilvia placed the bottle of Champaign down on to the bar, and then she placed her hands on to her hips and asked, "Goldie, where have you been? You just disappeared."

"Yeah, Baby, I know, I had a few things come up that needed my immediate attention, and I'm sure you can dig that!"

She dropped her hands down at her side, in a relaxed manner, and smiled {she was just so happy to see him). She replied, "Yeah, I know how that is."

"Hey, I did try to call you a few times, though, but the only thing I was able to get was your answering machine. I didn't leave a message. I hate those damn things."

"So you're the one that has been calling the house and not leaving a message."

He dropped his head, and replied, "Yeah Baby, like, I'm the one."

Now Goldie didn't know whether or not, Cilvia actually had an answering machine. He never used the telephone number that she had given to him. He took a chance on the answering machine line because he believed in the times that we live in, who didn't have an answering machine. If she would have said, 'that she didn't have an answering machine.' He could have always said, 'that he must have the wrong telephone number.'

Hollywood retrieved his glass of champagne off the bar and raised it into the air, and Goldie and Cilvia followed suit. They all tapped glasses and drank.

Cilvia asked, "So Goldie, what are your plans for later on tonight?"

Goldie reached over the bar and took her hand in his, "Baby, I'll be leaving town tonight. I only stopped by here to see you before I left because if I hadn't....I would have never been able to live myself."

Cilvia's....face clearly displayed her disappointment, she said, "Awe Goldie, I was looking forward to spending some time with you."

He released the hold that he had on her hand and placed it underneath her chin and replied, "Hey Sunshine, we have a lifetime."

"I was hoping more like this time."

As he leaned forward and kissed her on the mouth, he replied, "Baby, I promise you next time."

After Goldie's encounter with Cilvia, she went back to serving drinks, however, not before telling Goldie to see her before he left the club.

Hollywood sat there, shaking his head, "Goldie, I don't know what it is with you and women."

Goldie took a sip out of his champagne glass and sat it back down on to the bar and replied, "Hollywood, there's a couple of things that women and I share in common. We both want to be loved, we both need guidance at times, but even more important than that -there's a need to be understood. We don't always want to have to understand, you dig.

As Hollywood slapped Goldie five, he replied, "Yeah, man, I can dig it."

After a brief dialogue, Goldie and Hollywood got into the Jazz band and dug the set."

Chapter Forty Three

As Goldie made his way into Sheila's place, he moved straight to the living room closet, where he retrieved two identical suitcases from Sheila's set of luggage. One he filled with clothing, and the other he filled with the money for travel.

Now Sheila heard Goldie as he entered the house and made her way into the archway of the living room. She stood there, not knowing what to say, as she watched him move swiftly through the house, packing his things.

After which he placed both of the suitcases down at the front door in the living room, and then, he made himself comfortable. He sat there on the sofa, watching her, watch him, in silence. He motioned her over, and she eased over and sat down on the sofa beside him. She looked up into his eyes and asked, "Goldie, do you have to leave tonight?"

He pulled her close and kissed her on the forehead and replied, "Baby, " I'm afraid so."

Sheila snuggled in silence. She knew there was nothing that she could do that would persuade him to change his mind about leaving. They ended up spending the majority of the evening together, listening to music, and planning a future that they both knew would never flourish, at-least that is until Sheila had talked herself out and had fallen asleep on the sofa.

Goldie watched her as she slept for a few moments. He knew that it was time for him to make his exit. He also knew if he would have awakened her that she would have made leaving even more difficult for him. So he reached over on to the end table and retrieved the telephone receiver, and after getting Theresa on the line. He found out what hotel Uncle Smitty was staying at, and then, he got Uncle Smitty on the line and informed him that they should meet out in front of the Comfort Inn, in an hour.

Uncle Smitty tried to give Goldie a hard time, because of the time. It was four-thirty in the morning, but Goldie politely reminded him that he was the one who signed the paychecks and that when it came down to business, there was no family.

After Goldie's telephone call to Uncle Smitty, he leaned over and kissed Sheila on the forehead. Then, he walked over and retrieved the two suitcases that he had placed down at the front door earlier that evening, and then, he left the house headed for the Comfort Inn.

When Goldie arrived at the Comfort Inn, he noticed that Uncle Smitty was parked out in front of the hotel and that he had brought his two girlfriends with him.

Uncle Smitty spotted Goldie as he approached the car with his suitcases in tow, and he got out of the car and opened the trunk for him.

Goldie placed the suitcases into the trunk of the car and slammed it shut. Then, he walked around and opened the passenger side door of the car and told Uncle Smitty's women to step out of the car. He reached into his pants pocket and retrieved his bankroll, and he handed each of the women a hundred dollar bill, and then, he told them that he hoped they had a good time.

After which, Goldie got into the front seat of the car and slumped down into it. He was filled with disappointment.

Uncle Smitty started the engine of the car and asked, "Goldie, why did you do that."

He looked over at Uncle Smitty with contempt, and replied, "Let's get moving, this isn't the time or the place. It's six o'clock in the morning, and I need to be in town by two o'clock this afternoon {Uncle Smitty started moving the car}.

As Goldie made himself comfortable, he looked over at Uncle Smitty and said, "But now that you have asked, I'm going to tell you. How do you know that the chicks you were partying with weren't the police, trying to pump you for information? How do you know that they weren't jacker's?"

Goldie wanted to go on, but he knew that it wouldn't have made a-bit of difference, and any damage that could have been done was already done. Even if the women were only confidential informants, he knew that it wouldn't be long before the car that he was riding in would have been stopped by the law. He was sure that Uncle Smitty had better sense than he had been displaying, but then again, he guessed not. Goldie shrugged his shoulder's and thought {fuck it}. He was going to ride this one out. He figured that he had always been true to the game and that the game had owed him one."

After a few moments, Goldie told Uncle Smitty, don't sweat it, everything is cool, and he extended his hand.

Uncle Smitty shook Goldie's hand and replied, "I dig where you're coming from."

Now, that's all Goldie wanted to hear. He knew better than to talk to much shit to old -Uncle Smitty, because those old jokers will kill you, and this definitely wasn't the time or the place for a war.

Chapter Forty Four

AFTER about five hours of driving, Goldie and Uncle Smitty were about forty-five minutes or so away from Theresa's house, at a filling station on the outskirts of town {New Brunswick}. Uncle Smitty filled the car with gas, while Goldie made an important telephone call.

Uncle Smitty turned the large car off Route One, on to a jughandle that would take them into New Brunswick.

As he moved the car through traffic, Goldie sat up in the front seat and removed his shades. He informed Uncle Smitty of having to make a stop {Goldie's mother's house}. Yet, he never let Uncle Smitty know where he intended to make that stop. He also turned the directions to his mother's house into a maze. So that Uncle Smitty would never be able to find that area of the city, again. Goldie has never given any of his affiliates in the life that he led -the opportunity to meet the washer {Momma}. Theresa hadn't even had the privilege of meeting Goldie's mother.

Now when they arrived at Goldie's mother's house he had Uncle Smitty park down the street from the actual house, and to wait in the car until he returned for him. Goldie retrieved one of the suitcases out of the trunk of the car and told Uncle Smitty that he wanted to have a few things washed and pressed. Yet, the whole time he had taken the suitcase with him, with the paper in it.

As he made his way into Momma's house, he found her sitting in her favorite chair in the living room. He walked over and placed the bag down beside the chair and kissed her on the forehead. Then he eased over and sat down on to the contemporary love seat that had been arranged in the living room near Momma's favorite chair.

She asked, "Goldie, are you okay?"

He gave her a slight smile, "Momma, I'm fine. I just don't know about all of this."

Momma returned his smile, and it was the first time that she had ever seen her son uncertain about anything. She said, "Hey, I have supported you in everything that you have ever done. Please, do not miss out on this opportunity. This experience, and remember understanding life, is often measured in the level of one's experience(s). Goldie....if it doesn't work, you can always come home."

Goldie knew where Momma was coming from. He also knew that an opportunity like this would probably only come once in his lifetime, before prison or death had caught up with him. He replied, "Well since you put it like that....my decision making has become a lot easier."

He stood.

Momma stood and placed her arms around his neck and hugged him tightly.

She said, "Son, I love you so much, and I need you to take care of yourself."

Goldie returned her embrace, "Momma, I loved you too. He assured her that he

would give her a call upon arriving at his destination.

As Goldie prepared to leave Momma's house, he stopped and looked around the place. Then, he looked over at Momma, "You take care of yourself, and always remember I'm just a telephone call away, which reminds me, keep your cell -telephone with you. I believe that this would be a great time to test the system that we have in place."

Momma smiled, "Boy....get on out of here. Momma will be just fine."

Goldie squeezed her tightly and kissed her on the cheek before leaving the house.

As he made his way down the walkway, Momma made her way over to the screen door with tears streaming down her brown cheeks. She watched him as he got into an awaiting car and rode off out of sight.

Uncle Smitty noticed the change in Goldie immediately after he had returned to the car. Goldie's face was full of emotion, Yet, Uncle Smitty said, nothing.

As Uncle Smitty pulled his car into the parking lot of Theresa's development, he blew the horn. Goldie and Uncle Smitty both exited the car and moved to the rear of it. Uncle Smitty opened the trunk.

Theresa made her way out into the parking lot, looking jazzy as ever, wearing something form-fitting, seductive, and very revealing.

Goldie retrieved his suitcase from out of the trunk and set it down at the rear of the car. So, he could greet Theresa, and he quickly took her into his arms.

All of a sudden, a blue Ford Granada began backing out of a parking spot about four or five cars links away from where Uncle Smitty had parked in the lot. In passing, the driver of the Granada had slammed on its brakes, and two gentlemen jumped out of the car with their pistols drawn. Goldie pushed Theresa back away from him and turned to face his attackers, but the two gentlemen already had the drop on him. One of the gentlemen hollered, "Nobody move, and no one will get hurt." The other gentlemen quickly grabbed Goldie and slammed him up against

Uncle Smitty's car, placing the pistol to his head while the other gentlemen retrieved the suitcase.

Theresa began screaming and crying, "No, no, no, not my Goldie, as the gentlemen had began putting Goldie into the back seat of the Granada at gunpoint, and then they sped away. She didn't know what to think or to feel. She felt as though she was drowning.

Uncle Smitty grabbed her and held her tightly, trying to calm her down, but Theresa fought him. He was trying to ask her if there was a gun in the house. He wanted to follow the kidnappers. Yet it was like she couldn't comprehend what he was saying. He also knew that he couldn't leave her in that state of mind, so he carried her into the house.

Mean while Goldie and the two gentlemen of the blue Granada had changed vehicles, and were now riding in a red Chevy Van, on Route One, proceeding North toward Newark International Airport.

Goldie told Robert to push it.

He replied, "Will do Boss."

Stone slapped Goldie and Robert, five, and said, "We got that shit off."

Goldie gave Stone an intense stare, "Yeah, man, and you slammed me up against that damn car pretty hard to. I started to make you shoot me."

Stone reached over and tapped Robert, "Then we would have all been in trouble cause the guns weren't loaded."

Robert looked back at Goldie and smiled, "Now I know you didn't think that we would be using the real thing fucking with you, did you."

Goldie returned Roberts smile, "Yeah, you right man, I can dig it.

Now Goldie didn't know whether the guns were loaded or not, and he sure as hell wouldn't have put anything past the two of them. He also knew that if Robert and Stone thought 'that his suitcase was loaded with money that he wouldn't have a life.'

They arrived at Newark International Airport, right on schedule. Goldie got out of the van and thanked Robert and Stone for their role in his exit plan. Then, he handed Robert an envelope that contained payment for services rendered, after which he turned with his suitcase in hand and walked away.

Now on the inside of the airport, after Goldie had cleared the checkpoint, he moved slowly toward the gate that his flight was to depart from and noticed that Carla was nowhere in sight. He walked over to a stewardess and described Carla, and the stewardess, replied, "That she hadn't seen any such person."

As the passengers had began to board the flight, Goldie picked up his suitcase and started to walk away from the departure gate.

Carla eased up and asked, "Are you going somewhere?"

Goldie turned toward the direction that the voice seemed to be coming from, and there she stood. He eased over and pulled Carla close to him and replied, "Yeah, I'm going somewhere, and I'm taking my baby with me."

Carla asked, "Is this baby of yours someone that I should know about?"

Goldie smiled and kissed her on the mouth, "Of course you know my baby. Baby, don't be silly."

As Goldie and Carla approached the gate which their flight was to depart from, he stopped and retrieved his cell-telephone off his belt clip. He opened it and dialed -three numbers on the telephone. He pressed the talk button, and after a few seconds, he closed the cell-telephone and placed it back on to his belt clip.

Carla handed Goldie the passports and the airline tickets and asked, "Is there something wrong. Why didn't you complete your telephone call?"

Goldie smiled as he handed Carla his cell-telephone, "Baby, I'm fine, no more cell-telephones either. Now let's get on to our new island home. He retrieved his suitcase, and she placed her arm in his, and they began making their way toward the flight attendant.

As Goldie attempted to hand the passports and the airline tickets to the flight attendant {It seemed as if the airport had come to life}. Carla reached out and cuffed the arm that he extended. She hollered, "Freeze, FBI." Agents and guns were everywhere, passengers were FBI agents, baggage handlers were FBI agents, the flight attendant was an FBI agent, and the pilot and co-pilot were FBI agents also. It all seemed to Goldie, as being surreal.

As Carla began to read him his rights, "You have the right to remain silent."

Goldie looked directly into her eyes as she spoke in total amazement.

Chapter Forty Five

NOW by this time, Theresa was somewhat calm, sitting there on the living room, sofa, with her knees shaking, tears still streaming down her brown cheeks, and very deep in thought.

Uncle Smitty wanted to call the police.

Theresa told him that they needed to give Goldie some time. He may have been able to work the situation out or possibly even get away, and in their line of business, she didn't think that it would be wise, at least not at that point.

Uncle Smitty thought damn. Goldie hadn't even gotten the opportunity to pay him. He just knew that the kidnappers, robbers, or both had taken all of the money that was in Goldie's suitcase. That in it-self hurt Uncle Smitty's heart.

Theresa had called Jose but decided that she would wait a while before calling Cathy, and informing the crew to keep their ears to the ground for information concerning Goldie, and at that point, Theresa still really didn't know what to do, but she did know that she would never give up hope.

Mean while after receiving Theresa's call, Jose stepped out on to the terrace of another one of his, New York Estates. He was hurt and upset, contemplating a few things that had taken place over the last week or so concerning Goldie, but more so about the money. He wondered if Goldie was trying to put shit on him, but that thought he dismissed immediately. Jose believed that he and Goldie had come too far for bullshit to come between them, but he did decide that he would investigate this matter and get himself some answers.

Chapter Forty Six

A few moments after Goldie had closed his cell-telephone in the Newark International Airport. Momma had received the special ring tone on her cell-telephone that constituted an emergency.

At that moment, Momma had no idea whether or not this was a test or the real thing. Yet, she decided to act out the procedure and process implemented by Goldie during such a time.

Momma quickly moved into her bedroom and sat down to the vanity dresser, where she removed, eyelashes, a slightly graying wig, and added a carrot ear-ring to each ear that complimented the well-styled short haircut that Momma actually wore. She moved over to a hamper in the room, where she removed a housecoat, gown, and thirty pounds of padding.

Momma slipped into a two-piece pants suit, with a silk blouse, pearls, and a designer handbag, pair of glasses, and shoes. Despite her heart beating fast and her palms sweating, she looked over into a full-length mirror and mustered a slight smile. Then, she quickly moved over to the safe in her bedroom and emptied it.

As Momma made her way through what one would have considered being her home. She wiped down the area's of the house that she frequented, and made her way into an office that was rarely used in the house, where she removed about twenty pieces of personal paper-work and some outgoing mail.

Finally, Momma moved through the lower level of the house and out into the garage, where she got into a two-seated Benz {not known by the public}, like the house also brought and registered under an assumed name. That assumed name just so happens to be Goldie's, Mother's real name, who leased the house to the imposter Momma, who were actually the same person. If this drill wasn't a test, when and if Momma was ever caught up with, detained, or accosted by the law. They would find her at another one of her homes in the country, and they would be dealing with an entirely different person {yet the same}.

Chapter Forty Seven

CARLA pushed the door slowly open to Lieutenant Charles's office. She called out, "Lieutenant Charles." He looked up from behind his desk and quickly closed the file concerning Goldie that laid on top of it.

Carla stated, "You wanted to see me, Sir?"

Lieutenant Charles stood, "Yes, yes, come right in."

She made her way over to his desk.

He extended his hand and said, "I just wanted to commend you on a job well done, and I'll be the first to say that I had my doubts about you and this case. However, like always, you have come through with flying colors. Carla, your Dad, would truly be proud of you. I'm proud of you, and the bureau sincerely thanks you."

All of a sudden, the door to the office burst open, and in came Hank and Jill.

The Lieutenant hollered, "Does anyone believe in knocking on doors anymore around here?"

Hank curtly replied, "Boss, we apologize. We are just a little excited."

Lieutenant Charles gave Hank the look of knowing that he was bullshitting him and replied, "Well, let's not get that damn excited around here ever again."

Hank extended his hand, "You got it, Boss."

He accepted Hank's hand, and then he quickly scooped up the file on Goldie off the top of his desk and made his way out of the office. He said, "I'll give you guys a few minutes."

Hank eased over and kissed Carla on the cheek and said, "Girl, you should be a whole lot happier than you look at this stage of the game."

Tears began to stream down Carl's face.

Jill took Carla into her arms in an attempt to console her.

Hank stood there with his hands out at his side, and asked, "What did I say? What did I do?"

Jill looked over at him, "It's nothing that you said or done. We just need a little girl time together, alone."

Hank snapped his fingers and rotated his hips and replied, "Hello, and just what do I look like standing here chopped liver?"

Jill smiled, "Now you of all people know just what I mean."

He threw his arms around both of them and kissed Carla on the forehead before turning and walking out of the office.

Carla cried out, "Jill, this was the hardest thing I ever had to do."

Jill eased her back over near the desk, where they both had taken a seat in the office chairs. Carla removed a couple of tissues off the Lieutenant's desk. Jill said, "Remember it's not personal.... what you did out there was handle your business."

Carla looked up into her eyes and said, "You explain that shit to my heart."

"Well, let's look at the bright side of things. It's over and done with."

"You're right! It's over, but my heart won't let it be done. Jill, I don't know if I can do this shit anymore."

"Well, Carla, let's weigh it all out. Is this man worth your identity, your lively hood, your accomplishments, and all that you built?"

"Look, Jill, right now. I believe I just need some time to think, alone."

Jill stood and started toward the office door.

Carla called out, "Jill. I would have never been able to put Goldie behind bars had you and Hank not been there, had I not known that you guys were counting on me."

Jill gave her an affectionate and comforting smile.

Carla sat there in silence for a few moments, and then all of a sudden. She stood and snatched her pistol out of the small of her back and clutched her weapon tightly. She removed her credentials and laid the gun, and the small leather fold upon Lieutenant Charles's desk.

Chapter Forty Eight

A few months later, somewhere in New Jersey, at one of the States, Federal Prison Facilities. Carla, who had resigned from the FBI agency, had used those credentials and prior connections to enter this particular Facility. She was about to encounter Goldie for the first time since his arrest.

Goldie sat there in the holding cell, deep in thought, wondering who it could have been that wanted to see him. He wasn't expecting anyone and had fired his lawyer two days prior.

All of a sudden, Goldie stood as the main door opened and shut to the holding area. He watched Carla as she slowly eased-up close to the holding cell and placed her hands upon the bars.

Goldie sat back down on to a bench in the holding cell.

Carla was extremely emotionally. She said, "Hello, Goldie."

He maintained his silence

She asked, 'the guard that escorted her into the holding area to excuse himself.'

Carla continued, "Goldie to be honest with you. I really don't know what to say, I just knew that I had to see you. Goldie, you have to know if you don't give the government what they want that they will go after everything and everyone close to you. There's only one person who seems to have disappeared off the face of the earth and that's your mother. Goldie, it was very intelligent on your part to have given me your cell-telephone at the airport."

Goldie stood, "Did you turn my cell-telephone over to the government?"

She quickly replied, "No, of course not."

He gave a sigh of relief, "Carla…then, what the fuck do you want? Haven't you done enough to me? The government has already seized the little bit of shit that I did have, and are trying to give me twenty to life on top of it."

"Goldie, I want to help you."

"Why?"

As tears began to run down her cheeks, she stated, "Cause I love you."

"Oh, it's obvious that you don't love me."

Carla unbuttoned her overcoat, revealing her midsection and said, "I'm pregnant."

This pained Goldie in the area of his stomach, he sat back down on to the bench in the holding cell in somewhat of a stupor.

Carla continued to express herself to Goldie for the next five minutes or so.

He sat there listening to her in silence, and had come to terms with the fact -that do to the baby. Carla would never turn his cell-telephone over to the government.

She fell silent.

Goldie asked, "Would you like to hear a poem that I recently wrote?"

She mustered a slight smile, "Yes, Goldie, I really would."

Poem

I once lived the life of a millionaire.
I spent my money, I didn't care, and when it was gone.
,
I tried to find a friend, and guess what, there was no-one there, but with this experience, and where I've been.

I promise you all that I'll be back again, and when those same people need a friend, then you'll know in your heart that I win.

The End